Dolce Agonia

Dolce Agonia

A NOVEL

NANCY HUSTON

STEERFORTH PRESS
SOUTH ROYALTON, VERMONT

For information about permission to reproduce
selections from this book, write to:
Steerforth Press L.C., P.O. Box 70,
South Royalton, Vermont 05068

Written in English.
First published in French in 2001 by Actes Sud, Arles.

Library of Congress Cataloging-in-Publication Data

Huston, Nancy, 1953-
[Dolce agonia. English]
Dolce agonia : a novel / Nancy Huston.— 1st U.S. ed.
p. cm.
ISBN 1-58642-028-3
I. Title.
PQ3919.2.H87 D6513 2001

2001002169

FIRST U.S. EDITION

For my friends,
the living and the dead

For you, G., who so recently
made the leap

This is the common air that bathes the globe.

WALT WHITMAN

"A final try," said God. "Now, LOVE."
Crow convulsed, gaped, retched and
Man's bodiless prodigious head
Bulbed out onto the earth, with swivelling eyes,
Jabbering protest —

TED HUGHES, "Crow's First Lesson"

Contents

PROLOGUE IN HEAVEN

When I meet with the creators of other universes, I always make an effort to be modest. Rather than boasting about my work, I compliment them on the beauty and complexity of theirs. But privately, I can't help feeling mine's superior, for I'm the only one to have come up with something as unpredictable as mankind.

What a species! As I watch them living out their destinies upon the Earth, I often get carried away almost to the point of believing in them. Yes, they give me the uncanny impression of being endowed with autonomy, freedom of choice, a will of their own. I know it's merely an illusion, a preposterous notion. I'm the only one who's free! Every twist and turn of their fates has been decided on in advance; I alone know where they're headed and what paths they'll take to get there; I alone know their secret hopes and fears, their genetic makeups, the innermost workings of their hearts . . . And yet, and yet . . . they never cease to amaze me.

Ah, my sweet humans. It so tickles me to watch them flail and flounder. Blind, blind . . . perpetually hoping and groping, striving to believe in my goodness, make sense of their destinies, understand my plans. They simply can't help hankering after meaning. All I need do is give them a brush with birth or death and they think they've caught a whiff of it. Bowled over every time. Shaken to the core.

Take this gathering of men and women, come together at the home of Sean Farrell. Nothing unusual about them, though all consider themselves (this is one hilarious specificity of the human race) to be the center of the universe. They're not especially nice or strange or crazy. Most of them are white, most are no longer young, most are Jews and Christians oscillating between agnosticism and atheism. Though a number of them were born elsewhere on the planet, they have gathered for the evening near the eastern limit of the splotch of land that, for the finger snap of a couple of hundred years or so, has called itself the United States of America.

Why this particular story? Why these people, why this place and time? The fact that I've read my own work backward and forward an incalculable number of times by no means implies I don't have my prized moments, my favorite episodes in the history of mankind. The Hundred Years' War, for example. The Death of Cleopatra. Thanksgiving dinner at Sean Farrell's, circa 2000 . . . There's no point looking for reasons. All I can say is that a multitude of minor coincidences and unexpected undercurrents in the conversation made this dinner party into a poem. Suddenly beauty. Suddenly drama. Flames of fury, gales of laughter.

So here they are and, rather than plunging in medias res into a group of perfect strangers, allow me to provide a list of who is who to assist with orientation at the outset.

First of all, Sean Farrell. Born 1953, County Cork, Ireland. A poet, and a professor of poetry at the university.

The inner circle is made up of people who know and love Sean. Two are fellow professors — Hal Hetherington, a novelist, b. 1945 in Cincinnati, Ohio, and Charles Jackson, a poet and polemicist, b. 1960 in Chicago, Illinois. Two are Sean's former lovers — Patrizia Mendino, a secretary, b. 1965 in South Boston, and Rachel, a philosophy professor b. 1955 in New York City. Three had business dealings with Sean that evolved into friendships of varying intensity — his lawyer Brian, b. 1953 in Los Angeles, California, his house-painter Leonid Korotkov, b. 1933 in Shudiany, Belarus, and his baker Aron Zabotinsky, b. 1914 in Odessa, Ukraine.

The remainder of the guests, those who make up the outer circle, have come to Sean's place for Thanksgiving mainly because their partners were invited. These are Leonid's wife Katie, b. 1948 in Pennsylvania (who runs a crafts shop); Rachel's husband Derek, b. 1954 in Metuchen, New Jersey (who also teaches philosophy); Brian's wife Beth Raymondson, b. 1957 in Hammondsville, Alabama (a medical doctor); Hal's new wife Chloe, b. 1977 in Vancouver (whose profession I'll reveal in all good time), and their son aged eleven months, Hal Junior.

So here they are, brought together in a story a novelist would tell the way human beings like stories to be told — with protagonists and antagonists, a climax and a denouement, a happy or a tragic ending. But from where I stand, nothing ever "happens," there's only a sort of swirling, a vibrating, infinitely intricate chaos of causes and effects. For obvious reasons, storytelling isn't in my nature. I'm not the least bit gifted at drawing out the action, revealing this, withholding that, building up suspense. Since time was my invention, all moments in time are simultaneously present to me and I can skim-read from one end of eternity to the other in the twinkling of an eye. Moreover, it's a terrible strain on me to adapt to human sequentiality — it implies slowing down, brakes screeching, and squeezing out one word after the other. A devilish clumsy tool, language . . .

Still, I'd like to try.

Okay . . . .

Let's have some light, please.

Mehr licht!

Fiat lux!

Dinner Preparations

The odor like an ache throughout the house — it's always been this way, thinks Sean, hurtful, the smell of good food cooking, worse since Jody left but it's always been this way, in every house I've known, the meat especially, Gran's beef stews up in Galway, Ma's chicken soups in Somerville, Jody's exquisite osso bucos, the smell of meat cooking an acute pain, a stab of nostalgia, it's all right to walk into a house and eat a meal of meat but to be forced to smell it cooking hours in advance is torture, not because of hunger no but because of the idea, constantly conveyed and reconveyed to the gut, of the turkey slowly browning in its juices in the oven — insinuating, tantalizing, perversely promising warmth, goodness, happiness, simple family pleasures, all the things one can never have, has never had, not even as a child . . .

Been so long since anyone cooked here. What you could call cooking. The smell, the smell again, the smell. How to concentrate on anything, Jaysus, two o'clock, four hours to go, the bird's a big one, twenty-six pounds, "Big as a three-year-old child!" Patrizia had said as she whumped it proudly onto the table and spread its thighs and thrust fistfuls of stuffing into it. Katie and Patrizia are looking after the food part of the evening and Sean is jittery, jittery, hadn't planned on this lengthy limbo in the excruciating heavenly fragrance of the turkey cooking as they wait for night to fall.

Must get back to the mellowness somehow. Right, dose it just right. No counting, no more counting ever, but keep it at the right level, mellow, all the time. A finger, a couple, three, there we are.

Golden liquid calm. Good harsh cigarette. Good. A sigh. A cough. A riffle through *The New Yorker.* One of the cartoons makes him laugh out loud, and Patchouli pads over to nuzzle up to his knee and be scratched behind the ear. Once Sean had thought to send in a joke of his own to the magazine, about people having a weenie roast: "they ate their meal with frank relish" was the joke — but Jody had talked him out of it, saying there was no way of illustrating such a silly pun. This was near the end; during their first months together she would never have used the word *silly* about him or anything he wrote, conceived, whispered, in the day or in the night. Also toward the end, he'd punched her in the eye for calling his mother a professional masochist, then wept at her feet in remorse (this image comes to him unbidden and makes him cringe with shame — only time he'd ever raised his hand against a woman, or anyone; calamitous effect). Gone, five years gone. Now he's got no idea which continent she's on.

Nothing left in the glass; he sets it down and stares out the window at the steel-gray sky, a sky no poet in history ever attempted to approach with verse, nor any filmmaker with camera, a sky that defies definition, mocks metaphor, confounds hope, a nasty November sky so blank it turns the trees and fence and shed to dun. When all is shed and dun, thinks Sean and laughs again, but silently, wondering if this might perhaps become part of a poem. Null, null, was all the sky kept saying, and no one seemed prepared to argue with it. Black will be an improvement, thinks Sean. Black is a known quantity. You can do things with black. When you switch the lamps on and it's black outside, it makes a difference. A cozy, homey . . . The odor is bothering him again.

Take the bull by the horns. He ambles towards the kitchen, thinking "horns of the dilemma," used to know where that came from, don't anymore, hello Alzheimer nice to meet you, oh you say we've met before? Hm, guess that slipped my mind, haha! Slippery ground this mind of mine is getting to be, now why should a dilemma have horns? Is it some sort of mythological beast, a chimera, di-lemma, double llama, bull of the Cretan labyrinth, gaily tossing Ariadne upon its sharp, pointed excrescences? Surely not. Oh, it matters not, Ma. I won't have time to beat your forgetting record.

He finds Patrizia alone in the kitchen with her back to him, the white ribbons of her apron looped in a bow around her tight little Italian waist, her long black hair twisted up in a bun to keep it from falling in the food, her tight black mini skirt with the other buns distinctly perceptible underneath, Katie must have gone off to the bathroom, how serendipitous to come upon Patrizia alone like this, Sean's sex stirs in his trousers, he moves up to her and slides his hands, both free, over her pelvic bones and onto her abdomen, he's always considered that Patrizia had the most wonderful pelvic bones in the history of womankind, they jut out gently through the black material of her skirt. ("Love your breasts too, don't get me wrong," he'd told her once when they were lovers, he knew that women who'd nursed could be sensitive on the subject of breasts and Patrizia had had her two kids by then, both boys, whereas no boys were Sean's, nor any girls, nor would be, Jody having killed . . . "Your breasts are lovely but your pelvic bones are unique, a gift from God.")

She moves against him to feel him harden a bit more and he, nibbling the nape of her neck where the hairs are moist from the steam of her cooking, leans over her shoulder to see what's in the saucepan. Cranberries with grated orange rind. The berries are just beginning to pop. Like popcorn only softly, wetly, redly, all but inaudibly. When the popping ends (Sean recalls Jody having told him once, when she still hoped he might learn to cook), you stop heating the sauce and start cooling it. Then, for some unfathomable reason, it jells.

"Smells good," he breathes, his lips grazing the fuzzy lobe of Patrizia's left ear.

"*Secret d'un vieux livre*," says Patrizia. "A new French perfume I'm trying. You like the name?"

"I meant the food," says Sean. "The food smells good."

"Oh!" says Patrizia, feigning vexation and stamping gently on his foot with one of her spike heels. In heels she's just his height — not a gloriously tall height for a man — and barefoot she comes up to his eyebrows. He likes her lacy blouses and tight skirts, her old-fashioned femininity, American women don't dress that way anymore. Hearing Katie flush the toilet down the hallway he draws away slightly, politely, from Patrizia's body, which is still young and firm (though not as young and firm, naturally, as seven or eight years ago when she was first hired as a secretary by the Romance Languages Department and he'd gone sauntering past the doorway of her office and halted abruptly in the hallway and taken three steps in reverse and turned to train his irresistible sad brown gaze upon her; she was still married at the time, he wasn't yet, now she's divorced and so is he, to say the least) — and, caressing her buttocks lingeringly as he draws away, he admonishes his sad peter to go back to sleep, even slipping a hand into his pocket to push it over to one side with a peremptory pat.

"Everything's under control," says Katie, tucking in her exaggeratedly purple shirt as she enters the room, and grinning, her face beneath her white hair as ruddy and crinkled as an old leather cushion. "Stuffing's in the turkey, turkey's in the oven, oven's in the house, house is in the forest . . . And now" — with a flourish she draws a rather shriveled jack-o'-lantern from a paper shopping bag (*dead*, thinks Sean, odd how everything seems dead to me these days) "for the pumpkin pie!"

"You sure that guy's still edible?" Hands on shapely hips, Patrizia leans over the ridgy orange globe and sniffs at it.

"Course he is! He was my granddaughter's masterpiece, just look at that evil grin, look at the scar on his temple, isn't he gorgeous?"

"Gorgeous is one thing, edible's another," says Patrizia, not unkindly.

"I've kept him in cold storage since Hallowe'en," says Katie. "He should be fine. All I've got to do is scrape the candle wax off the inside, then I'll boil him and peel him and mash him and cook him and stir him and sweeten him into a dessert. Talk about witchcraft. Like kissing toads. My poor Leo. I've been kissing him for thirty years and he still hasn't turned into a handsome prince!"

Sean and Patrizia laugh, though not so loudly as to make Katie think it might be the first time they've heard this joke. Is this the sort of evening it will be? wonders Sean, instantly feeling the need for a glass in his hand, the golden burn at the back of his throat, the warm cloud rising in his brain.

"Oh, wow! Did you see Patrizia's cranberry sauce, Sean?" asks Katie.

"Yeh," says Sean. "As a matter of fact I was admiring Patrizia's everything in general and her cranberry sauce in particular when you walked in."

"Patrizia, I'm going to write an ode to your cranberry sauce," says Katie.

"Is that a promise or a threat?" says Patrizia.

"Look at it!" says Katie. "Did you ever see anything so beautiful in your life? Poured into glass molds, flecked with glints of orange, the thousand liquid rubies trembling in the light, dubious jewels of a blood-earned crown. O, the deep red of Persephone's pomegranate, so much more sinlike than the pale apple of poor Eve! How'm I doing, Sean?"

She laughs loudly, mirthfully, tosses back her mane of white hair and, seizing a meat cleaver, splits the poor dead jack-o'-lantern down the middle. Sean refrains from crying out — but no, no guts spill from it, it is empty. He leaves the room to get his glass, bottle, cigarettes, ashtray, the essential indispensable accoutrements of his being.

When he returns moments later, Katie is busy assembling the other ingredients. She has taken the jars of cinnamon, nutmeg, ginger and cloves down from the spice rack. Their tops are grimy, Theresa never cleans that sort of thing, Sean is cut to the quick by the sight of these spice jars with their grimy tops, no one ever uses them, not since Jody — wonderful cook Jody, unforgettable cook — spice jars dating back to, Jaysus, they'll outlive me for sure, I'll be putrescent in the earth and this ridiculous rustic mail-order spice rack Ma gave us as a wedding gift will still be sitting where it is now, saying parsley leaves, garlic salt, cardamon, crap.

"Oh dear," says Katie all at once. "I meant to bring maple syrup and it slipped my mind. Got any maple syrup, Sean?"

"Good question."

Cooperatively, he opens the refrigerator. Patrizia is now sifting flours for the corn bread, a mixture of all-purpose and cornmeal, where do women learn these things, do they hide the recipes in their corsages and sneak a peek at them when our backs are turned? (What Ma liked best about America were the TV dinners and the shopping freedom, frozen fish sticks freedom, instant chop suey freedom, preprepared Thousand Island dressing, saves you time, gives you all the time you need in order to live your real life, right Ma what was I looking for what was I bloody well looking for, ah the maple syrup. He spies a small graceful bottle of Vermont maple syrup at the very back of the fridge, a gift from that smart redheaded Vermont novelist — Lizzy? Zoë? I'm sure there was a *z* in her name somewhere — who'd given a smart redheaded reading on campus a couple of years ago and then come home with him, attracted by his name and fame if not by, whatever, and performed an extraordinary fellation upon him by candlelight though she'd refused to let him reciprocate in any way, he can't quite recall why, did she have her period or a special boyfriend or what, then made him pancakes for breakfast and was indignant to discover there wasn't a drop of maple syrup in the house.) He seizes the graceful bottle and brings it out at last, blushing to have spent five minutes staring stupidly into the refrigerator, but the women have noticed neither the delay nor his discomfiture, they're cooking, happy, happy cooking. How can Katie be happy again? wonders Sean. But there she is, happy again, laughing, joking, outwardly her old self, making jack-o'-lanterns with her grandchildren and throwing her pots and running her crafts shop and writing her godawful poems, the only palpable trace of the horror being her suddenly all-white hair.

"Hey," Patrizia says to him, "what are you hanging around in the kitchen for, anyway? Can't you see you're in the way, underfoot, too many brews spoil the cook? Have you nothing better to do? Why don't you go perform some manly task — lay the fire, for instance?"

Fire, the word *fire,* followed by the visualization of the gestures inherent to the laying of a fire, produce a sickening sinking sensation in Sean's intestines. Grate's empty, bin's empty, nothing in the shed but kindling and a few humongous logs rolled over in a corner, shite.

"Shite," he says aloud. "Dammit to hell," he adds for good measure. "I forgot to ask Daniel to order more firewood. He was here Tuesday, there'd have been plenty of time . . ."

"What? There's no wood at all?" says Katie.

"Bunch of big logs is all."

"Well go chop them up into a bunch of little logs!" says Patrizia. "The exercise'll do you good."

"Yeah," says Katie. "Chopping wood wasn't beneath Tolstoy."

Sean looks at them, their faces beaming and humid with the kitchen warmth, he has no wish to leave them, to be sent away, chased out into the icy mean cold and gray, go suffer Sean, go suffer like a man, go on you little pansy poet, they think it's funny, they think it's cute. He shrugs into his parka, angry, resentful.

"Take Patchouli with you," says Patrizia, "I bet you haven't let him out all day!"

And he slams the door like a child, knowing they're thinking "like a child," "dear Sean," "he'll never change," "we love him the way he is." Stomping down the path to the woodshed he can feel his hands shaking, not for the cold, not for the whiskey either, he simply hadn't wanted to be alone tonight, especially not in the freezing woodshed with a heavy unwieldy ax in his hand, staring at a bunch of dusty logs, Jaysus, Jaysus bloody Christ.

"Dear Sean," says Katie, now deftly peeling the thick skin away from the chunks of soft cooked pumpkin.

Patrizia hums as she kneads the dough for the corn bread, reveling in the grainy gritty texture of the yellow mixture beneath her palms, humming with a certain deliberateness because the psychologist at the hospital had advised her not to worry ("Worrying won't help your son, Mrs. Mendino, and it won't help you. What Gino needs is for his mom to be cheerful and optimistic, that's the best thing in the world you can do for his health"), so she's humming and kneading the bread dough and conscientiously directing her thoughts elsewhere, toward the sensation of Sean's hands just now as they crossed on her stomach to grip her by the hips, and how warm and firm his body was as he pressed her to him, and how swoon-deeply she used to be in love with that body. She's had other men in her life, before and since Sean, but Sean was the only one who'd truly loved making love to women, other men used their penises like clubs or chimney pokers or credit cards whereas Sean would moan with each slow thrust, his body arching, his face contracted in ecstasy, it was as if his whole self was moving inside you. Still, both had known from day one that their affair was more a matter of friendship than of passion. Patrizia loved life too much to put up with Sean's lengthy bouts of sulking, and Sean was put off by Patrizia's naive enthusiasm for everything that grew, twittered, and twinkled in nature. "Nature is for hicks," he'd told her once, unequivocally, "and birds are birdbrains." She'd spend hours lavishing her culinary attentions on an eggplant casserole au gratin and by the time they sat down to eat he'd be dead drunk, staggering beneath the weight of ancient memories, oblivious to what was on his plate. To make matters worse, he snored at night. On the other hand, he sang quite marvelously in the shower. That pseudo-cowboy song he'd made up for her one day — how did it go? *"I'm a ramblin' gamblin' man, jes amblin' down your heartroads babe . . ."*

"How's Gino doing?" says Katie, now meticulously mashing the pumpkin flesh with a fork, squashing the squash, preferring not to disturb the vibrant harmony of the room by dumping the stuff into a blender and allowing its electric scream to frazzle their brains for thirty seconds.

"The x rays are pretty scary," says Patrizia without looking up. "He's got a tumor the size of a walnut."

"Oh dear," says Katie.

"Least it's his calf bone and not his brain," says Patrizia, whose best friend died of brain cancer some years ago. "Easier to live with half a leg than half a brain, huh?"

"More fun, too," says Katie.

"So now we're waiting for the biopsy results." Thanks for asking, she thinks but doesn't say aloud. Katie could have behaved as if Gino's problem were a minor one compared to the death of her own son, but minor problems don't exist where children are concerned, everything's important, no comparisons allowed. She knows how much you love your son's calves. You're amazed to see them grow so long so fast. You marvel at the way they turn brown in the summertime, get covered with bruises and mosquito bites. Sprawled on the couch watching an old film on TV, you melt at the way they go suddenly heavy on your lap as your child sinks into sleep.

"Must be a tough thing to go through alone," says Katie, certain that she herself wouldn't be able to endure the anguish, amazed as always by the grit, the grim determination, the stick-to-itiveness of solitary mothers.

"Oh, I'm used to it," says Patrizia. "And at the office everyone's incredibly understanding. I don't know how many half days I've taken off." (For some reason this morning's dream jumps into her head — a dream in which, instead of planting flowers and vegetables in the ground, she'd *buried* them. A little earth helps them to live, too much destroys them, she says to herself. An interesting problem of degree.) "'Bout time I basted that bird again, don't you think?"

She bends to the oven, inches out the pan and spoons drippings over the bird, which is beginning to brown and sizzle. ("As a matter of fact," says *Joy of Cooking* after a lengthy discussion of the various schools of thought on turkey roasting, "in cooking any bird you are faced with a real and built-in problem." Patrizia had laughed out loud upon reading that sentence this morning — the breasts are done before the legs is the problem, and by the time the legs are done the breasts are overdone. Problems like that I can handle, she says to herself now. Give me as many of those problems as you like, dear God.)

Where does her strength come from? wonders Katie. Why is it I'm not strong? The women of Belarus are strong, the ones who watched their radiated husbands swell or shrivel, blacken, bleed and die, their children faint and collapse and lose their hair and die, the ones who've miscarried over and over again, the ones who don't dare make love anymore for fear of conceiving a monster, the ones who make love and give birth to monsters and shower them with love and affection until they die at age seven. Strong women. Brave women. Katie has no idea how they do what they do. She needs her husband Leo, more and more needs him since David's death, all the time needs him, she can feel the tension of his absence even now, even here, in Sean's house a mere two miles from theirs, though she knows exactly what he's doing (getting the storm windows on for the winter); since David's death she can't bear not to know where the members of her family are at any given moment, they could be whisked away, struck down, malevolent forces are at large, roaming, foaming at the mouth, she wishes Leo were here right now, wishes she could eliminate the time and space that separate them, make it be six o'clock at once and hear his tread on the front porch, she'd recognize the step of that man among a million, the specific shape and weight of that body treading, oh tread forever my beloved, never end, sixty-seven now, not old really, lots of years left still together, hey hon? Lots of years. This was the first year they'd had no children at all on Thanksgiving — two married, one buried (she winces at the rhyme), even Sylvia off to Philadelphia with her boyfriend — Katie whips the pumpkin flesh into a smooth thick consistency, scoops it into a double boiler, begins to measure in the spices and sugars — but I wish Leo were here, *here*, in the room with me.

Sweat drenches her suddenly, her blouse is soaked through — good thing it's so hot in the kitchen, she thinks, shrugging, my face is already red.

Sean too is drenched in sweat. He's removed his parka and hung it on a wooden peg on the back of the shed door. Hands still shaking, arms shaking now too, legs shaking — he hates having to pretend he's a strong man. I'm a weak man, I admit it, what more do you want, my ancestors were measly potato-fed pablum-skinned beer-blooded peasants from County Cork and you expect me to behave like a muscle-bound New England lumberjack? I earn enough money to pay strong men to do this for me. Who needs a fire in the fireplace anyway, bunch of wannabe-rustic stuck-up artists, the house has central heating, dammit to hell.

He's done nothing but splinter the log at which he's been hacking for the past ten minutes. The ax never seems to land twice in the same place. It bites into the wood and gets stuck, he wrenches it out again, panting, sweating, hefts its weight with shaking arms and brings it down in yet another place. Perhaps it's dry enough — did *you* know how to do this, Da? Did you ever chop wood in the course of your nasty brutish short existence? No, eh? They can take Tolstoy and shove him — perhaps it's dry enough to saw. Where's the feckin' saw? (He virtually never sets foot inside the shed. The tools have been here since he bought the house twenty-four years ago, immediately the university, proud of having captured this prizewinning precocious genius of a poet, gave him tenure at the unprecedented age of twenty-three.) That's what I'm good at, Da — good at and good for. Not chopping wood, not basting turkey, not having a successful marriage — *writing poems*, had you ever been around to read them. Who knows, old man, perhaps we'd have drunk and thunk together, the two of us, perhaps you too had a bent for poetry, though Ma never mentioned it — pubsong poetry, broken violin poetry, the sweet lilting Irish tradition of despair, eh?

(Sean's father cuffing his ears in affectionate greeting. The dark dank smell of the pubs where Sean would be sent to ferret him out and bring him home for supper. "Ay, let's go, me boy. Hadn't seen the hour it had gotten to be." Staggering, muttering his name. "Me little Sean. Me only wee boy." Hugging him to him in the wet dark streets. The wavering lamplights. The glistening slickness of the fishermen's raincoats as they prepared to go out before dawn. The smell of fish, the curve of nets strung carefully along the beach, untangled, ready to be swirled back into the boats. The piss stench in the corridor of their home. The brownness and the wetness of things. His mother's breasts jiggling strangely against his chest as she hugged him to her, proud of his marks at school, proud of the way he'd learned his Bible verses at Sunday school. *"Are not two sparrows sold for a farthing? And one of them shall not fall on the ground without your Father."* Sean had been perplexed by this: did it imply that God was responsible for the death of sparrows? That he made them fall on purpose? *"But the very hairs of your head are all numbered. Fear ye not therefore, ye are of more value than many sparrows."* Thanks, God. You bet my hairs are numbered. I sure hope You're keeping track of the ones I've lost so far.)

"Aaaah! Shite, shite, shite, Jaysus feckin' Christ oh bloody God!" The saw — angrily, jerkily maneuvered by his right hand — has sliced through the soft flesh next to his left thumbnail. Bright blood wells. Sean brings his left hand to his chest, fingers clenched on bleeding thumb, curves his right hand around his left for protection, bends his head, his knees, crumples to the earthen floor and sobs. Pomegranate gem. Cranberry color. The inside of my body. And I'll go back to the house and the women will laugh at me, sweetly, condescendingly, not unkindly, but they'll laugh at me, not understanding, the inside of my body . . . "Not good, Mr. Farrell" — two weeks since that day at the clinic when the doctor's words had come rolling slowly through the air, clear and detached as white round pearls, then sliced brutally into his brain like the sawteeth just now into his thumbflesh — "Doesn't look good to me, Mr. Farrell. Does not look good to me." "Am I going to die fairly soon, Doctor?" "I'm not God, Mr. Farrell." "Okay." Numbered hairs, numbered days.

The fine brown rich turkey aroma hits him like a kick in the soul as he opens the door. The women see the scowl of despair on his face — they know Sean, love Sean, know better than to laugh. They minister to his wound like mothers (yes, thinks Sean, the way mothers used to do, or be purported to do, in some fairy tale or other), they ask no questions because the answer is clear — no logs will be coming out of that shed tonight.

Katie sees how to kill two birds. She takes out her stone. "You know what?" she says. "I'll call Leo and tell him to fill the trunk with wood — we've got piles of it right in the garage." She flushes with pleasure and hormonal imbalance, face ablaze beneath her shock of white hair, an excuse to call Leo, hear his voice, joy, joy.

Her hand on the telephone. Sean sees Katie's hand on the phone and thinks oh, the fascinating life that receiver has led over the years! All the hands that have grasped and squeezed and stroked it, their sweat and smell wiped off twice weekly by Theresa. All the mouths that have breathed into it. The murmured tendernesses and whined reproaches it has absorbed. His pleading with Jody through the holes in the gray graphite, begging her to come home until his voice cracked, "I can't live without you! Jody! Jody, I swear it! Nothing in my life on this earth appeals to me, not one thing, not even my work, if you're not going to be here to share it with me." "Don't be maudlin, Sean . . ."

"Did you want a drop, hon?" asks Patrizia. "Might serve as an anesthetic for that thumb of yours." Thank God for Sean's dinner party, she thinks — a stroke of luck for her — she'd have been crawling the walls at home alone, with Gino and Tomas at their father's for the long weekend. "Their father," Roberto has become.

(Roberto at age nineteen, choosing eggs with her at the Haymarket, his long brown fingers skimming over them, such grace. His black eyes promising her everything she'd ever longed for. The way he'd French-kissed her in front of the whole church as — stiff and thrilled and terrified in her wedding dress of white taffeta — she stood there next to her father and the priest, his sudden warm thrust of tongue into her mouth such a surprise that she'd all but wet her panties. The way his curly head used to lie heavy on her naked breast, his face in sleep like that of a young child. Roberto picking up Tomas for the first time, his son, his newborn son, staring at him and bursting into tears. Roberto giving Gino a miniature baseball bat for his third birthday and teaching him how to swing it. Roberto slumped in an armchair the day he'd gotten laid off, watching midafternoon TV and drinking beer. Roberto snarling at her instead of celebrating when the Romance Languages Department hired her as a secretary . . . It wasn't her salary he envied but her happiness. Born in the town, she knew its inhabitants and resources like the palm of her hand — and it thrilled her to sit at the center of a whirling maelstrom of professors and students and come up with quick elegant solutions for their invariably urgent problems. Roberto had never forgiven her. He'd taken no notice of her affair with Sean or the men who came after. He'd ceased touching her in the daytime and coming to her at night. Then he'd started snapping at his sons, then bashing them in the face, then bashing her in the face, until at last she told him she'd hired a lawyer. Yet — the same person. His graceful brown fingers on the eggs.)

"Don't mind if I do," says Sean, his thumb now washed and swabbed with disinfectant and copiously bandaged, so Patrizia fetches the whiskey bottle and glass from the living room and pours him the drink, deft, neat, up, straight, the way he likes it — and before moving away again she kisses him, brushing his noble sweating balding brow with her soft lips.

A strand of dark hair has escaped from Patrizia's bun and curves down around her chin like a question mark, a lovely Modigliani stroke half framing her face, and as her eyelids close Sean succeeds at last in shoving the lung cancer back into a corner of his brain, a large corner but nonetheless a corner, leaving room to exult in the momentary pressure of her lips on his forehead.

"Leo will be over around five to start the fire," says Katie, hanging up the telephone with a grin, not even pretending to conceal her delight. "Oh mý God, the pie filling!" In an instant she's flown across the kitchen, grabbed the wooden spoon and begun to stir. It's like clay: there's only one right thickness to the mixture. Too thick or too thin: no pot, no pie. The rotating motion is the same, too. (Ah the peace of throwing pots, shaping smooth gray matter with her hands. Gray matter yes, as if it were her very brain, as if her hands were smoothing and shaping her own thought processes, making them round and regular and symmetrical as her right foot kicks gently to keep the wheel speed constant and she leans over, at once intent and absent, losing her gaze in the wet gray clay, watching it rise and ripple beneath her fingers, dipping her hands into water, just the amount she needs to keep the clay moist, it's something you know instinctively, don't need to think about, your fingers do it all by themselves.)

She pours the filling into the piecrust. Sean seems even more brooding and erratic than usual this evening, she thinks. Strange he should have chosen Thanksgiving for a dinner party — the most familial of holidays for the least familial of men. No relatives left, none at all since his mother died last summer. No kids, not a fatherly type. Though I shouldn't say that, he was brokenhearted when Jody had an abortion without telling him. Sobbing in Leo's arms. "Ma's only chance to have a grandchild! Her single remaining dream and hope — pulverized." He tended toward exaggeration. It's true, though, that he worshiped his mother. We never met her but he described her decline to us in hair-raising detail. Her mind like a cliff — and at first, just a few pebbles rolling down its side to be engulfed by the waves of oblivion. Then rocks, boulders, tumbling faster and faster, carrying chunks of earth with them, until eventually the cliff itself collapsed and there was no one there anymore. Long evenings of black humor and gin fizz. Maisie, her name was. Sean described his new writing project to us, a long poem cycle listing everything his mother had forgotten. Leo suggested a title, *Maisie's Lost World*. No, said Sean. *What Maisie No Longer Knew*. The first poems would contain the mundane details of her life as an elderly lady in a Boston suburb: where she'd put her keys, when she'd last washed her hair, which subdivision of her complicated pocketbook her change purse was in. Then, as the cycle wore on, the forgotten details would grow increasingly moving and significant — the names of her friends and siblings, the name of the country she lived in, the year of her husband's death. And the final group of poems, searingly rich in color and feeling, would deal with the most deeply etched, hitherto ineffaceable impressions — her childhood memories. A grease fire in the kitchen when she was two, a neighbor boy who shoved his grubby hand into her underpants and left a toad there, a Protestant shot dead in the street in Galway, his head blood mixing with the gutter mud and rain. Could be a lovely book, thinks Katie, if he ever gets around to writing it . . .

"I'll have to use the microwave oven for the pie," she says aloud. "Otherwise it'll taste like turkey."

Sean nods without hearing her. Half-moon glasses on his nose, he in turn is bent over *The Joy of Cooking*, running through the list of ingredients for his own contribution to the meal. The recipe calls for fresh pineapple (he bought canned), fresh strawberries (he bought frozen), two cups of dark rum, two cups of lemon juice, one and a half cups of orange juice, one cup of grenadine, two bottles of brandy and two quarts of ginger ale. He wants all his guests to be thoroughly inebriated by the evening's end — no exceptions, not even Beth the virtuous, Beth the quasi-teetotaler — and nothing can compete with punch for the unwitting consumption of large amounts of alcohol. Oh, the sweet slip of a cashier who'd rung it all up for him at the supermarket! "Having a party, Mr. Farrell?" she'd asked. "You bet your pretty pink pantyhose, Janice," he'd replied, learning her name from her name tag, not for the first or the second time. "Like to come? Consider yourself invited." And she'd giggled, without even bothering to answer him. He must be joking, of course! He couldn't seriously entertain the idea that a silky seventeen-year-old like herself might crawl between the sheets with a balding old dodderer like him. Och, never mind.

Turning his back to the women so they won't offer to help, he attacks the can of pineapple with the can opener, his fumbling worsened by the bandage on his left thumb. Women are so bloody helpful, he thinks, as pineapple juice spurts onto the kitchen table and Patrizia rushes to wipe it up with a sponge. Why do they always feel compelled to help people? Can they not mind their own business rather than leaping into other people's lives to tidy them up, straighten them out, scrub them clean, iron the creases out of them? Where would I be without my creases? I'm a creasy person. I write creasy poems. Creases are my raison d'être, my calling, my sacred vocation. Sean "Crease" Farrell, they should call me. He slides the crushed pineapple out of the can into the punch bowl, wishing his hands weren't shaking quite so visibly, trying to forget, forget, forget. Lend me your memory, Ma. Some of those black holes of yours would come in handy just now.

Patrizia has bent to baste the dead bird again. The shapely thigh flesh thus exposed reminds him of some of the redeeming features of the female sex.

"Does Patchouli eat turkey bones?" she asks, but he doesn't hear because her head is still halfway inside the oven — like the witch, she says to herself, just before Gretel gives her the fatal shove. Do all children long to topple their mothers headfirst into the oven and bake them to a crisp?

"What?" says Sean, now struggling with the strawberries. (They've frozen so hard that they refuse to come out of the box, so he has begun peeling away the cardboard, strip by sticky strip.)

"Does Patchouli eat turkey bones?" repeats Patrizia, straightening now, turning, smiling, charmingly lifting the stray strand of hair back away from her face, whence it promptly falls down again.

"I don't know, I never made turkey before," says Sean, as if it were he who were making it. "Doesn't it splinter and stick in their throats and cause them to choke to death or something?" The image of splintering revives in his brain his recent unpleasant experience with the log.

"Nah," says Katie. "That's for cats. Poultry bones are no problem for dogs, they just gulp them down without even chewing them. Patchouli will have the feast of his life."

(The Patchouli joke, not really a joke, the Patchouli story, has been going on for decades. When Sean's father died in 1962 and his mother decided to try her luck in America on the pretext that she had a second or third cousin somewhere in the greater Boston area, Patchouli materialized on the boat during the crossing. Since then he has neither aged nor changed in any way; he's still a rambunctious affectionate tail-wagging black-and-white mongrel pup who, in his enthusiasm to be loved, tends to knock things over and mess things up. Sean has written countless poems about his dog. He feeds it bones and leftovers, walks it twice a day and pats it as he sits at his desk, typing poetry and drinking whiskey late into the night. None of his friends has ever seen Patchouli but all respect him and defer to Sean's belief in him.)

III

PATRIZIA

Ah, my beloved flowers. Aren't they cute? Budding, blooming, or withering, all of them must eventually come to meet their maker. So ... shall we begin with, ah, Patrizia Mendino? Let me set your mind at rest by telling you I have no intention of meddling with her son Gino for the nonce. He'll be all right. The surgeons will remove the benign tumor on his calf bone and there will be an end to it. He'll lead a normal life — become a jewelry maker — settle down in New Mexico — get married and have a son whom he will name Roberto, after his father. Tomas, on the other hand, I'll spirit away at age twenty-six in a pileup on the treacherous Highway 128, the Boston Ring Road.

When she hears the news of her son's death, a strange thing happens to Patrizia. She begins to lactate. At age fifty, her breasts swell painfully with milk. She finds this at once distressing and acutely embarrassing. There are no babies around to relieve her and she doesn't have the nerve, at her age, to walk into the local drugstore and ask for a breast pump. Cold baths, hot compresses, nothing helps ... After a few weeks the swelling goes down, but now her destiny sets up shop there — in her shapely breasts, in the form of a tumor. Patrizia pays no attention. Time passes. Calmly, nonchalantly the illness makes inroads in her body. It feels at home there.

Patrizia retires at sixty and it's then, only then, that she discovers her calling in life. She's meant to feed the birds. She feeds them. Coos and croons to them. Wishes she could nurse them. Her breasts ache. Pains shoot out to her shoulders and armpits, then her arms, chest, back. She doesn't go to see a doctor. She sees no one.

Her hair grays and thins. Her dark eyes grow beady and suspicious. She loses touch with every facet of reality except for birds. They flock to her garden and love it there. The minute she steps out of the house, they swoop and flutter around her, settle on her head, arms and shoulders, hopping and chirping, a mass of twitters. She works hard to feed them. Knows which ones need crushed insects, which seeds, which orange rind, which margarine. Cooks for them, as her grandmother used to cook for the family. Says grace with them, sings them snatches of opera and Sicilian love songs. Recovers the long-lost language of her childhood, chatters to them in Italian as she scatters their seeds and crumbs. *Venite, carissimi miei, uccelli miei, bellissimi miei, mangiate, mangiate, buon appetito . . .*

This lasts a number of years. To the neighborhood children Patrizia is the bird lady, the crazy woman, the witch. She screams at them if they approach, for fear they'll frighten her birds away. The cancer continues to spread, claws its way into her brain, gnaws at her reason; she can no longer clean house, shop or cook for herself; neighbors begin to worry at the smell; they make a few phone calls and an efficient employee of West Surburban Social Services is sent to do a frailty assessment; after filling out her questionnaire she deems there is sufficient frailty in this individual to justify her immediate removal to an institution; there, standard medical tests are performed and the doctors' eyebrows shoot up at the results; by this time Patrizia is thoroughly demented, praying aloud to Saint Francis of Assisi but screaming at everyone else; the young doctors are awed by the foulness of her tongue; she insults them in a startling mixture of English and Italian, screeching at them until she goes hoarse, until her voice is nothing but a whimper.

After only three days in the institution, three days during which she loses what little foothold she had left in reality, I can't take it anymore. Yes, sometimes even I feel sorry for people. No doubt about it — Patrizia will be better off with me. Okay, time's up, *ragazza.* Come along.

IV

Greetings

Glancing out the window, Sean sees with relief that the sinister metallic gray of the November sky has given way to black.

Katie moves at a leisurely pace around the living room, switching on lamps to create warm intersecting circles of gold and ochre. Hardwood floors gleam, rugs and cushions fairly purr, patchwork quilts hum a tune about another era — when, of a winter's night, women would sit and sew and sigh together around the fire, murmuring sad secrets to one another. Katie glances at the empty grate, then at her watch. Nearly five. She wills for Leo to come. Her thoughts go skittering from Alice to Sylvia to Marty, then to Alice's two boys, then to Marty's little girl Sheila, the one she'd helped carve out the jack-o'-lantern and who, when she'd turned five last September, had confessed to her in a whisper, "It's tough being five, Grandma. People expect so much of you." Katie tries to recall how she'd responded to this but fails because David is there now too, in her mind's eye, his blue jeans slipping down around his hips . . . It'd be easier if there were a fire in the grate, she thinks. A fire gives you something to look at instead of your thoughts.

Sean sets the punch bowl out on the porch — there being no room for it in the refrigerator, what with the cranberry sauce now jelling there in twelve individual molds.

"So who all's coming?" asks Patrizia.

Raising the awesome knife she brought with her this afternoon, she wields it over the bright tight motley shapes of the vegetables heaped upon the table — sweet potatoes and corn, red and green peppers, zucchini, green beans, onions, garlic, parsley. All of women's aggressiveness goes into cooking, thinks Sean, dragging deeply on a cigarette as he watches her stab into the particolored flesh, peel and slice and chop, reducing it to cubes, to julienne, to utter helpless conformity.

"You'll see," he says.

"You don't want to tell me?"

"I don't like lists."

"So it's a surprise?"

"Mm-hm."

"A dozen of us?"

"Baker's dozen."

"Thirteen? You only gave me twelve molds. Hey, Sean, I'm a superstitious Italian, my mama always told me thirteen at the table was bad luck."

"There'll only be twelve at the table. The thirteenth guest, being underage, will be sent upstairs to bed."

"Underage? *Id est?*"

"Under the age of one."

"There's a *baby* coming?"

"No, an eleven-month-old adult."

"Whose?"

"You'll see."

When Tomas was eleven months old and just learning to walk, Patrizia remembers, he lost his balance, fell forward and hit his brow on the sharp edge of a wall, a deep dig spurting blood — instant panic, screaming child whisked into arms and rushed to bathroom, water, sponging, washcloths, water, rinsing, compresses, holding, pressing, rocking, oh my God, oh my God — but Tomas went on spouting blood and screaming and Roberto was God knows where; at some point she must have gotten her little boy into the hands of a doctor, there were stitches, now there's a pale sickle-shaped mid-forehead scar, the doctor and Roberto and Tomas have erased the incident from their memories, but Patrizia . . .

"There's Leo!" cries Katie, trying to make her dash for the porch look like normal walking.

"Got a wheelbarrow or something, Sean?"

The wood is brought in and stacked, the fire is lit, time-honored gestures of virility in which Sean does not even feign to take part, his wounded bandaged thumb being excuse enough, no need for more, no need for sarcasm and superciliousness, be a good host tonight, affable . . .

"Join you?"

"Sure."

The men in the living room drinking whiskey, the women in the kitchen making succotash — too bad if it's a cliché, thinks Sean, deep down we all prefer it this way. Clink of the glasses, clink of his brown eyes against Leonid's gray ones that are getting hard to reach through his old-age disguise, the glasses, the wrinkles, sagging jowls, bushy eyebrows and the rest. Old age always looks like a disguise, thinks Sean, you're convinced that people will at some point rip off their masks and laugh, revealing their true, young faces underneath — yes youth is truth, which is why the Bible tells us we'll be resurrected on Judgment Day with every hair on our head — me too, right God? I'll wake up with every one of my numbered hairs grown back, my cheeks filled out, my hands steady and my legs capable of taking me places at a run. But will I still be able to write good poems? Och, that is the question.

"Chin-chin."

They don't talk much, don't need to, friends all these years, this half-life of Sean's in the course of which Leonid has gradually eased his way out of middle age — but still he's strong and muscular, never would it occur to Sean to put up his own storm windows or carry six armloads of logs up the front steps. They don't talk much because they've known each other so long that they're comfortable together, and even if they don't recall with perfect accuracy all the facts they've learned about each other's lives they know the main ones, how many children each of them has or used to have or would have liked to have had, where their own childhoods unfolded, the ways in which their parents died.

(Leonid's died a year apart almost to the day, his father in 1984 and his mother in '85, and though his father died in his bed and his mother in a riverbed, still, they'd died more or less the way elderly Belarussian peasants were supposed to die, the way generations of their own ancestors had died, in the village of Shudiany where they'd lived all their lives, not suspecting that less than a year later the air of Shudiany would be zinging with a hundred and forty-nine curies and that its inhabitants would be contracting fatal diseases by eating the lettuce that grew in their gardens or camping out along the Pripiat River. Leonid hadn't gone home for his parents' funerals — an expensive trip. He's been home since, however. Once.)

"Looks like snow out there."

"Yeh?" Sean turns his head toward the window only to be polite. As he has no intention of venturing out of doors again this evening, the weather report leaves him indifferent. "Ah yes."

Leonid wrenched his back this afternoon carrying one of the storm windows up the ladder — almost fell, didn't fall thank God, but now the pain is there, familiar and abominable, part of the nucleus pulposus slipped into the fissured annulus, something to that effect was what the doctor had explained to him when it happened two years ago, and now he's thinking dear God not that again, please, please spare me the lumbago, the cortisone, the fogginess and grogginess, being dragged down and down by the pain, perhaps Sean's Chivas Regal will do the trick.

"Turkey sure as hell smells good."

"Can't stand it," says Sean.

Leonid booms with laughter, on the off chance that the powerful vibration of his voice in his rib cage might help to numb the pain in his lower back.

"How come you're celebrating Thanksgiving if you don't like turkey?"

"Oh, ah likes turkey all right," says Sean, imitating a southern drawl for some reason obscure even to himself. "Ah jes' don' like the smell o' turkey cookin'. Makes me all sad, know what ah mean? Hurts mah stomach, hurts mah soul, smellin' so warm an' cozy an' all. Git mah meanin'?"

"Yeah, I do," says Leonid. "I used to feel that way myself, as a child. Every Sunday we'd go over to my grandmother's for lunch and she'd be frying bacon . . . It was only bacon, I mean it wasn't roast beef or anything . . . But every time I'd walk into her house and smell that bacon frying, I'd feel . . ."

"How about some music?" As he sets his glass on the coffee table, Sean upsets the ashtray; a dozen Winston filters and a cloud of ashes drop and drift to the rug at varying speeds. "Goddammit, Patch!" he says. "Can't you watch where you're going? Look what you've gone and done! Dogs are nice," he adds, addressing Leonid. "In lots of ways they're nicer than kids, but they simply can't be trained to clean up their own messes."

Leonid laughs again, more softly this time because the booming hadn't done his lumbago any good. He knows better than to start fooling around with a broom and dustpan. There are limits to his altruism. Carrying the wood inside was already a major piece of stupidity.

"That Patchouli," he chuckles, shaking his head.

With his bare hands, Sean scoops up what he can of the ashtray's contents and tosses it into the fire; then he wipes his hands on his trousers and scuffs the remaining ashes into the carpet with his shoe. Jody had hated his smoking; she herself had quit after a single session of group hypnosis in Manhattan, and boasted about it to all who would listen. "It's easy, Sean. You should do it, Sean. Do you want to be wheezing and coughing twenty years down the line? If you don't love yourself enough to do it for yourself, do it for *me*, because *I* love you." "Bloody right, you love me, provided I consent to undergo hypnosis and psychotherapy and daily jogging and a graduate course in feminist theory — provided, in other words, I turn into a different person." That had been one of their favorite fights. They'd covered that territory fifty or sixty times by the time she left.

"What'll it be? Miles?"

"Great."

Leonid shifts a cushion under his lower back to ease the pain, you've got to relax into it instead of stiffening against it, the important thing is to not *feel* the pain, because it gets worse if your muscles start bunching up to fight it. He'd taken a handful of aspirins before leaving the house but so far they hadn't done any good. "Shouldn't be hefting heavy weights anymore, Mr. Korotkov," the doctor had told him. (David's body had been weightless when he picked it up, the most amazing thing, a feather — and he, Leonid, a man of infinite power. Bending down like God from heaven, he'd effortlessly lifted the long body of his youngest son and slung it over his shoulder like a cape, a feather cape, no strength had been lacking in him that day.)

"Nice, eh?" says Sean.

"*Bitches Brew*, hm?"

"Yeh. That's one thing that'll be nice forever. When the people of the thirty-first century study the twentieth with its towering mountains of corpses, at least there'll be Miles to redeem us. At least we can say, well we came up with Miles, didn't we? That's something, isn't it? For Billie and Chet and Miles, the human race is worth saving, don't You think so, God?"

"You bet."

Some time goes by.

"Someone once told me," says Leonid when it has gone, "that if Miles was working and the phone rang he'd pick up the receiver and go 'Wha-wha-wha?!' then hang up again. He didn't even know what *dimension* he was in."

"Right," says Sean appreciatively.

Did I ever know that sort of trance, painting? wonders Leonid.

Nah. Even when I believed in it, when I first came to New York and thought I had half a chance of being good — even then I was easily distracted. Friends would drop by unannounced and instead of being pissed off I'd be glad. Always preferred to talk to them. Go out for a bite, a drink, sit down, have a cup of coffee, how's tricks, whatever, chew the rag. Didn't mind. Painting could wait, people couldn't. As soon as one of the twins walked in I'd set down my palette and turn to her — "What's up?" (Since David's death Leonid has set down his palette for good; he paints only other people's houses — that way things are clear, square, four walls and a ceiling, doors, window frames, water-based, oil-based, sanding, preparation, mixing and stirring colors, you know what's required of you and you improve with practice. That's how he met Sean in the first place, repainting his house for him some fifteen years ago, could use another coat, could use another coat, they keep telling each other, not absolutely sure they'll get around to doing it someday.)

Sean half stands, pours them each another drink and sits down again, it's better now, almost bearable, he's grown accustomed to the turkey smell, and instead of the day waning the night has begun to dawn, no, can't say night's dawning can you, why not, maybe even night could dawn if it set its mind to it . . . Nascent night . . . He can feel the way Miles's music is wrapping itself around his brain, the way his thoughts slip into the grooves and rhythms of the trumpet line, the jolts and jars of it . . . Jody liked only baroque, she did her best to convert me and I tried, God knows I tried, spent hours driving around the state with Monteverdi and Frescobaldi on the tape deck, practically nodding off at the wheel, but I can't bear for things to be harmonious and symmetrical. Crease is my middle name.

"Something I've been meaning to ask you," says Leonid.

"Hm?" says Sean.

"Where do you get your socks?"

"My socks?"

"Yeah. They look like good socks. Are they good socks?"

"These ones? Er . . ."

"You see, because I don't know how to buy socks anymore. I just can't get used to the idea that good socks are an extinct species. It depresses me! You buy a pair of socks, you wear them two or three times and you see your big toe sticking out. I wouldn't mind spending more money if I was sure they'd last me more than a week."

"Built-in obsolescence," says Sean, not proud of his originality.

"It's depressing," Leonid insists. "I stand there at Woolworth's studying the labels on the socks, and what I see is: 'mostly acrylic.' That's a tragedy, Sean, you know what I mean? Not even 'mostly cotton' or 'mostly wool,' 'mostly acrylic'! If that's the best they can claim, makes you wonder what the *non*acrylic ingredients are."

Sean laughs. The doorbell rings and he looks at his watch: ten to six. "Hundred to one that's Derek and Rachel," he says.

"You recognize the car?"

"No. But Rachel is a ten-minutes-early person."

"Oh yeah?"

"Used to drive me up the wall."

He rises, waits for his brain to settle, heads for the kitchen.

"I'll stay put," says Leonid, dreading the moment when he'll have to extract himself from the armchair.

"Stay put."

(Not that Sean's a late sort of individual — he's got nothing to be late about and little to be late for, as his graduate poetry seminar meets only once a week, Wednesdays from two to four, and the rest of the week is something that must be gotten through to the best of his ability — but Rachel's obsession with time had been a torture to him. They simply hadn't been compatible. They'd be in Boston together for example, romantically wandering down Charles Street — and Rachel, seeing the WALK sign start to blink, would leap forward, dragging Sean with her, intent upon dashing across the street before it changed to DON'T WALK — "Hey, Rache," Sean would protest. "It says *walk*, not *run!*" "If you didn't smoke so much, you'd be able to run." No, that wasn't Rachel, that was Jody — bouncing up the front steps bright-eyed and glowy-skinned after an hour of jogging through the woods and finding her husband seated at the typewriter, nursing his sixth coffee-and-a-cigarette of the day. No, Rachel had never berated him for smoking. I love you, Rache, I really do. We just weren't compatible, that's all.)

"Hey."

"Sean!" Rachel's skin. "Sean," she says again in a whisper at his ear, her cheek a shock of softness brushing his. She blushes, as she does every time they embrace in front of her husband.

"Hi, Sean," says Derek.

The two men hug. (Sean doesn't particularly feel like hugging Derek. He wouldn't do so spontaneously, of his own volition, in another context, but he can hardly do otherwise given that over the years, annoyingly to them both, they've been in love with the same woman on two different occasions. Lin Lhomond, Derek's first wife — spurred, Sean is convinced, by the intensity of his belief in her as a dancer — had flown away to Mexico to launch an international career, dumping their two daughters in Derek's lap. And Rachel, Lin's best friend since high school and for a brief time Sean's despair-mate, had married Derek the minute his Mexican divorce came through. Sean has never been able to fathom how two exceptional women like Lin and Rachel could fall for a typical Jewish academic grind like Derek; nonetheless, he clasps the tall man's over-coated body to his own, waiting for the moment of compulsory closeness to be past.)

"Cold out there," says Derek, stamping his feet as if his shoes were already covered with snow. "Gonna snow." Sean looks sick, he thinks. Not aging well. Eyes too bright. Already fairly pissed. Bad sign he started drinking so early in the day. Oh God, spare us one of his scenes, please.

"About time," says Rachel. "It's rare to have had no snow at all by Thanksgiving. Hi, Katie!"

The kissing and hugging and handshaking go on for a while. Then Rachel whips out her chocolate cake — the only thing she ever learned to bake, but scrumptious. Famous.

"Who's running things here?" she asks. "Where should I put this?"

"Set it out on the porch," says Patrizia. "The fridge is full."

"Won't it freeze?"

Rachel goes back out to the porch with her cake. They'd made love on this porch once, she remembers, without blankets or sheets, the rough floorboards scraping their skin, they'd wept in each other's arms on this porch, she remembers, more than once . . . Patrizia's eyes are red, she thinks — is there something wrong? Don't dare ask her. Theresa told me one of her boys has a health problem, fairly serious. Might be just her contact lenses, though. Or slaving over a hot stove all afternoon . . .

"Want me to bring in the punch bowl?"

"Yeh," says Sean, "the time is ripe."

Rachel's short hair is more salt than pepper now, he notices, and close up it's impossible not to see that her skin is crisscrossed with fine lines, but the delicate sharp-angled bones of her face haven't budged; she's still got that waify Audrey Hepburn look — at, what is she now, two years younger than me, forty-five. ("Will I make it to fifty, Doctor?" "I'm not God, Mr. Farrell." "Okay.")

Rachel carries the large crystal bowl inside, fake staggering with the weight of it . . . Wouldn't it be funny if, no it wouldn't be funny at all, about as funny as the time Sean threw a glass of whiskey in my face, or the time he shook a champagne bottle then uncorked it between his legs and aimed it at me like a fizzing cock . . . Did he indulge in that sort of behavior with his other women, or did I have a monopoly on his dark humor? She sets the bowl down on the kitchen table and, crossing over to the cupboard, begins lifting down punch glasses.

No hesitation, Derek notices. After all these years she still knows where Sean keeps his glasses. And I'm still jealous. Tired of being

jealous. Sean's a wreck. Look at that posture. Never gets any exercise. You've got to keep on the move, that's what I tell Violet down
in Florida. ("Don't just lie around all day, Mother — go swimming!"
"Me, swimming? You must be *meshugga*, I spent my whole life in
Metuchen, New Jersey, surrounded by freeways and factories, and
now my son expects me to be a bathing beauty! Look at me, I'd look
like what in a bathing suit? Like a ridiculous, that's what. One of
those crazy fat Polar Bear ladies who strip to the skin and toss
leather balls back and forth on Coney Island beach in the middle of
winter. Swimming is for the birds, Derek. A joke. But I'm bored.
Klezmer music I can put up with once a year, not every day." "Why
don't you try reading?" "Reading? Me? When did I ever have time
to read? You're the reader in the family, you're the man of books, your
father never read, he was too busy making dresses in the factory so
you could go to college and get your degree and read as much as you
like until he had a heart attack and you could attend a colloquium
while he died. So for you it's good — read, read! But for me, no.")

"Hey Charles," says Sean.

Derek, who had been leaning against the porch door, at a remove
from the others, watching them fill punch glasses but not listening
to their banter — pleading, rather, with his mother Violet down in
Florida — bounds away from the door as the next guest comes in.

This man Sean clasps willingly and warmly to his body —
Charles Jackson, a tense and elegant black man, barely forty, new to
the department, to whom he'd taken an instant liking because,
though celebrated from coast to coast for a sizzling collection of
essays titled *Black on White*, he'd refused to teach a course in African
American poetry. Insisted on teaching the poets he loved, from
Catullus to Césaire and from Whitman to Walcott.

"Hey," says Charles, barely glancing at the others as he shakes their
hands. "Good to see you." Meeting, greeting, he knows a number of
them already but is paying no attention to names and faces because his
brain is still in an uproar from the fight he has just had over the tele-

phone with his wife, hideous, Myrna sitting there screaming at him from the house he still hasn't finished paying for in Chicago. "No you won't get them at Christmas either, the settlement's a month in summer and that's *it*, you *bastard*, no weekends, you *bastard*," *bastard* now seeming to be the only word she knew, "I'm gonna throw the *book* at you!" "You act as if I'd committed a murder or something!" "Yes, you *did* commit a murder! You murdered *me! You murdered my *life!* You murdered my *love* for you! It's *dead!* It's *over*, Charlie!" "Don't call me Charlie." "Charlie Charlie Charlie! It's over, man! You're a dead duck. You're a dead fuckin' duck, man. I'll send you the kids by plane but I don't want to ever see you here, is that clear? Don't you ever *dare* set foot in this house again . . ." From that to this. From *that* — a single afternoon spent in a hotel room exploring the luscious brown body of Anita Darven, the young writer the university had brought up from South Carolina for a series of poetry workshops — to *this* — a new job at a new university, nine hundred miles away from his sons Randall and Ralph — and especially, especially, his daughter Toni, apple of his eye, jewel of his heart, named Toni because Myrna, unlike Charles, revered the novelist Toni Morrison, tiny Toni won't even remember me, she's only three, won't remember I ever lived with her, I'll be faraway daddy for her, *the bastard*. Though it's been nearly a year, he can't get over having been ripped away from that wife, that house, those plans, that future — he's still reeling from the shock of it.

He downs a couple of glasses of punch without noticing or speaking to anyone, standing motionless in a corner of the kitchen reliving the hideous fight, and then he notices Derek heading toward him in a beeline, the way white people come over to black people when they see them standing alone, for fear they might start feeling left out, so coming over and saying,

"Hi again."

If he asks me how I'm liking the university, thinks Charles, how I'm getting used to it, if it's very different from Chicago, I'll go into the next room. Or if he says anything at all about the punch.

"Are you all right?" says Derek. "Forgive me for asking, I hardly know you, but you look . . ."

"Oh," says Charles, disarmed by the sincerity. "I've got problems with my kids."

"Are they big or little?"

"Little."

"Little kids, big problems."

"What about you?"

"Yeah, as a matter of fact I've got problems with my kids, too."

"Are they little or big?" says Charles.

"Big," says Derek.

"Big kids, big problems," says Charles.

Derek laughs. "Mine are girls," he says. "Eighteen and twenty-one. Angela, the older one, is in Manhattan . . . doing what a million other young women are doing in Manhattan."

"Trying to become an actress," says Charles.

"You got it."

"And waiting on tables in the meantime."

"On the nose."

"And the eighteen-year-old?"

"Marina. She's the one I'm worried about. She doesn't eat."

"Takes after her mother?" says Charles, glancing at emaciated Rachel on the far side of the kitchen, who has just put two cigarettes in her mouth, lit both, and handed one to Sean.

"No," says Derek, "that's not her mother. Her mother split when she was three."

"Oh."

"Marina fainted in class the other day, giving a paper," Derek goes on. "She's in Bronxville, at Sarah Lawrence. Majoring in Holocaust Studies."

"Holocaust Studies?"

"Uh-huh."

"Mm-mh. Reminds me — don't you think we should have a

Slavery Department up here? Seriously. Give doctorates in Advanced Slavery?"

"Good idea," says Derek.

"You know . . . 'I took an intensive course last summer and finally managed to get enough credits for my B.A. in Torture. Eventually I hope to get a master's in Genocide.'"

Both men sip punch for a while.

If he wants to tell me what the problem with his children is, thinks Derek, he'll tell me. Now or later. Or never. Not.

The doorbell rings again: it's Beth and Brian (the Hairy Ones, as Sean privately refers to them because of Brian's leftist-lawyer beard and Beth's long hippie frizz) — and suddenly the kitchen seems very full, their copious stomachs, loud voices and forced laughter take up room, produce a shift in mood — don't spoil it, Beth, thinks Sean, it was starting to feel good there for a minute. With them, kindly brought by them, is Aron Zabotinsky, the gaunt and aged baker, a man who is both silent and hard of hearing but whose sparkling sapphire eyes speak volumes — early eighties, thinks Sean, no, not so early anymore, must be well into his eighties now, born in Odessa before the revolution, cherished by all in town for his perfect bagels and rye bread, but he's also a connoisseur of poetry: Brodsky, Milosz, me.

Now there is a flurry of coats and scarves and gloves, "Getting seriously chilly out there," everyone is saying, "feels like snow, feels like snow." Whatever would we do if we didn't have the weather to talk about? thinks Sean. Once he'd had a brief affair with a girl from Port-au-Prince — and when, calling her on the phone for the first time, he'd said, "My house is shrouded in thick fog . . . What's the weather like down there?" she'd burst out laughing. "Sorry, Sean, that won't work. In Haiti we don't talk about the weather, it's hot and sunny every day of the year." "What do you use for small talk, then?" he'd asked. "Political murders. You hear they just lynched So-and-So in Cité Soleil?" He's forgotten the name of the politician assassinated that day. The girl had a lovely name, though — Clarisse. Remembered that one, Ma. *You can't take that away from me.*

Beth is pulling bags out of bags — ah the appetizers — nacho chips, guacamole dip, mixed nuts, pretzels, all of it marked low-fat, low-calorie, low-cholesterol, low-salt. Sean meets Rachel's eyes, which flicker with irony as she turns to lift down bowls for these insipid sins, these diluted dangers, these calibrated transgressions.

Beth glances around the kitchen in controlled dismay and uncontrolled anticipation — oh God, an enormous meal ahead and what what what will she manage to refuse? Her eyes register the pumpkin pie on the counter, her nostrils register turkey and sweet potatoes, Aron has brought fresh bread and rolls from his bakery and I saw Rachel's chocolate cake out on the porch, by midnight I'll have absorbed some ten thousand calories and gained three pounds, I'll be nauseous, disgusted with myself, hoping never to see anything edible again, Vanessa doesn't want me to come and visit her at school anymore, says she loves me but she's ashamed, doesn't want people to know I'm her mother, oh God I should never have accepted this invitation, don't like Sean Farrell anyhow, never have, bulimics and alcoholics have too much in common, but at least I don't get nasty when I overeat, just miserable, just want to withdraw, be alone in the dark, hibernate forever in my cave of fat.

Patrizia forgives Beth all her faults, physical and moral — because she'd turned to Beth for advice, week after week, throughout the terrible illness of her friend Daniela, and again now, with Gino's tumor — and whenever they talked, whether over the phone or in a coffee shop or standing in line at the supermarket, Beth gave Patrizia calm, clear information as to what was going on in the bodies of her loved ones. At such times you don't want to hear platitudes like "Everything will turn out fine" or "There's nothing to worry about." You want your problem to be taken seriously, given careful attention by somebody who both knows you and knows what they're talking about. If necessary, you want to prepare yourself for the worst.

Poor Beth, thinks Rachel. Look how she avoids meeting people's eyes, and how her own eyes go darting anxiously about, looking at the food — *is she going to eat it? Is she going to eat it all?* Oh I know her fear. Of all the women present, though she'd never believe it, I'm the one who knows it best. Starving yourself is essentially the same thing as stuffing yourself — the main thing being the absolute, permanent and implacable animosity between you and food. Lin and I at age seventeen, competing to see who could survive on the lowest number of daily calories. Nothing for breakfast. Half an apple for lunch. A yogurt for supper. Mastery. Mastery. We would have loved to swallow one end of a long ribbon, as Indian yogis do, inching it through the digestive tract and expelling it through the anus, then pulling the ribbon back and forth to clean out every last impurity. We yearned for lucidity, limpidity, mind over matter. I may not count calories anymore but I still derive a perverse pleasure from handling junk food in the certain knowledge that not one iota of it will be entering my body.

As she transfers the various chips and dips into bowls, Rachel notices that Derek has deliberately moved into the living room so as not to torment himself with the sight of how familiar the kitchen still is to her, how her hands still reach automatically to the right cupboard for the right bowl. (Some of the things she and Sean purchased together fifteen years ago are still here — the sea-green water tumblers from Rockport, the black plates from Soho — objects acquired during their brief weeks of pretending they could make each other happy despite overwhelming evidence to the contrary, specifically the fact that both of them had been flailing in the murky waters of melancholy since childhood and were unlikely to turn into lighthearted hedonists overnight, no matter how powerful Love was touted out to be. "*Love,*" said God in the Ted Hughes poem Sean had read to her one night, one of the sinister black nights in the course of which they'd mixed gin and vodka and sperm and tears until not only their heads but their very souls were aching, splitting, spinning — and Crow, God's imbecilic student, instead of repeating "*Love*," had gaped and retched, thus engendering Man. Gaped and retched, raped and getched . . . RACHE! had been Sean's triumphant phonetic conclusion to the night. And I'd have to get up three hours later to teach a class on Aristotle, thinks Rachel now; Sean never needed to get up early but I did, and then he'd fall asleep and start to snore.)

She carries the tray laden with appetizer bowls into the living room, passing Charles and Patrizia on the way, bowing slightly, ironically, as she proffers and they take, partake, seeing them lick their lips involuntarily to get at the salt — and *becoming*, strangely, ephemerally, the salt on their lips as they lick it — but this is an elusive image; she can't quite get at it, so it dissolves.

"How come *you* guys haven't got any kids tonight?" Patrizia asks Brian and Beth, filling their punch glasses with the flair of a professional cocktail waitress or a priest serving wine at mass.

Brian downs his in one gulp, wipes his beard and holds out his glass for more while Beth sips suspiciously at hers: "Is there alcohol in it?"

"Oh, scarcely a drop! " Patrizia lies brazenly. "So how come you guys are childless on Thanksgiving?" she repeats. "You're not divorced! You don't even look separated!"

Is that supposed to be a joke? thinks Brian, gulping again, wiping his beard, longing to be tipsy and quickly so, hoping that the liquor buzz will take the edge off his tinnitus, the perpetual maddening ringing in his right ear. In the first place, she forgets I *am* divorced, my eldest daughter Cher is thirty and lives in Palo Alto California and hasn't deigned to speak to me in about eight years. In the second place, Jordan's in jail again. Well, that much I can tell her, I guess.

"Jordan's in jail again," he says out loud.

"Oh," says Patrizia, her eyes darkening in sympathy. "That's a drag."

And in the third place, Vanessa had preferred to go down to

Manhattan with a friend of hers from school, rather than have to deal with Beth's food problem on Thanksgiving.

"And Nessa's spending the weekend with a friend," he adds lamely — as if this were normal, as if two hundred and fifty million Americans hadn't traveled miles by plane, car, and train to be with instead of away from their families this evening.

Rachel crosses the living room and holds out the tray to Aron Zabotinsky, "the Old One," who has settled into Sean's rocking chair. He looks up at her and smiles, recognizing her, then shakes his head. Rachel is one of his most faithful customers. Every Sunday morning at ten, regular as clockwork, she opens the door to his bakery — called Tinsky's because Aron had rapidly tired of spelling his name to incredulous Americans — purchases three bagels and a loaf of rye bread, and wishes him a good day. (Aron has told no one in town, no one in the state, in fact no one in the Northern Hemisphere, that he was not always a baker but became one only fairly recently, twenty years ago, when he retired from teaching Social Anthropology at the University of Natal in Durban and came to the United States: first to Connecticut where he had relatives, then here. *I am not one of those who departed my homeland . . .* As the words of Anna Akhmatova thudded through his brain at night, tormenting him, he'd resolved to revive the gestures learned earlier still — decades ago, before his first exile, back at his father's side in Odessa: braiding the bread for Passach, shaping the bagel dough into thick rings, dropping them into salt water to boil before they were baked, sprinkling them afterward with sesame or poppy seeds or finely chopped onions, stacking apples, walnuts, raisins and paper-thin layers of dough for wedding strudel. Oh, the way his father's large red hands used to draw the hot trays out of the oven, sliding a wooden paddle beneath the loaves and rolls and whooshing them into the tall wicker basket, then waiting for the rabbi to come and bless them . . . In 1931, when Aron was sixteen, the family had managed to escape from Odessa thanks to cunning and bribery and the convenient proximity of the Black Sea. His father knew nothing about South Africa at the time, apart from the fact that his brother was already established there, running a watch factory in Pretoria — but given that Ukraine was suffering severe economic and stomach pains as a result of wheat requisitioning, he'd been more than willing to wash his floury hands of the place and go off to join his brother.)

"How's business?" asks Leonid, attempting to draw Aron into the conversation he's been having with Sean next to the fire, but for the moment Aron feels like saying nothing. (Their native towns of Odessa and Shudiany are no farther apart than Boston and Detroit and there's a bond between Aron and Leonid because of this — the ambiguous bond that connects all those born in the shadow of the Soviet Union during those tense bleak murderous years; Aron knows Leonid isn't Jewish — and, given the long-standing tradition of anti-Semitism in Belarus, this is all he wants to know about his past; they've never discussed their youth in detail because they know how unpleasant details can be in these matters, and Aron is a silent man in any case, in fact Leonid is a bit surprised to see him here tonight — no, come to think of it, it's not so surprising because Aron is known by all to be a lover of good poetry; entering Tinsky's, Leonid has more than once caught sight of a volume of Sean's poems sticking out of the baker's pocket. Leonid himself is poetically illiterate: he loves his wife's poems because he loves his wife, and there is an end to it.)

"Good, good," says Aron. It's true, business is good and he wishes to add nothing — wishes, now that he's in his final years, to rest and refrain from small talk, renounce everything superfluous and superficial — these munchies Rachel is passing around, for instance. (Though an atheist, he's always felt there was something beautiful in having one's food prepared in accordance with sacred laws, blessed by the rabbi — the cows and sheep slaughtered like this, the wheat ground like that, all well in the eyes of God. His wife

Nicole, raised a perfunctory Catholic on the island of Groix in Brittany and converted to leftist ideals by her years spent studying philosophy at the Sorbonne in the 1930s, had never understood Aron's respect for religious ritual. To her mind, religion was mere hocus-pocus — a ploy for distracting the poor from their suffering. "But what's so bad about that?" Aron would ask her. "All human minds, not only those of the oppressed and downtrodden, need periodic relief from reality . . . Should we deprive the proletariat of the only happiness they have — the capacity to levitate, to sacralize?" Yes, Aron has never forgotten the breathtaking beauty of that moment every Friday evening when his mother would light the candles . . .)

"Can I get you some more punch, Aron?" asks Katie. But the baker has scarcely touched his glass; he shakes his head and smiles and utters not a word, so Katie moves away.

"A stroke of genius," says Derek, coming over to squat down next to Aron's rocking chair. "I mean it. A real stroke of genius, to set up a shtetl bake shop on Main Street in this yuppie WASP town. I never realized how much I'd been missing real bagels until you came along. It's true, you don't notice! You let people impose things on you. Puffy bagels. Chocolate bagels. Low-fat bagels. The day comes when you stoop so low as to buy a doughnut! And then when the genuine article comes back, it makes you so happy you could weep. Rachel and I can no longer leave our bed of a Sunday morning without the promise of brunch from Tinsky's."

Aron smiles indulgently. He sees that Derek has grown rapidly uncomfortable in his squatting position — Zulus can squat for hours on end, even the oldest and most decrepit among them, but in whites it's a position that denotes youth and Derek isn't young anymore; he can pretend to be young for a minute or two but then his thigh muscles start feeling the strain and his belt starts cutting into his gut and now it's getting urgent that he change position, either sitting down on the rug or standing up, it will depend on how Aron responds to his compliments, but Aron is responding not at all, he's merely smiling and rocking back and forth like a very old man, taking a mildly perverse pleasure in the spectacle of the younger man's discomfort.

At last Derek gets to his feet, so painfully that Aron can almost hear his knees creak, repeating, "Seriously, a stroke of genius."

Deafer than I thought, thinks Derek as he turns away. Or could be he's decided to turn down his hearing aid and enjoy the silence for the duration. He's earned it — has the right to it, I imagine. Wish I could have given my father a few years of silence before he died. Some French writer — Queneau? Quignard? — pointed out that there's no such thing as earlids. You can shut your eyes, but you can't shut your ears. Our ears make us vulnerable, put us at the mercy of other people's insolence and bad taste. Poor Dad. What would you have liked to listen to, instead of dawn-to-dusk sewing machines at the factory and dusk-to-dawn Violet at home? Music? I wonder . . . Not this music, anyway. You never did like jazz — said it was vulgar. Look at Sean's record collection, must be a thousand titles in jazz alone. Didn't much like Irishmen either, did you? Thought they were *schnorrers*. "If they want to loaf around in pubs and sing songs all day, more power to them. I don't have the time. I've got work to do." Sean *is* a *schnorrer*, as a matter of fact. Good thing he snores, or Rachel might not have worked up the courage to leave him and I might not have had a second wife. She says she was prepared to die for him but not to listen to him snore at three o'clock in the morning. It wasn't fair, she said — they'd fight for half the night, then he'd fall asleep and start snoring and she wouldn't get a wink of sleep; the next day he'd be prepared to turn over a new leaf and she'd be a wreck, wasted, suicidal.

"What about you, Derek? Can you use a refill?" says Katie. He looks at her and grins, hands her his glass.

"How've you been, Katie? Feels like ages — when did we last see each other?" He hopes it wasn't at David's funeral. How many years ago was that? Derek wonders. Couple or three already. (Time flies on campus, especially since the girls left home and the years are no longer colored by the grades they're inching through at school. All the years seem the same, the calendar of exams and holidays just keeps spinning around, as inexorably and inanely as a gerbil in its wheel, freshman classes keep popping up, blonder and blander every year, having read less and reflected less and being less inclined to make an effort to comprehend Spinoza — "He should have laid claim to his Jewishness" is what they say nowadays.)

"No, not that long ago," says Katie. "We ran into you at the Fourth of July bash last summer, remember?"

"Oh, sure, that's right," says Derek.

"You even danced with me!" says Katie.

Derek remembers that, too — but, smile as he might, nod as he might, he can't repress a surge of pity for the Korotkovs. (*The worst thing, the worst possible thing,* the words come back to him — their son David had been in high school with his daughter Angela, he'd even played violin at one of her dance performances, then gone on to study musicology in Boston at the Berkley College of Music and then suddenly he was *dead.* Derek was among the first to hear the news, Theresa the cleaning lady had told him, the day after the body was found — "David Korotkov is dead" — the word a thud in Derek's gut, his whole body recoiling from the force of it, incredulous, convulsed, knowing that this, *this,* losing a child, was the worst thing that could happen to anyone, instantly and wildly extrapolating to his own children, wondering if they too were fooling around with drugs — what if Marina was injecting heroin into her veins at this very minute? — and then, as he repeated the sentence *David Korotkov is dead,* sharing the news with their friends one by one, he'd observed to his dismay how the emotion drained from the words, how the repetition transformed them into a story, a piece of fiction, he kept saying "the worst possible thing, the worst thing that can happen," but he couldn't feel the *truth* of it anymore, within a matter of hours the pain had ceased to affect him, he watched the others recoil in shock and horror and could only envy them their feelings, ashamed at how rapidly his own had detached themselves from the event itself to hide behind the words — *how was this possible?* And tonight — no pain at all — nothing but pity.)

Katie is now bending over her husband, the man of her life, kissing the gray-white hairs that frizz at the reddish nape of his neck — "What about you, hon? Something more to drink? Oh — you guys are doing whiskey, better not to mix."

Leonid raises a hand behind him and firmly grasps his wife's head with it, frames her jawbone, slips his fingers into her thick white hair and squeezes her scalp, saying with his fingertips *I'm here, it's okay.*

"Yeah, I'm a bit soused already," he says out loud. "Between the music and the Chivas and Sean's sparkling conversation . . ."

"Scintillating, not sparkling," says Katie.

"To me it's sparkling, like sparkling wine," Leonid insists, always on the defensive about the way he uses the English language. "What time is it, anyhow? I'm starving. Is everybody here?"

His deep rich voice carries out to the kitchen, causing Patrizia to protest, "Not yet! We're not ready! The table isn't even set!"

$$\overline{\text{V}}$$

CHARLES

Charles will be the last to go. He's got four whole decades ahead of him. Wealth, fame, *und so weiter*. His three children estranged from him, coming to visit him only because they have to, coming less and less often, stilted in their behavior, all of them ill at ease, unfamiliar to each other in their words and ways. He'll remarry a couple of times but there'll be no more children. Never again a child living in the house in which he lives, laughing crying playing, pounding up and down the stairs or waking sweaty and feverish in the middle of the night. Perhaps to compensate for this loss, he'll publish a number of excellent books on the possibility of love, desire and passion between whites and blacks, not always rape, not always perversion, even in centuries past, even under the institution of slavery. A plea for light brown skin (such as that of his children) sometimes bespeaking, rather than suicidal splitting and self-hatred, a double inheritance of love.

An unhappy man, on the whole.

He won't feel a thing. At one fell swoop, his third wife will be a widow; and the messy pile of papers on his desk, a posthumous volume of poems.

Grand, genteel house in the posher part of New Orleans. (It was Tulane University that ultimately made him the offer he couldn't refuse.) He used to enjoy sitting at the desk in his study, staring out at the slave's shack in the backyard that now contained only garden tools for the gardener, daydreaming as he prepared his classes, consulted books of poetry and history, jotted down notes. Window open, gentle breeze blowing through the curtains onto his desk, riffling the pages of his books . . . Lush green plants dripping and lapping out of doors. A pair of slippers outside on the front deck for him to slip into when he comes home. Only this time there will be no homecoming. He's lying facedown on the burning pavement. His glasses were knocked several yards away by the impact of the motorcycle that hit him, then sped off down the street. Shouldn't have stepped off that curb, my boy! But the sensation of pain — jolt — crash — didn't have time to register on his brain. Indeed, the sudden release of a massive amount of glutamate in his brain annihilated every neuronal trace of the previous ten minutes, during which Charles had absentmindedly packed his briefcase, gone to the toilet, locked the front door of his house and walked toward the street. His skull cracked on the pavement, if anyone had been around to hear it crack. A number of small thoughts for a poem were still drifting around inside of it, waiting to be seized upon and followed through. They spilled out onto the hot pavement — the image of his shoehorn, the memory of his mother's gingham apron and his grandmother's crab apple jelly, the rolling creases in the red earth of Canyon de Chelly — exposed, evaporated, gone.

VI

The Latecomers

"We're still waiting for Hal and Chloe," says Sean at the same time.

"Who's Chloe?" says Katie. "Don't tell me Hal has gone and found himself yet another sweet young thing!"

"I'll set the table," says Charles, whom Myrna in the course of their ten years of marriage had initiated into the joys of daily life — shopping and cooking and above all looking after young children — only to snatch them away from him at his very first misstep. "Just tell me where everything is, I'll be happy to set the table." It will remind him of before, of then, the days when he had a family to feed and a wife to love and all those things that, he now realizes, were incommensurably more important to him than tenure and book sales and his name in the *New York Times*. He's not paying attention to the other conversation because he's never met Hal Hetherington and does not yet care a whit about the ins and outs of the novelist's love life.

"Yeh," says Sean. "Only this time he's also married her and given her a child."

"No!" says Patrizia. "That's the underage person you were telling me about? *Hal Hetherington has a baby?* I don't believe it."

"I hate the expression *given her a child,*" says Beth. "As if it was his to give. As if he had the child in him in the first place, and then generously agreed to pass it over to his wife."

"No speeches tonight, luv," says Sean.

"Don't call me luv," says Beth, turning pink with anger. "I forbid you to call me luv."

"Would you guys stop bickering?" says Patrizia. "We're in the middle of a juicy piece of gossip and I want to know the details. Seriously, Sean. Tell us."

"He's too old to be a father," mutters Beth.

"The bare bones of it are all I know," says Sean. "You remember Hal was on sabbatical a couple of years ago, doing research for a new novel out in Vancouver. Well, destiny was awaiting him there, in the shape — a rather pleasing shape, I gather — of a certain Chloe. So once he had wooed her and wed her, he wangled an extra year's leave out of the university and took her on a fabulous honeymoon trip down the West Coast. Their son was born in Santa Barbara, apparently."

"And you haven't met this Chloe yet?" asks Leonid.

"No, he's been hiding her from me."

"How old is she?" asks Rachel.

"Twenty-three."

"*Twenty-three?*" cries Beth in dismay. "What's Hal, fifty-five or something? Good Lord, he could be her father!"

"I thought you said he was too old to be a father," says Sean.

"Ah, go to hell," mutters Beth.

A pensive moment follows, during which all of them (all except Aron Zabotinsky, who isn't listening but staring into the fire with his hearing aid turned down and recalling the Pushkin poem his mother used to recite to him when he was little, rocking him next to the fireplace and whispering the horrific warning into his ear as sweetly as if it were a lullaby: *O gore, gore nam! Vy deti, ty zhena! / Skazal ja, vedajte: moja dusha polna / Toskoj i uzhasom; muchitel'noe bremja / Tjagchit menja. Idjët! uzh blizko, blizko vremja: / Nash gorod plameni i vetrom obrechën; / On v ugli i zolu vdrug budet obrashchën, / I my pogibnem vse, kol' ne uspeem vskore / Obrest' ubezhishcha; a gde? o gore, gore!* — ah, he thinks now, so she knew we'd eventually be forced

---

* "Woe to us all! Dear children! Darling wife!" / I cried. "Know this! My soul is full of strife / And fear! A grievous burden weighs me down: / The hour is close at hand: unhappy town! / Too soon in roaring flame shall all be burned! / Through fire and wind to dust and ashes turned . . . / And all are doomed to perish in a day / Unless we flee . . . But where? O grief! . . . I dare not stay!"

flee the city, flee the country . . .) variously readjust their mental processes to prepare for the arrival of someone young. Wondering, uneasily, what they'll look like to her. Knowing the answer: old. Even Patrizia, the baby of the group, is half again Chloe's age. Whereas they're *not* old, and among themselves agree, understand that they are not. Over the years they've watched each another develop wrinkles and sags and rings, pockets and pouches and extra chins — but when they look at each other they magnanimously erase them, forget them, go back, get in, under, down to the essence and the soul. Now they learn they'll be condemned to be their bodies this evening after all, their decaying bodies, objectified and judged. Oh God, Sean. How unkind of you to spring this on us.

(Yet how could Sean not have invited Hal? Both of them oldtimers and big names on campus, with two decades of students and meetings and theses and literary do's in common, the frail intense trembling alcoholic Irish poet and the big boisterous best-selling novelist from Ohio had become close friends almost in spite of themselves. Secretly each resented the other for having witnessed his lack of gumption and initiative over the years — holding up, hiding out, sitting on their laurels in this cushy job in the middle of nowhere, not really living, preferring not to actually get out there and live, taking an occasional stab at concubinary bliss and failing lamentably and returning to their respective books. Indeed they cared little for each other's work — Sean found Hal's novels verbose, overblown and hopelessly realistic; Hal found Sean's poetry deliberately, perversely opaque — still less for each other's girlfriends — Sean was bored stiff by the dumb blondes with whom Hal was forever falling in love and Hal was intimidated by the brilliant neurotic ladies who appealed to Sean — and yet, willy-nilly, they cared for each other.)

Katie, her forehead bathed in sweat, is now sitting on the rug, leaning against her husband's thigh, and Leonid is stroking her hair with his rough right hand. He knows she's thinking twenty-three, that's just Alice's age, and twenty-three, that was David's age when he died, he would have been twenty-five now but having died he'll be twenty-three forever, that's the definitive curve of his destiny, from zero to twenty-three, a small curve, cradled within the larger curves of his parents' lives instead of intersecting and leaping beyond them as it should have done. And now this stranger will walk in here, a false note in tonight's music, so carefully concocted and conducted by Sean — this twenty-three-year-old Chloe, the only one who knows nothing of any of us, the only one unaware that Sean's mother died of Alzheimer's last summer, that our son OD'd in the most gruesome way two years ago, that Rachel's aunts and uncles were gassed at Birkenau, that Brian and Beth's adopted son Jordan is in jail for petty theft, that Charles is in the throes of a divorce . . . And the presence among us of a young person, innocent and full of hope, will of necessity drive the conversation up to its most inane level — weather and politics, with perhaps a few movies thrown in by way of cultural spice. A mistake, Sean, thinks Katie, to have invited this Chloe to join us tonight — or a mistake, Hal, to have married her and brought her here — for now the women will grow catty and self-critical, while the men will fall over themselves in an effort to impress and delight the girl — oh, let her not come, please God, let their lateness mean their child is ill — no no, never wish for children to be ill; then let it mean that some emergency has come up, Chloe's father is dying and they had to jump on a plane for Vancouver — no no, never wish for parents to die; but you get the idea, God, do what You can to prevent that girl from entering this room.

"It's nearly seven," says Rachel without consulting her watch. "Maybe we should start without them?"

"Yes," giggles Patrizia, "or the turkey will be overdone. The breasts *and* the legs." (No one else giggles, as no one else is aware of the *Joy of Cooking* conundrum.)

Just then headlights glance in the driveway and a horn blares out: *TA, ta-ta TA-TA– TA-TA.*

"That's Hal!" says Katie.

"That must be them," says Charles, half to himself. He's steeling his nerves, anguished at the perspective of seeing a baby this evening, with his own children so far away, changing without him, growing up without him, *you bastard* — whereas he'd sworn he would not be like his own father, forever absent, traveling, busy, working for the Cause, writing speeches for the King, "Please don't go away again Daddy, please play with me, please Daddy" — every day with Randall and Ralph precious, irreplaceable, his continual awareness of that, the tentative questions murmured at bedtime, "Daddy, did *you* used to be afraid of the dark when you were little?" and the laughter around the breakfast table, tiny Toni feeding her stuffed dolphin with her baby bottle, and the problems that arose suddenly, seeming insurmountable, then just as suddenly dissolving — you miss a day, you've missed it — it's gone, gone.

Sean gets to his feet, the world slides to the right, he puts out a hand to grip the back of Leonid's armchair and steady it, make it stop moving, glances at the whiskey bottle, about three-fifths empty, not too bad, I opened it at two P.M. and have been sharing it, I've seen worse, much worse — "Shhh!" he says. "Patchouli, shut up, will you? That's no way to welcome our new friend Chloe. You'll scare the wits out of her, barking like that!"

Everyone laughs. A burst of relief at the silence being broken, the evening being carried on to its next stage.

As he crosses the kitchen — not staggering, not tripping, not bumping into chairs, not yet, no, quite proud, on the contrary, of the relatively straight line he's walking — Sean glimpses Patrizia's vegetable knife lying on the counter where she left it. Wiped clean. Shining. Scalpel. They'll cut through the skin on his side, the doctor had told him. They'll slice a long arc through his flesh, severing the intercostal muscles and prying the ribs apart so as to expose the pleura, then excising the affected lobe of his left lung. Or perhaps the entire lung. "It all depends. We'll need to do more tests. The first thing is, stop smoking, Mr. Farrell. Stop smoking, can you do that much for yourself? Stop smoking." As he walks past the counter, Sean picks up the knife and slips it between his teeth, pirate fashion. Biting into the handle and grinning dementedly, he steps out onto the porch to welcome the latecomers.

It has begun to snow. The first stinging clear-cut flakes are drifting through the porch lamp's shaft of yellow light. And this is what Chloe sees — as, her baby cradled in her arms, swaddled against the cold, she moves up the walk to meet her new husband's friends for Thanksgiving dinner — a madman; a slightly bent personage with a gleaming knife blade between his teeth. Is this a joke or what, Hal? Is this the kind of humor your friends appreciate? She stops dead in her tracks.

"Is that Sean?" she whispers under her breath.

"Yeah."

"How 'bout if we just go home?"

As it was, she'd been apprehensive about coming. As it was, she'd dreaded being introduced to these people who were familiar with Hal's foibles and had met the whole string of his other girlfriends. She'd braced herself to face their condescension, their superciliousness, their politely concealed smirks: "So here's number Twenty-One" . . . but this . . . no, this she *hadn't* expected. She's on the point of turning back, heading for the car — but Hal is laughing raucously and giving Sean a bear hug, crushing the smaller man to his chest, saying in a low pleading voice between plosions of laughter — "Hey man, put that thing away, are you fuckin' crazy or something? What are you, pissed out of your mind before dinner? Come on, Sean, straighten up, I want Chloe to *like* you, man, it's *important* to me," talking fast and low, then laughing again, loudly, then turning, making a broad gesture with one arm to draw his wife and child up the porch steps — "Don't be afraid, Chloe, it's just a joke, come on" — and Chloe at last, reluctantly, eyes lowered, mounting the steps with the baby in her arms — his wife and child! The ineffable beauty of

the pair! Hal is so proud he fairly shouts out the introductions —
"Sean, this is Chloe! And this is our son, Hal Junior!"

"My most humble apologies." Switching from pirate to prince
mode, Sean gallantly grasps Chloe's right hand with both of his and
bends to press his lips to it. "I don't know what came over me."

"Did you cut yourself with the knife or what?" says Chloe confusedly, noticing his bandaged thumb.

"Oh, that . . . no, no, no," says Sean, embarrassed, angry with himself for his move, which is clearly connected to the cancer but also,
more obscurely, to Phil Green his first stepfather, the man his
mother had married when Sean was eleven and who'd always found
ways to spoil occasions like birthdays and Christmas — either by
insulting Sean's mother with obscenities or by whacking Sean across
the head with the flat of his hand, even once whipping out a gun and
announcing his intention of blowing out everyone's brains including
his own. Where are you now, Phil Green? thinks Sean as he presses
his lips to the soft scented flesh of Chloe's right hand. Rotting on
Death Row in some Texas jail, I sincerely hope. "Please come in," he
says, looking at Chloe so insistently that she's forced to raise her
eyes, and relents. "Everyone is impatient to make your acquaintance
— partly because you're Hal's wife and partly because they're getting
very hungry."

Hal has the feeling he's lived through this moment before. Not
with another woman, with Chloe. The removal of coats and hats and
scarves in Sean's hallway, the catch in his throat at the sight of his
wife's delicate beauty, the way her deep red calf-length dress clings
to her slender body and parts at the throat, so that her throat is a
graceful cream-colored corolla rising from the bloodred flower of
her body and culminating in a golden crown of short wispy hair, the
way her uncertain eyes lock with his, then plunge into the soft folds
of the baby's blankets in her arms — he's lived through all of this
before, the impression renews itself infuriatingly, second by second,
until they reach the living room. Then it vanishes.

The child is awakened by the flood of warmth, odors, voices — it makes a startled sound and stirs in its mother's arms. Pushing aside the blankets, Chloe reveals its large white head. The adults move in close, smiling and nodding at Hal and Chloe, vying for a glimpse of the little one. Hal Junior glances around and, recognizing nothing, freezes; his long-lashed eyes widen in amazement. He turns to his mother — true north — gets his bearings, then turns again to stare at the rest of the world. His mouth drops open in such a quintessential expression of bewilderment that the adults burst out laughing. This harsh ruckus causes him to turn convulsively back to his mother and bury his face in her chest, which sets off a fresh wave of laughter, which causes him to burst into a wail.

He looks human the way a chimpanzee looks human, thinks Sean as he leads the little family upstairs to the spare bedroom, where Theresa the cleaning lady set up a makeshift bed for him that morning.

You forget, thinks Patrizia. Even if you think you remember, you forget what it's like to actually hold a baby, hug and feed and love a little baby of your own. There's nothing like it in all the world. (She herself had suffered at the hands of a distraught, overworked mother. She'd been the youngest child, the afterthought, and her mother — already exhausted by her own eight, not to mention the children she took in to make ends meet — never had time for her. No time, no room, no patience, the house a bedlam. Luckily, her *nonna* lived with them and Patrizia was her favorite. It was at her grandmother's side that she'd learned to cook meticulously, with generosity and . . . "What's the most important ingredient in every recipe?" "Salt?" "No, love! *L'amore* . . . ," how to mince onions and parsley and garlic using a *mezzaluna,* how to grasp the true meaning of Christ's parables: "When love is present, *always* there is enough to eat. It's love that multiplies the loaves and the fishes, *capito?*" how to tell a swallow from a sparrow: "*Venite, venite bellissimi, mangiate!*" and a hibiscus from a hyacinth: "*Ma si,* you can talk to the flowers, too, the good Lord made them beautiful just like you!" It was through her *nonna,* born in Agrigente, Sicily, that Patrizia had dreamed the land of her ancestors — little church *piazze,* ancient temples ideal for playing hide-and-seek, puppet shows, dry scorching heat, olive trees and cicadas . . . Finally, it was thanks to her *nonna* that she'd acquired a passion for the opera, and the habit of turning on Puccini or Verdi full blast when she did the housework, singing along with La Callas at the top of her lungs as she vacuumed one room after the other . . . She sang to her sons as well — old Sicilian tunes — sure, she yelled at them but she sang to them, too; they had the works, the whole gamut of mammas from good fairy to evil witch — and if they didn't like it, too bad, *è così* — but oh, how wonderfully you spoiled me, darling *nonna!*)

Katie, too, is looking at the child in his mother's arms with something that resembles longing. What an unsurpassable sexual experience giving birth had been! All four times, the moment of expelling the child suffused with orgasmic strength-joy — *there* — a *human being* — coming out of *me* — strong enough to do *that!* — and the sense of perfect peace and serenity in the ensuing days because you'd done something so incredible — and the shock of leaving the hospital, staring at the swarming human throngs in the streets of Manhattan and thinking good Lord, each and every one of these people was once . . . BORN!

Tiny Toni, thinks Charles, is one hell of a lot prettier than this chalky bald dwarf. Oh the silkysoftness of her lightbrown skin and darkbrown curls. ("Black may be beautiful," Myrna had said to him once, when their son Ralph was but twelve months old, "but nothing can beat *café au lait.*" "Black on white," Charles had said, moving onto her and entering her, loving her, fucking her with gusto, "Black on white," he'd breathed into her face — and she'd laughed, licking his throat and knotting her legs behind his back, for this was already the title of his book.)

At that age they're still okay, thinks Leonid, but then they hit the terrible twos and start drinking your turpentine and chewing on your paintbrushes and trying to imitate your creativity by smearing blue paint all over the living room couch. Boy, am I glad to be out of *that* period. (This morning he'd called Selma, one of his twin daughters from his first marriage — and, hearing the sounds of toddler chaos in the background, been catapulted back into those years when he was a young father struggling to be a painter in Lower Manhattan, unable to afford a studio, inviting artists better established than himself to see his work in hopes of somehow connecting through them to a gallery, serving them coffee in his studio corner of the living room and being distracted from their talk of modern art by the need to prevent Selma and Melissa from upsetting the coffee cups, banging their heads on a corner of the table or getting their grubby hands into the sugar bowl. "Those who display contempt for material existence will be condemned to drown in it," Birgitta his then-wife had told him — was it a quote from somewhere or had she made it up herself? — and over the years he's resigned himself to the fact that he must indeed *not* have been a true artist, that he hadn't had the ruthlessness, the single-mindedness, the cruel egotism that being an artist required; the family's claims on his energy had always seemed more important, more valid than his own. Now it was his daughter Selma who, seven times in the course of their five-minute phone call — he'd counted — had been summoned to deal with tiny emergencies — "He pulled my hair!" "Look out!" "Don't do that!" "She peed on the floor!" "Hey, don't touch that!" — wailing, banging — "How many times do I have to tell you?" "Can't you sit still for *three seconds?*")

"Who's going to carve the turkey?" he says now, rising at last from his armchair, anticipating then feeling then recovering from the burning flash of pain in his lumbar region, after having ascertained that Katie was in the kitchen and wouldn't see his face contort, his hand move up involuntarily to support his lower back.

Patrizia lights candles — recalling how, as an adolescent, she used to steal votive candles from the cathedral and then, alone in her bedroom, test her ability to endure pain by dripping melted wax onto the naked skin of her breasts and stomach.

And the feast is carried in; the feast foods are carefully, lovingly laid out on the table. Cornucopia! Horn of plenty! *Corn* and *horn* are the same word, thinks Sean, returning momentarily to his earlier speculations about the horns of the dilemma, a cornet is a kind of horn but a hornet is not a kind of corn, and moreover to be horny is definitely not the same thing as to be corny . . .

All of them are seated now, all twelve of them around the table, taking in the glistening brown glazed skin of the bird that spurts juices when pricked with a fork, the green salads dotted with garlic croutons — no danger here, thinks Leonid, as he watches Katie toss one of the salads, American lettuce is safe to eat. In the United States, thinks Katie, it's all right to eat lettuce and tomatoes and cucumber, we don't need to worry about thyroid cancer, or giving birth to a baby who resembles a bag, completely sealed, with no apertures. Hal is now wielding a knife (not Patrizia's vegetable knife but an electric carving knife, purchased for Sean's thirtieth birthday by his mother Maisie through a mail-order catalog and never once used until tonight), dexterously severing the string that was holding the bird's legs together, splaying them wide then sawing them off, drawing out great spoonfuls of dressing in which the bird's body juices have brought all the other ingredients into harmony, bread crumbs and onions, celery and giblets, liver and walnuts and spices. The glass cranberry molds sparkle with rubysweet promise; Sean has opened three bottles of the excellent French wine brought by Charles — and there's more of it in the kitchen, much more; Aron's rye bread and Patrizia's corn bread have been sliced and stacked in baskets along with crusty caraway-seed rolls; bowls full of brightly colored vegetables are being passed around, succotash and brussels sprouts, yams sweetened with maple syrup and mashed potatoes gilded with butter — oh my God thinks Beth, bursting with pleasure and alarm, do we really need all this food, is there no end to it? — and there are relishes, chutneys, condiments, tiny dishes of pickled beets and cucumbers, there's wild rice shot through with toasted slivered almonds, there's salt, there's pepper.

"What did we bring?" Chloe whispers to Hal, having gathered that this is to some extent a potluck meal; and Hal replies, squeezing her red velvet knee beneath the table, "We brought youth, sweetheart. We brought beauty." Chloe looks down in embarrassment and at once her brain begins to wend its way through the paisley patterns on the tablecloth — just as, at the age of five or six, in the Vancouver coffee shops where her mother occasionally got waitressing jobs, she used to love retracing in black ink the patterns of shells and curlicues embossed in subtle white-on-white relief on the paper napkins. Go into it, she thinks now, meandering amid the swirling reds and oranges and greens of the cotton print. Get lost in it, she thinks. Never come out.

Seated between Aron and Derek, Rachel feels a twinge of pain at the base of her skull and thinks: Oh no not that, not a migraine this evening, please spare me, God; she sees Aron draw a small silver box from his pocket and discreetly extract a selection of three or four little pills; this reminds Derek that before embarking on such a heavy meal he should protect his sensitive stomach lining by taking some calcium; several other guests surreptitiously swallow their respective medications. Good thing Prozac is a morning pill, thinks Rachel. Sean had always hated the word Prozac, "a combination of prosaic and Muzak" — and he'd hated the idea of her taking it, too. "How do I know if I'm relating to you or to your Prozac?" he'd yelled at her once. "Well, how do I know if I'm relating to you or your Scotch?" she'd yelled back. "You've got a point there," Sean had said, in an abruptly normal tone of voice. "Maybe the real question is, *can your Prozac relate to my Scotch?*" Now she meets her former lover's eyes across the table and raises her glass to him in a silent toast. He's smoking a cigarette, allowing Patrizia who is at his left to heap food on his plate as he smokes and drinks and looks around intently at his guests and admires the slimness of Patrizia's thighs, even when not crossed.

Funny, thinks Sean, looking around the table, when you're in your twenties you've got a set of friends you think will be your friends forever — but in fact they won't be, in fact there's virtually no one in the room today left over from the set of yesteryear, things just keep shifting and sliding and slipping away, you win a few and you lose a few but mostly you lose and lose . . .

What kind of a meal do Boston prison inmates get on Thanksgiving? wonders Brian. What's Jord having for supper tonight? No, what *did* he have, it's seven-thirty, he probably finished eating long since . . .

Then Katie gets to her feet. Face crimson. Menopause, excitement, shyness, all at once.

Poor white people, thinks Charles. Their skin makes them open books.

"I just — I know we're not all of us believers," she says, "and even if we were, we wouldn't have the same God. But I wanted — well, you know, I thought it was so great we'd be getting together tonight, I wrote this little, this, sort of grace, you don't mind? Don't kill me, Sean."

Aron turns up his hearing aid.

"Hi, God," Katie begins. "We've come here to give thanks. Well You might ask what we have left to be thankful for. True, it's been a rough haul. We weep to see how imperfect You've made us. We haven't been able to figure out much of anything. Your flock has scattered every which way and our brains are fairly scattered too, to say nothing of our souls. Yet here we are. Not only that, but whether You happen to be around or not, love will be here, too."

"Thank you, Katie, that was a nice grace," says Aron. "Thanksgiving is the only all-American holiday because whatever their religion, everybody in this country loves to eat."

"Though it can hardly be said that the turkey is our totem,"

Derek points out. "Its demise and consumption don't constitute a sacrifice for us. We have no special feelings about turkeys, no myths and legends in which turkeys play a major role."

"We just think their flesh tastes good," says Charles, "and we shoot it full of hormones to make it taste even better."

"True," says Hal sententiously. "The Turkey is to the people of the United States of America neither what the Lamb was to the people of Israel nor what the Cow is to the people of India."

"Nor even," puts in Rachel, "what the Frog is to the people of France."

"Maybe it means something to the people of Turkey?" says Patrizia facetiously.

"The word does come from there," says Sean.

"No!" says Beth.

"Yeh, it used to refer to a sort of guinea fowl imported through Turkey."

"Where did you get that?" says Rachel.

"From the dictionary."

"I hadn't finished," says Katie.

"Shut up, you guys," says Leonid.

"Well anyway, God, what I wanted to say was — if You can — bless us. Bless this food. Bless our lives as they stretch behind us and before us. And while You're at it, bless the whole shebang."

"I'll drink to that," says Leonid.

"Amen," says Patrizia, and "Amen" say one or two of the others in mild obedient echo.

VII

DEREK

It's nice of them to include me in their thoughts from time to time, even if they tend to make me in their own image. They think I love them, for example. What a misunderstanding! What could a feeling like love possibly mean to an omnipotent, omniscient being like me? Love can arise only where there are gaps, losses, lacks, weaknesses, myopia. To tell you the truth, love was an unplanned by-product of the human species. It seems obvious now, in retrospect, but for some reason it didn't occur to me at the time — if you make physically and psychically imperfect creatures, they'll tend to reach out to one another. They'll have an unquenchable thirst for wholeness, an ineradicable hope of completing one another. Only humans (and a few animals tamed by humans) know how to love. Maybe that's what gives me the uncanny impression that they're free — that something, somehow, is being *exchanged* among them independently of me, this thing called love . . . I can feel it in their eyes . . . the contact of their skins . . . the incoherent jumble of their words . . . Even if it's nothing but a chemical reaction, reproducible under laboratory conditions, I find it thrilling to watch it happen and bask in the illusion that something, at least, escapes my control.

Anyway. Like Charles, Derek will be lucky. He'll have no idea what hit him. He'd be stunned were someone to inform him that he's got a mere five years to go.

That spring, he decides to take a jaunt down to Manhattan to see his daughters Marina and Angela, and help the latter celebrate her son Gabriel's second birthday. The toddler's father happens to be married to a woman by whom he has five legimate offspring, so to him Gabriel is an unfortunate accident, a shameful secret, virtually a ghost. He spends only two or three days a month with him — and even then, for fear of being discovered and denounced, he never takes him out to play in parks or zoos. Derek, on the other hand, thinks Gabriel is the most wonderful thing in the world. He's mad about his grandson. Spoils him silly. Can't get enough of him. Whether it's because his own father Sidney was away from dawn to dusk supervising the manufacture and sale of flimsy women's dresses, so that he never got to know him until it was too late, or because Derek himself never had a son, his love for this child is so overpowering that it shames him somewhat and he tries to conceal it as best he can, which is not well at all.

Today, after spending most of the afternoon shopping for a birthday present, he finally stumbles upon a life-sized Big Bird in the toy department of Macy's and decides to splurge on it (Angela had told him Gabriel was crazy about her old *Sesame Street* tapes). The bright yellow, six-foot-tall stuffed animal costs more than four hundred dollars and turns out to be unwrappable; Derek knows Angela will berate him for bringing something so extravagantly large and visible into the cramped quarters of her apartment in Union Square; but he also knows that Gabriel's mouth will drop open in thrilled disbelief when his TV friend materializes before his eyes.

He takes the R-train at 34th Street, his mind a tangle of conflicting emotions including embarrassment and anticipation, dread and love. He opted for the subway after calculating that at this time of day (five P.M.) the sight of a gray-haired philosophy professor waltzing down Broadway with Big Bird would cause roughly fifteen thousand heads to turn, whereas in a moving train the figure would be considerably lower. He shouldn't have cared so much what people would think. He's been living out in the sticks for too long; he should have remembered that New Yorkers are inured to eccentricity and pride themselves on not batting an eyelash even when faced with major displays of madness.

Now it just so happens (as the saying goes, though of course I had all these events planned out long in advance, arranged and integrated into my scheme of things, so that what, seen close up, may appear to humans as an imperfection actually turns out, with sufficient distance, to have been an essential detail of my universe) that in the fifth car of the R-train on this balmy spring afternoon, there's a shoot-out between a couple of rival pimps. They keep bobbing up and down, taking aim at each other around Derek who, like all the other passengers, is reading the *Times* and pretending that nothing is going on.

And it just so happens (as the saying goes) that Derek's heart finds itself right smack on the trajectory of one of the bullets as it travels from the gun of Pimp No. 1 toward the head of Pimp No. 2 — a tiny Puerto Rican, barely five foot five. "No!" "Oh my God!" "Oh God!" "No, no!" "I don't believe it!" "Jesus Christ!" Such are the cries emitted by some of the passengers as the train screams to a halt at Union Square, the doors slide open, and the pimps melt into the rush-hour throng, leaving Derek — whose soul is already waltzing down the Milky Way in my direction — to spout great gouts of hot heart blood all over Big Bird's soft synthetic yellow fur.

VIII

First Helpings

Throats are cleared, bowls are passed, smiles exchanged, wine-glasses filled, knives and forks picked up and aimed; the eating commences.

"That was a nice grace, Katie," says Patrizia. Maybe I should start going to church again, she thinks. I miss the stained-glass windows that throw color on the walls, the flickering candle flames that pass our thoughts on to the dead, the singing at the top of your lungs, the heavenly little midmorning snack, and being able to daydream while the preacher drones away. I mean, why should you be deprived of church just because you doubt there's Anyone up there?

"Terrific turkey," says Hal, sinking his incisors deeply into the soft flesh of the bird's left leg. "Delectable." He notes with relief that the flesh is tender, because he acquired three false teeth last week — two on the left and one on the right side of his mouth — and is leery of eating anything stringy or tough. Chloe doesn't even know about the teeth; he can remove, clean and reinsert them when she's not around. No reason for her to see my dentures, he thinks, remembering to his annoyance the joke about the aging couple — Gee honey, says the wife when they go to bed one night, it's been so long since we made love, you used to bite me, you used to be all wild and passionate! Leave me alone, the guy says, I'm tired. Come on, honey, please, the wife says. Oh, all right, the guy says, heaving a sigh. Hand me my teeth! "Delectable," repeats Hal, having polished off the piece of leg and now reaching across the table to stab a slice of back, wishing he could forget the goddamn joke.

Compliments are murmured. "Wonderful succotash." "Great bread, Aron." "This cranberry sauce is heavenly." Mandibles chomp, taste buds jubilate, tongues dart, epiglottises flap, esophagi flex their muscles involuntarily. Beth is making a conscious effort not to gobble down her turkey but to chew each mouthful slowly and thoroughly, the way she learned to do at Weight Watchers years ago. Aron is merely picking absently at the contents of his plate. Sean isn't eating much either. He rises often, surreptitiously refilling people's glasses as soon as they're half empty. Wants to push . . . this evening . . . somewhere . . .

Once their first, most urgent hunger has been appeased (in fact more gustatory curiosity than real hunger), people begin casting about for a subject of conversation.

"That's one beautiful little boy you guys have got there," says Patrizia.

"Thanks," says Hal, wolfing down a forkful of brussels sprouts.

"Hm! So you get all the credit?" says Beth.

"So you're from Vancouver, are you?" Brian asks Chloe.

"How old is he?" asks Beth.

"I lived in Vancouver, actually, for almost a year," says Brian.

"Eleven months," says Chloe to Beth.

"Nice city," says Brian. "Beautiful scenery. Rained a lot, though. Bunch of us went up there in '71 to get away from Uncle Sam."

"Uh-huh," says Chloe.

"Bastards nabbed me anyhow — on *Christmas Day*, believe it or not! I'd just gone down to L.A. to spend the day with my folks."

"Brian," says Beth. "She doesn't know what you're talking about. She wasn't even born."

"Oh my God, that's right. You weren't born yet. Did you ever hear of the Vietnam War?"

"Uh-huh. Sure, I heard of it," says Chloe, and she isn't lying, though she'd be hard put to distinguish between the Tet Offensive and Pearl Harbor.

"Were you a student out there?" Rachel asks Chloe, searching for the common ground they might be able to tread with this vapid-eyed childmother, who probably blossomed into pregnancy the minute Hal so much as looked at her. Unfair that some women can conceive so effortlessly, whereas Rachel's own womb has remained obstinately babyless despite years of careful timing, temperature charts and hormone injections . . . Three years ago, she and Derek renounced taking the in vitro leap: she was forty-two by then and the expectant mothers in the gynecologists' waiting rooms had begun to stare at her in perplexity, deciding she must have come in with premenopausal complaints. ("What's with your new wife?" Derek's mother Violet had asked him once when Rachel was within hearing distance in the next room. "I was sure she'd give you a son, at last a son, I'm dying for a grandson, the years are passing . . ." "It wasn't written into our marriage contract, Mother.")

"More yams, Aron?" she adds in a low voice.

"I beg your pardon?"

"A little more sweet potato?"

"Oh! Oh no, no, thank you."

"Nah," says Chloe. "I didn't even finish high school." Not gonna pretend, she thinks. Either Hal loves me or he doesn't. Not gonna lie my way through the evening, through our whole life here. Too bad if he's ashamed. No I did *not* happen to be working on a master's degree when I met Professor Hetherington. Though I did occasion-ally specialize in mastery . . .

(Chloe's mother had been a free woman of the 1970s — too free, too woman, not enough mother; she'd had two babies in quick suc-cession by two different fathers, a boy and a girl, Colin and Chloe, without ever really believing in either of them. It was Vancouver, it was poverty, a dismal little place on East Hastings Street, the sort of place in which it's hard to even imagine what to hope for. The children had grown up with the sense that their house was a toy house, one cardboard box set askew on top of another and teetering and tottering there, the cheap disparate furniture in the living room never managing to create the sense that it was actually meant for *living* . . . Drugs and an inordinate amount of sex went on in that place — and as if this weren't enough, when Colin was nine and Chloe eight their mother started shacking up with an Ecstasy freak and offering her children's bodies to him for his pleasure. His pleasure, as it turned out, involved — among other things — sophisticated experiments in strangulation. This lasted for several years and did a fair amount of damage to the children's sense of reality. They took refuge in playing cards, cat's cradle, checkers, tic-tac-toe, any sort of game with strict rules and a firm structure to it — and at last, in their early teens, they worked up the nerve to go to the police. This led to their mother's arrest and their placement in foster homes — different ones, on opposite sides of the city, which led to their running away so as to be together again, neglecting school and other social obligations such as coming home for supper, which led to their being nabbed and sent to different homes again, which led their to running away and stealing food from supermarkets and sleeping out on park benches, which led to their being locked up in different institutions for juvenile delinquents. When they were released at last, aged eighteen and seventeen respectively, they set up housekeeping together and started selling their bodies on the streets.)

"I wasn't teaching out there," says Hal, coming to her rescue with a loud laugh. "I just met her, that's all. I saw her walking down Homer Street and I threw myself at her feet and begged her to trample me."

"Hal," says Chloe, frowning, disliking the metaphor.

(Homer Street was generally worked by gays — but being androgynous in appearance, Colin and Chloe sometimes enjoyed switching roles like twins in a Shakespeare comedy and telling each other how they'd boggled the minds and bodies of their customers when they came home in the morning for breakfast. This — their shared words and laughter — was the thin layer of humanity that protected them from the raw violence of their daily lives. Despite the discouragement Chloe felt as she learned the monotonous alphabet of human perversity, in particular the incredible amount of pain otherwise normal human males were prepared to inflict or endure merely to relieve themselves of a teaspoonful of semen, it was a period she would later look back upon as happy — because she and Colin were together, and in control of their fates. Then Colin was stabbed to death by a client who'd lost track of what was fantasy and what wasn't, and Chloe found herself alone. The comforting buffer of her brother's words and laughter was replaced first by whiskey, then by cocaine. At twenty-one she was well on her way to becoming an addict when Hal Hetherington, wandering around the city ostensibly to research his novel on the gold rush, caught sight of her slim boybody and fell for it, hard. As usual, his impulse after paying for her flesh was to save her soul by asking her to marry him, come home with him and settle down into a normal family life — but to his astonishment, Chloe, unlike the many other androgynous hookers to whom he'd offered similar sinecures over the years, had said yes.)

"Homer Street!" says Hal. "Can you believe that? American novelist meets love of his life on Homer Street!"

"Don't go jumping to poetic conclusions," says Rachel. "It's probably some Randolph Homer who invented salmon canning back in 1862."

"So what do you do, Beth?" asks Charles from across the table.

"I'm a surgeon," says Beth. "A generalist."

"Oh, really? That must be . . ."

"Actually I work nights at Welham Hospital. Emergencies."

"Wow," says Charles. "That must be . . ." (He's suddenly in an ambulance in downtown Chicago, the previous summer, with his mother in a diabetic coma, his hands freezing, his forehead dripping with sweat as the ambulance dodges and swerves its way through midtown traffic, "Hang on, Mama, we'll get you there, don't leave me Mama, hang on." He remembers how clear-cut every car and building had appeared to him in that instant, how ineffably lovely the colors of people's summer clothes, how moving the message of each individual face he glimpsed from the ambulance — *life, life* — impressions pouring into his heart, crowding and jostling there, merging into one other, filling his eyes and brain to overflowing, until they reached the emergency room.)

"Yeah, you must see some pretty hair-raising stuff," says Derek. (He recalls the bedlam that had reigned at Saint Luke's Hospital in Manhattan the night he went there after breaking his baby finger in a silly student brawl in the Columbia University dormitory. Since people were called up according to the seriousness of their problem, he'd waited half the night. Young black men would rush in bleeding profusely from the head, or be brought in, supported by their friends, with half an arm shot off; there were old ladies doubled over in pain, old men gasping on stretchers, children feverish and glassy-eyed in the arms of their anguished parents . . . "Guess I'll just go home and put a splint on my own finger," Derek had decided at four in the morning, unable to take it anymore.)

"Yes, I do," says Beth, but she's so busy chewing a mouthful of turkey dressing that Brian has chipped in before she can go any farther.

"Actually there aren't that many violent crimes in Welham," he says. "But last week a couple of old farmers got into a tiff, one of them picked up a pitchfork and wham! Right through the other guy's head."

"Ugh!" says Katie.

"The guy was DOA," Beth manages to put in, "but we did an x ray anyhow; it's mandatory."

"It was amazing," Brian goes on. "The pitchfork was literally buried in the guy's head. The four prongs went right through his brain from back to front."

"I found the x ray really moving," says Beth in a soft voice.

"Oh, yeah, the dental work," says Brian, spoiling her story.

"That's the other thing that shows up on x rays," says Beth, swallowing an unchewed mouthful of dressing and giving Brian an angry dig in the ribs. "He'd had seven or eight of his teeth filled, you know? I mean, he'd lavished a certain amount of care on his body. He'd spent a considerable sum of money. He wanted his teeth to last him a long time. And then one day — one insult too many . . ."

"Anybody read the new Philip Roth?" says Hal, uncomfortable with the subject of teeth.

"Reminds me of a guy I defended once," says Brian.

"Oh, Brian, don't tell that knife story again," says Beth. "Everybody's heard it already."

"I haven't heard it," says Charles, made hypsersentive to anything that resembles uppitiness in women by his recent phone battle with Myrna. "What's the knife story, Brian?"

"Do the short version then," sighs Beth.

So Brian tells the story of one of his clients, a traveling salesman into whose skull an irate customer had plunged a knife — vertically, from fontanel to chin. Miraculously, the blade had passed between the two cerebral hemispheres and the man had survived with a slight stammer as the only sequela. He'd taken his assailant to court for the stammer, though — because, wanting glibness of tongue, he could no longer ply his trade.

Everybody laughs except Chloe, who rises abruptly and leaves the table. They hear her rapid step ascending the staircase.

"Did I say something?" asks Brian, his right ear ringing more insistently than usual, as it always does when he's embarrassed.

"She probably just wants to check on the kid," says Hal.

Chloe has never told Hal about her brother, so he can't imagine why knives should be so upsetting to her. She hasn't told him about her attachment to cocaine, either, so it doesn't occur to him she might be doing a line in the upstairs bathroom. There's a great deal she has not told Hal, and will never tell Hal, or anyone, about her past.

"Haven't heard a peep out of him," says Patrizia.

"Maybe she's squeamish," says Rachel.

"Yeah," says Derek. "You never know, knives and pitchforks in brains might not be everybody's idea of a perfect Thanksgiving dinner conversation."

"Right," says Brian. "Sorry about that." (Yes, they should change the subject. He longs to fill his mind with something other than the files that clutter his desk and shelves, the dreary repetitive tales of breaking and entering, infringing and striking, battering and raping and dealing — oh God the smoke the coke the guns and the continual obscenity, the lean unhealthy bodies, shifty eyes, nervous hands, resentful voices, metal bars, judge's mallet, "Ladies and gentlemen of the jury" — and his own efforts to explain, reason, stave off chaos, contain the pain, prevent property and body boundaries from being crossed — this is you and yours, this is not, don't touch don't penetrate don't stab don't steal — but the pain always welled up and flowed over anyway, taboos were transgressed, barriers stoven in, hymens perforated, brains clubbed, locks picked, windows smashed to smithereens . . . Just this morning he'd been in forensics down at Roxbury, staring at a Harley-Davidson sweatshirt, stained and still moist with heart blood, a bullet hole plumb through the eagle's head on the back, the victim was sixteen years old and the perpetrator, Brian's client, seventeen. THE LEGEND LIVES ON, proclaimed the sweatshirt, yes the legend undeniably lived on but the kid was dead and Brian was not allowed to weep for him, you've got no choice but to joke about these things, it's the only way to survive, just as you joke about the framed series of blood spatter patterns that decorate the hallway in forensics, saying they remind you of Monet's *Water Lilies*, or joke with the morgue employees about whether the worms in today's corpses were of the jumping or the crawling variety.)

"You guys are so lucky to have a baby," sighs Beth. "Sometimes I go up to the maternity ward on my coffee break just to see the babies. They make me feel better. You know . . . each and every one of them a total miracle, a total hope . . ."

"Yeh," says Sean. "Amazing, isn't it, the way hope keeps renewing itself? The way people manage to blind themselves to the shape of human destiny — up, then down . . . with the peak at a national average of age three?"

"You just want to live in hell, don't you?" Beth says to Sean with her sweetest smile. "And drag as many of us down with you as you can. Have you ever actually believed in anything?"

"Of course," says Sean. "I believe in dog."

"I know what he means though," says Rachel, coming to Sean's defense. "Some days I can't bear the sight of young people. Especially in groups."

"Don't you think it's because we're jealous?" says Katie.

"No, it isn't that," says Rachel. "It's their . . . arrogance. They're so sure of themselves. Hanging out in bars and coffee shops around town, talking in big brash voices, just dripping with testosterone and ready-made ideas, 'The world is ours' . . . whereas they don't know the first thing about it! There's something frightening about youth." Schopenhauer was right, she goes on in her mind. The idea that life has its own force, its own exigencies. The new comes in like a steam-roller and innocently, gleefully crushes the old. No matter what we think or want, this is the way things have always been and will always be.

"I still think part of the reason we resent youth," says Katie, "is because we haven't got it anymore. It's scary getting old." You didn't get old, Mother, she thinks. You'll be young forever.

"What's scary about it?" says Sean. "All you do is die."

"My son's afraid of aging, too," says Patrizia at the same time.

"Your *son?*" says Charles. "How old is he?"

"Nine."

"He's nine years old and he's afraid of aging?"

"Yeah. Says he doesn't want to enter the two-digit numbers. He's had enough of growing. Wants to stay right where he is."

Brian and Hal burst out laughing.

"I was nine when my da died," says Sean, "and I will allow no one to insult the sensitivity of nine-year-olds."

"He says he can't believe this is his real life," Patrizia goes on. "He says everything he sees breaks his heart, because it reminds him of a former time he saw it, 'when he was happy.' Last summer, he refused to play badminton in August because it reminded him of how much fun he'd had playing badminton in July. 'It isn't happiness anymore,' he said, 'it's a pilgrimage to happiness.' And last week, realizing he was now tall enough to reach the glasses in the kitchen cupboard without the help of a stool, he was devastated. Told me he heard this little voice in his head saying, 'Never again.'"

"Amazing," says Sean. "Edgar Allen Poe didn't realize that until he was thirty-six."

"The other day," says Katie, "I came across a photo of Alice when *she* was nine. Our oldest daughter," she adds, for Charles's benefit. "On her library card or something. There she was — messy hair, braces, laid-back smile — the photo of someone who no longer exists."

I thought it was their son that died, thinks Charles, who has heard only shreds of town gossip concerning the Korotkov tragedy.

(Beth is remembering Vanessa when *she* was little — a red-cheeked, impish, affectionate four-year-old — ah yes she loved me then — unquestioningly, blindly, from the inside — she was still the flesh of my flesh — when did it change? When was the *day* on which your gaze upon my body became negative, disparaging, judgmental? Oh and to think how joyful I was, carrying you, what pleasure my flesh gave me throughout the nine months of pregnancy, loving food guiltlessly because I was eating to feed not myself but you — *you,* darling, to make you thrive — flesh of my flesh — earth mother — and when you were born I was in no hurry to shed the extra pounds because I wanted to be food for you — my breasts were huge and pendent, dripping, swollen tight with milk — I reveled in being there for you, enough for you — remember how you used to giggle and bury your face between my breasts — how old were you then, two, three? dreadful not to remember — we'd go rolling around on the bed together — you'd play with my hair, climb up on my stomach — I'd be a mountain for you, sweetheart — when did it stop ? And *why?* Now your diet is taped to the fridge, a slap in the face every time I want to snack — but I simply *have* to eat when I get home from work — after the tension of the hospital — a fresh form of suffering to be dealt with every few minutes, all night long — patients groaning, hysterical, prostrate — the old lady who came in last night with all the symptoms of intestinal blockage — abdomen puffed up, intense pain and vomiting — but when I asked if she'd passed wind in the course of the day, she burst into tears and was too ashamed to answer — "I've never been so humiliated in my life . . ." Or the ambulance driver at three in the morning — "I thought you said it was a *kid,* I was expecting to pick up a *kid*" — "No," says the guy's wife, "I said a *kidney* problem" — "I coulda sworn you said it was a kid, you just wanted to make me drive faster!" "Why would I tell you it's a kid when it's a kidney?" — almost coming to blows, the two of them, with the poor patient still lying there on the stretcher, waiting to be registered . . . Or the little girl who fell out of a sixth-floor window last summer . . . still alive when they brought her in, but broken, every bone in her body broken, for hours we tried to save her, knowing it was impossible, while her mother banged her head against the glass partition in desperation, over and over and over . . . When we lost her, a pall settled over the place — it was weeks before we could look each other in the eye . . . Oh Vanessa! Night after night I can feel the tension rising in my body, and the only way to defuse it is by making myself a hearty breakfast when I get home — food, food! I can feel the pleasure coursing through my veins, all the suffering being gradually washed away — can't you even *try* to understand?)

"She's a lovely girl," says Aron out of the blue.

"Who?" says Katie with a start.

"Chloe."

"Ever see Hal with a dog?" says Beth.

"No," acknowledges Aron. "But there's something special about Chloe."

"I couldn't agree with you more," says Hal.

"Speaking of dogs," says Leonid to Sean, "should we set our turkey bones aside for Patchouli?"

"We already asked him," says Katie.

"Who's Patchouli?" says Chloe, reentering the room.

"Sean's dog," says Hal. "How's the baby?"

"I didn't see a dog — is there a dog here?" says Chloe, visibly alarmed.

"Oh, Patchouli wouldn't hurt a flea," says Hal, and the others laugh.

"But is he in the house?" says Chloe.

"He's never been known to bite, has he?" Rachel can't resist putting in.

"Not blond women, anyhow," giggles Patrizia.

"Come on, you guys, will you lay off her?" says Beth.

"Pass the succotash, and ENOUGH!" roars Hal, pounding the table with his fist. But as Beth has polished off the succotash, he has to content himself with more sweet potatoes and brussels sprouts.

"So you're writing a novel about the gold rush, are you?" says Leonid. "That must have been a thrilling time to live."

Delighted, talking with his mouth full, Hal launches into a lengthy evocation of the Klondike in the 1890s, while Chloe withdraws into the private perfect world she still shares with her brother Colin.

Look at these old fogeys, Col, she says to herself. What the fuck have I gotten myself into? Well you may ask, well you may ask. Oh, I won't be spending much time with these friends of Hal's, I can tell you that. These are highfalutin folks, Col. High IQs, high salaries, high opinions of themselves. But *we* know. The truth ain't high, it's

low. Ground's where it's at, right? Even better underground — like
you. Just look at that old geezer over there. What's he doing here,
anyway? The others are *old* but he's frankly decrepit. Must be about
a hundred. Never opens his mouth. Empty blue eyes, empty brain.
Nothing goin' on in there. A hundred years on the earth and that's
his conclusion — nothing.

Chloe knows nothing about Sean, so she can't be expected to
understand how he made up his guest list — inviting all his local
friends and acquaintances who might be feeling lonely on this
evening of mandatory festivity. As for Aron's brain, it isn't empty, it's
merely far away.

(Impressed as always by the enormous quantities of food Americans
are capable of ingesting in the course of a single meal, he's suddenly
back in Pretoria on that scorching February afternoon of 1933 when,
scarcely a year and a half after their arrival, they'd learned about the
new famine in Ukraine — a famine entirely due to careful Soviet
planning. A first cousin of Aron's father, who'd managed to leave for
the United States after the first wave of pogroms in 1905, had
returned briefly to Odessa for his mother's funeral and been overwhelmed by what he'd seen. Aron was eighteen at the time, and he's
never forgotten the shock of seeing his father slumped sobbing over
his cousin's letter. As a baker he'd had regular dealings with wheat
farmers, and though the full extent of the tragedy wouldn't be known
until much later the effects were already there, palpable and horrific
— the Soviet regime had requisitioned virtually all the year's wheat
harvest; hundreds of thousands of peasants had been slaughtered or
deported to the east on the pretext that they were wealthy "kulaks" —
and now, to punish Ukraine for its nationalist deviationism, its lack
of enthusiasm for the communist regime, its reluctance to cooperate
with forced collectivization, six million Ukrainians would be allowed
— no, encouraged — no, helped, to starve to death, *yes, six million,
yes, to death* — ah, thinks Aron, but no one cares about *those* six million dead; virtually no one even knows about them; were I to walk

over to Sean's bookshelf, take down the encyclopedia and look up the word Ukraine, chances are they would not even be mentioned. After that day, the Zabotinskys had abandoned the Russian language, even in the home; the language that had symbolized culture and poetry to the Jews of Odessa was the language in which Ukraine had been humiliated and starved. In South Africa, Aron's mother had stopped reciting Pushkin and Akhmatova to her son. She had shed her lovely romantic poetic Jewish girl skin and emerged an aggressive white capitalist and a Zionist. Pragmatic, positivistic English had wedged itself between them, replacing Russian with its dark associations of intimacy and mystery . . .)

Rachel isn't listening to Hal either because she's never been keen on his novels and doubts she'll be reading this one when it appears. (Look at the way all of us are hardening and drying up, she muses. Sclerosis and skeletons — same word — *skeletos, sklêros* — dry hard things! And why is it so often *sadness* that comes to the surface in the faces of older people when they're not smiling or talking, not intent on expressing anything in particular? Sadness and defeat. A letter to the young. A warning. The way Leo's eyelids droop, his mouth turned down in two deep folds that reach almost to the jowls. Katie's knit brow. Worse than knit, crocheted, a permanent frown etched between her eyes. My own worry creases, crisscrossing every which way. Derek's forehead, furrowed as if from decades of unmitigated anguish. Aron's air of absence — almost dumb, almost imbecilic when he's not "looking" at what he's seeing. None of us is very attractive. Well, apart from Chloe — but she doesn't count, she's only attractive because she's young. Perhaps no one is truly attractive, in the final analysis. Perhaps human beauty is neither more nor less than a hormonal illusion useful to the perpetuation of the species. What would *true* beauty be, Plato?)

And Katie, as usual, as always, is being dragged back to the second day of August 1998, the day on which she'd realized that her life was about to change. And then it had changed. Forever. (David's phone

had been ringing obstinately, maddeningly busy for three days, causing Leonid and Katie to wonder, then worry, lose sleep, grind their
teeth, finally ring up the operator in desperation — "What's *wrong?*"
"I'm sorry, he must have left the phone off the hook, there's nothing I
can do." . . . . Katie: "Shouldn't we drive into town?" Leonid:
"He asked us to leave him alone." . . . . Leonid: "Maybe we
should drive into town?" Katie: "He *told* us to leave him alone." David
had been their youngest, the baby of the family until Sylvia came along
six years later, an afterthought. The photo albums showed a grinning,
good-natured, roly-poly little boy — until when? *Until when?* Where
had they gone wrong? Katie's grief gives her endless food for thought
on the subject, and all the food it serves is saprogenic; every shred of
memory can be fished out and studied anew from a different angle;
even the most luminous images can be tainted by doubt and suspicion
— wasn't there just a hint of mold, a whiff of putrefaction — wasn't it
already starting to turn blue? . . . On the verge of completing his doctorate in musicology, David had dropped out of the Berkley College of
Music and gotten strung out on heroin, holed away in a cruddy little
room on Power Street across from the roaring traffic of General
Pulaski Skyway. "Can't we help you?" "The only way you can help is by
letting me live my own life." "Isn't there anything we can do to help
you?" "I'll never grow up if you're helping me all the time." Where had
they taken a wrong turn? How had the first seeds of self-hatred and
self-destructiveness been planted in their son's brain?)

"Couldn't you have learned all that without going to Vancouver?"
asks Beth.

"What do you mean?" says Hal, disgruntled at being shot down
in full flight of eloquence.

"I dunno," says Beth. "Libraries, the Internet . . ."

"No," says Sean sharply. "There will be none of that. Not in my
home, thank you very much. Not this evening."

"Oh, come on, Sean," says Beth. "I hope you're not going to give
us your Luddite spiel again . . ."

"No. I'm simply going to request that people refrain from pronouncing that word tonight."

"Ah," says Beth. "And would you kindly enlighten us as to which other words you have deemed taboo?"

"I would suggest," says Sean after a hesitation, pushing his plate away and lighting a cigarette with badly shaking hands, "that each of us say now, at the evening's outset, which word they'd like to have excluded from the conversation. Think about it."

The silence startles Aron.

"What is it? What is it?" he asks, looking around.

". . . A word you'd prefer not to hear," Rachel tells him, leaning close and speaking directly into his ear.

"No, no, I can hear all right," says Aron, turning up his hearing aid.

"One word each," says Sean. "Katie?"

He's counting on Katie to stand by him, humor him, play along with him; and she does.

"Clones," she says. "No clones or cloning tonight, okay?"

"Right! " says Sean. "Leo?"

"Nuclear," says Leonid. "I'd prefer. If we can avoid it."

"All right!" says Sean. "No Internet, no clones, no nuclear. What else? Patrizia?"

"Cancer."

"Except as an astrological sign . . . Brian?"

"Palestine," says Brian, provoking a shout of laughter.

"If we censor Palestine," says Aron, catching on, "we'll have to censor Israel as well."

"Absolutely!" says Sean, draining his wineglass, enjoying the turn things are taking. "And you, Charles?"

"Perhaps we could try omitting all references to divorce?"

"Ohhh wow, that's a tough one," says Brian who, as always when he drinks, is laughing and sweating a great deal — glasses steaming up, nose and pate deep red with laughter. "Maybe we could call it . . . the D-word? Your turn, Beth," he adds, placatingly.

"You, too, have the right to declare a word off-limits for the night."

"This is ridiculous," says Beth, folding her arms across her ample chest and blushing, disliking the role she's always forced to play in Sean's company — moralizing, virtuous, judgmental — whereas that's not at all the person she feels she is, deep down.

"Come on," pleads Brian. "It's just a game."

"Well then . . . calories!"

Another shout of laughter.

"Woody Allen!" says Rachel.

"Saddam Hussein!" says Derek.

"Viagra!" says Hal — and several of them approve, applaud. "What about you, Chloe? " he asks, turning tenderly to his young wife. "Anything you don't feel like talking about?"

"Yes," says Chloe.

"What's that?" says Patrizia.

"Alfalfa," says Chloe with a defiant little half smile that endears her to Sean instantly and forever. (*Alfalfa* is a word she learned from one of her clients. She always asked them what line of work they were in, to make them think she was interested in them as individuals, it was better, quicker that way, and they invariably invented some prestigious job or other, getting hard by lying to her, thinking she believed they were wealthy doctors or lawyers or businessmen, but this one had told her he was an alfalfa farmer — he couldn't have made *that* up! — and since she'd smoked several joints that afternoon the word had made her shriek with laughter, "Alfalfafarmer alfalfafarmer," she'd stuttered, tucking his wad of ten-dollar bills into her bag — and luckily, instead of taking offense, the man had joined in her mirth, then informed her that the alfalfa plant had beautiful purple flowers, and that he owned enormous fields of it in the neighboring province of Alberta, acres of tiny purple flowers stretching as far as the eye could see, and this vision of soft mauve limitlessness had plunged Chloe into an unaccustomed sensation of peace.)

RACHEL

What will become of Rachel? Well, as a general rule, normal people tend to get depressed as they age, and depressed people tend to get more depressed. Rachel is no exception to the rule.

In grief, in mourning since birth for her Zykloned uncles and aunts, for all the Jews of Europe, and for the children she'd been unable to concieve — and then for Sean Farrell, whom she'd loved more than anyone in the world — and then for Derek, whom she'd not only loved but married, Rachel will, against her will, live to be extremely old. And the amazing thing is that she'll go on being an exceptional philosophy professor to the bitter end. Firing her students with her enthusiasm. Awakening their thirst for understanding — then slaking it somewhat — then making them realize how parched they still are. Bringing to green and vibrant life not only the dialogues of Plato, many of which she knows virtually by heart, but even the more arid thoughtscapes of Kant, Hegel, Leibniz. Her students worship her. They thank her. They dedicate their books and theses to her. They hold her in their hearts as a model of kindness and lucidity. Sixty-five comes and goes and no one even dreams of suggesting she retire. She's not merely a pillar of the department, she's virtually a national monument. Her mind stays sharp and her tongue limber; her gallows humor survives the decades unimpaired. At eighty-three she is still lecturing and her lecture halls are still packed.

There's another reason for which, despite her longing to do so, Rachel renounces rushing headlong into the ever-waiting, ever-welcoming arms of death. A double reason — Angela and Marina,

Lin and Derek's daughters. She feels that with their father dead and their mother as good as dead (out of touch these twenty, thirty, forty years), the girls have been orphaned enough as it is. They need her. Marina, especially, needs her. This, reflects Rachel, is one of the pleasant surprises in life — people actually do love and need one another. At sixty, Marina is more passionately attached than ever to her eloquent, illusionless, octogenarian stepmother. They meet in Manhattan once or twice a month for a drink, a meal, a film, a play, a ballet, an art exhibit . . .

The day I come to pluck Rachel, however, she is at home. Quite alone in the big old house purchased by Lin and Derek back in the 1970s, shortly after they were married. Rachel has seen the house undergo numerous transformations. Lin danced in its attic for years. Angela and Marina grew up there. Lin departed; Rachel moved in. Then Angela left, and then Marina. Then Derek died, and a memorial service was held for him in the big old house. Now Rachel has been living there by herself for ages. And now she is about to die there.

She's run herself a bath. Carefully, she hoists her thin knobby aged body over the edge of the tub. Recalls, for some reason, the bath Lin gave her many years ago, following her single serious attempt to end her life (she'd just realized that trying to fit her neuroses around Sean's might not be the shortest path to happiness) — ah, how soothing the warm water had felt that day, as the hands of her dearest friend sponged it over her skin caked with vomit and excrement . . . And now, all these years later — destabilized, perhaps, by this ancient memory that has flashed into her mind unbidden — she slips. Bangs her head on the cold-water tap. Faints from the pain. Sinks beneath the soapy scented surface of the water.

That's the end of Rachel's soul. The adventures of her body are not quite over, however. She's got a kindly next door neighbor named Sarah who, though, considerably younger than Rachel herself, only midseventies or thereabouts, is sliding swiftly down

Alzheimer's Slope. That evening, Sarah comes over with a letter for Rachel that was mistakenly delivered to her address. Knocks on the door, no answer, sees the lights are on, knocks harder, calls out, no answer, tries the door, finds it open — "Rachel? Rachel?" — checks out the different rooms — "Rachel?" — finally opens the bathroom door, sees the corpse in the bathtub, gasps in horror, rushes home, forgets what happened by the time she gets there. "Hey," says her husband, "why didn't you give Rachel her letter?" "Oh, yeah," says Sarah, blushing, flustered, aware and ashamed of the tricks her memory now likes to play on her. She turns around, goes back to Rachel's house, finds the front door open, walks in, sees the dead body in the bathtub, shrieks in horror, rushes home, still with the letter in her hand. "Don't tell me you forgot to deliver it again," says her husband with a tolerant smile, and so on, back and forth, half a dozen times — Sean and Rachel would probably have split their sides laughing, had they been around to watch.

Time Passes

The punch and wine are beginning to take effect, people are relaxing, their auras are spreading slowly around them and overlapping. Sean is proud of his own degree of inebriety — exactly right, the way he likes it, an inner heat, steadily fed throughout the afternoon, steadily fed, fedily stead, as even as peat fire, not the bloody furnaces they've got over here, hey Ma, that keep on breaking down right bang in the middle of winter, when out of doors all is raging freezing blizzard wind and ice, you never did get used to these cruel New England winters, did you Ma . . .

"That's a real snowstorm out there," says Chloe, as if she were sitting in Sean's mind reading his thoughts. "It's snowing cats and dogs."

"You can't say snowing cats and dogs," Hal corrects her gently. "It almost never snows in Vancouver," he explains to the others. "You could say it's snowing . . . I don't know . . . Moby Dicks, maybe . . . Or baby seals . . ."

But Chloe has stopped listening. (The cocaine is floating her back and back, she's in Vancouver again, 1996. A perfect June day. Colin is still alive. He's twenty, she's nineteen and they're living together in that time of their lives she'll later look back upon as the happy time. On this day as on many days, they sleep on their respective foldout couches until three in the afternoon. Awakening, they rise and shower — Chloe first, then Colin — to purify their bodies. Dress in white: she a simple summer shift, he an Indian shirt and baggy cotton pants. Bring out the expensive exciting white powder they save for special occasions. Bend to inhale it through their nostrils

— Chloe first, then Colin — to purify their minds. Now they're wholly immaculate, twin Indian gods. Standing face to face, they take each other's hands and stare into each other's eyes as their strength and purity gradually rise and intensify. Their hands begin to move. Slowly, softly, they slide up each other's arms, then over each other's necks, faces, chests. Sensation — all night long shoved down into the deepest recesses of their bodies for protection — rises to the surface and overflows their pores like molten gold. They are gods, twin gods, divinely stroking each other's hips, each other's backs. A mere grazing of the lips sparks off swoon, ecstasy, orgasm. The tongue is unbelievable in its wetness and sweetness. Their limbs stretched taut yet weightless, their brains flooded with light, they circle one another in a twining, twirling cocaine dance, two young gods in love and alone in the world, and the drug fills their hearts with a bright white tremolo melody, one pure shimmering note after the other, and their hands are pure as they free one another of their clothing, and the bobbing of Colin's member against Chloe's stomach is pure and the way he lifts his younger sister in his arms and lays her on his bed is pure and when, slowly, gravely, he moves onto her and into her, what locks their shining eyes together is the purest and the most innocent of loves.)

I won't I won't, thinks Beth. I will not be the one to ask him to put out his cigarette. I'm his guest, I've accepted his hospitality, he makes the rules in his own house . . . but he knows I suffer from asthma and emphysema, knows I hate the stink and choke of smoke, knows it spoils my appetite, I won't say it, he'd only joke about the favor he's doing me, spoiling my appetite, we've been through that number before, also the one about the hype the American Cancer Society puts over on us all, telling us that the health damage done by cigarettes costs the country billions of dollars a year — as if not smoking guaranteed you an inexpensive death! says Sean. As if non-smokers didn't die at all, didn't cost the country a red cent! (Jord smokes two packs a day, probably more when he's in jail, oh Jordan

my baby boy, my shiny-eyed child, my romping curly-haired toddler
— *what happened to you?*)

"I thought of you last week, Hal," says Rachel. "I took a late-night
shuttle to La Guardia, and the guy next to me was writing. Great big
guy, baseball cap, T-shirt, blue jeans, can of Coke. He kept madly
scribbling on a yellow legal pad, flipping over page after page and
heaving these terrible sighs . . . Never have I seen anyone write so
with such intensity — I tried to see what it was, but he kept hiding
it from me. Every time I'd lean forward to rummage in the seat
pocket and sort of slide my eyes over to the left, he'd shield his pad
with his big beefy arm so that I couldn't see a thing. After a while it
started getting on my nerves."

"Yeah," says Hal. "What business was it of his if you felt like
sticking your nose into his affairs?"

Sean and Brian laugh, but Derek is ill at ease. This scene in the
plane reminds him of something, that fateful flight to Wisconsin,
eight months ago. (He'd agreed to give a talk in Madison, at a colloquium on "The Epicurean Ideal in the Postmodern World." This
would have been fine except that his father Sidney was in the hospital just then, about to undergo a triple bypass operation. "It
should go smoothly," the surgeon had told Derek. "There's no reason to worry." "How can you leave your father alone at a time like
this?" his mother had shrieked. "And leave *me* to deal with everything, what's more? I've heard of selfishness, but *this* much selfishness, and from my own son — it's beyond me." Preferring to listen
to the doctor, Derek had decided not to cancel his trip. When he'd
gone to visit Sidney in the hospital the day before his departure,
he'd noticed that his hand was bizarrely limp and that his face was
gray, almost green in the ghastly neon light of his room. And yet,
even as he spoke to him in a calm, reassuring tone of voice, he
couldn't stop making up new paragraphs for his talk in Madison —
about the loss of pleasure brought about by the gain of time: "In
contemporary America, communication is instantaneous but it is

meaningless," for instance; or: "No one slaves over hot stoves any-more, but our food is tasteless." "What have we lost? The art of conversation, the art of letter writing, the art of preparing and shar-ing food — in a word, the art of *presence*." "I have to be going now, Dad." "Go ahead, son," Sidney had said, wheezing, averting his watery blue eyes to look out the window — had he been crying? no, there was no reason for him to cry, his eyes had just been watery — so Derek had boarded the plane for Madison, madly typing more notes into his laptop as he flew, notes about the loss of intensity, the loss of real contact, the loss of the acutely appreciative sense of the here and now that is the essence of Epicureanism — modern tech-nology allowing us to function with our minds in one place and our bodies in another so that we grow increasingly oblivious to the neighborhoods we drive through, the people we rush past in the street. Derek's seat companion in the plane, a black-bearded, white-turbaned Sikh in a business suit, had kept glancing over at his com-puter screen, trying to figure out what he was working on. This annoyed Derek no end — as did, at the back of his brain, the gnaw-ing awareness of the contradiction between the content of his lec-ture and the fact that his own father's thorax was being cut open as he wrote it . . . Indeed, he never saw Sidney again. Violet's phone call came the next morning, shortly before he was scheduled to speak, and he realized with sinking heart that he was going to get the worst of both worlds. He'd be allowed neither to have nor to eat his cake, neither give his lecture nor be present at his father's death — oh God! His mother was right *again!*)

"Anyway," says Rachel, "I finally gave up and went back to my book. But then . . . I heard him start to snore. Glancing to my left, I saw that the pad had slipped off his lap and the seat lamp was cast-ing a tiny spotlight on it, so I bent to study it more closely . . ."

"And what was it?" says Patrizia.

"Nothing," says Rachel.

"What do you mean, nothing?"

"Not a human language. Page after page of scrawls, doodles, scribbles — not a single decipherable word."

"And that made you think of me," says Hal. "I'm touched."

"Are you getting used to life in these parts, Charles?" asks Derek — just as Charles had feared he might, a couple of hours ago in the kitchen. "The locals aren't exactly famous for their hospitality."

"Oh, I had a fine example of their hospitality the other day," answers Charles. "I was in my kitchen — my sink's right in front of the window, like Sean's here — so there I am, doing the dishes, when all of a sudden I look up and see my next-door neighbor rushing up the walk toward me."

(Patrizia thinks of her own kitchen windowsill, lined with pots of growing things, flowers and herbs and even, in the summertime, cherry tomatoes — the kitchens of intellectuals are so dreary! Sean's fridge, ever since Jody left . . . there's nothing in it. And not a single bird feeder in his backyard . . .)

"She's this frizzy-haired blonde," Charles goes on. "Thirtyish; always in a tizzy, forever yelling at her son to practice the piano . . . Anyway here she is, headed straight for me, so I look down and pretend to be absorbed in coaxing the garlic out of the garlic crusher with a toothpick, but she raps on the window so I've got no choice but to open it — 'Excuse me,' she says."

Charles's perfect imitation of a Boston yuppie accent provokes hoots of laughter.

"'Excuse me, hi, I'm Maggie. I live next door.' 'Yes?' 'Well, you know, my mother always told me to welcome new neighbors with muffins, and I just realized you've already been here six months and I still haven't gotten around to baking muffins for you . . . Well anyway, that's all I wanted to tell you — please consider yourself muffined!'"

"Oh, TERRIFIC!" shouts Hal. "Do you mind if I use that in my novel?"

"Are you sure they had muffins up in the Klondike?" says Beth drily.

"Ah yes, time passes," says Leonid, with his faint but ineradicable

Slavic accent. "You want to make muffins, the days tick by, and all of a sudden it's too late to make muffins."

"I could be your grandfather," says Aron suddenly, turning to Chloe with a smile. "Do you realize that?"

"You could be my great-grandfather," says Chloe, accurately. "But you're not."

"No indeed I'm not," says Aron, wondering what it is about this girl that he finds so irresistible. Does she perhaps remind him of a woman he once knew or saw in the movies, but who, but no, no one, that must be it, he has *never* seen so fresh and pure a girl, pure as the driven snow, was that Shakespeare, fresher even than her own infant — he represses an impulse to reach past the fat belly of Chloe's husband and caress her smooth left hand as it rests swanlike on the table, poised and alert, a ruby glittering on her thin ring finger — but she'd surely snatch it away, revulsed by the contact of my scaly yellow parchment skin — no more skin-love for us, the elderly, no more stroking and caressing ... Might it be that she reminds me of my own mother? (Also blond and long-necked, back then, yes, in Odessa, before the exodus. That other world. The lilac scent of her as she sat on the bed next to me, her graceful shadow-hands clenched into wolf jaws or flittering as crows' wings in the shaky light of the oil lamp on my wall, while beyond the windows of our basement rooms, in the streets of Odessa, throughout the country, civil war raged. Such upheaval, such fear and confusion, so many questions squeezed out over lumps in my throat: "What's happening, Papa?" "Well, there are six different armies operating on Ukrainian territory," Aron's father had told him — and, all these decades later, he can still spell off the enemy armies on his fingers: the Ukrainians, the Bolsheviks, the Whites, the Entente, the Poles, and the Anarchists. "Each of them hates all of the others," his father went on, rolling out the dough, rolling out the dough, "but they all agree on one thing, namely that it's indispensable to slaughter all the Jews." "But *why?*" That question had never made it around the lump.)

"Besides, my grandfather committed suicide," Chloe adds, for the benefit of no one in particular.

"How dreadful." says Beth, a hundred images of successful and unsuccessful suicides in the emergency room crowding into her brain at the same time: blue faces, slashed wrists, bloated stomachs . . . "How awful."

"No. I mean for me it wasn't dreadful, 'cause I never even met him. It was just a story my mom used to tell. A pretty good story. He got depressed about being old and not having done anything with his life, so one day he decided to hang himself in the garage. But the funny thing was, he left a bunch of notes around the house saying how this thing worked and how that thing worked — he even stuck a note on the windshield of his car, saying watch out for the brake, it tends to stick."

"That was sweet of him," says Rachel under her breath, wondering if *she* will have the foresight, in her final moment of despair, to leave a note on the kitchen stove: *Right front burner on the blink.* (Rachel has never felt she had the right to walk the earth. The main problem, as she'd once confided to a psychiatrist, was that she was born. As far back as she could remember, this had been the message tacitly conveyed to her by her parents in Brooklyn: how dare she be born, when so many more worthy than she had died? You should have been a boy should have been a boy should have been a boy, how dare you not have masculine attributes — a prepuceless penis, forelocks and a yarmulke? And if you couldn't have been a boy, at the very least you could have *had* a boy — or two, or three, four boys, to replenish our decimated race — but no, not even *that* — totally useless! A superfluous human being! Not a man, and not a real woman either! A pseudo-man! Getting herself a bunch of fancy diplomas! Running around spouting Greek philosophy — as if God hadn't handed down His truth to *us*, once and for all. An "educated woman" — ha! No wonder you couldn't have babies! See what happens? Too much gray matter, not enough estrogen! Got what you deserved!

Wives are meant to be submissive to their husbands, their lords and masters, not discuss philosophy with them over the breakfast table! O those fine male minds steeped in study and tradition — the uncles and grandfathers, the knowledge and learning, the centuries-old beauty of scholarship, the endless commentary on the Book, the nodding, gray-haired, white-bearded heads, the wise eyes and wizened hands — reduced to ashes, to air! And *she,* a mere dark-haired girl baby, had the gumption and the presumption to *live?* Personally, Rachel feels nothing but animus for these God-fearing women-fearing life-fearing men, maniacally obsessed with the body, rules about food, sexual intercourse and personal cleanliness . . . but, being scrupulously honest, she can't help acknowledging the extent to which she resembles them.)

Boy, this is getting morbid, thinks Charles, rising to fetch three more bottles of red wine from the kitchen. November is the dying month, the month of decline and darkness. He resents having been forced to board the suicide train of thought, which always hurtles him straight back to the death of his brother Martin — also in November, how many years ago, fifteen already, I was twenty-five and Martin barely twenty, just a kid for Chrissake, he'd have had plenty of time to mend his ways, little nervous jivy punk Martin, named for the King and incapable of staying out of jail two months in a row, forever getting into stupid trouble, stealing cars (maybe Charles should have helped him escape from jail after he stole that car, maybe everything would have turned out differently), dealing dope, Martin the family disgrace, filthying the family name, source of shame to his father the speechwriter, the freedom fighter, making a mockery of his father's eloquence by raving about crime being legal in a country founded on genocide and slavery — and when, after getting himself mixed up in yet another pointless break-in, Martin had heard the cops pounding up the stairs to the apartment he and Charles were sharing on Sedgwick Street (chosen by Charles for its convenience to the Chicago campus of Northwestern where he was finishing his doctorate in Comparative Literature), he'd reached for his gun and put it in his mouth and pulled the trigger, sending his brains splattering all over the kitchen walls, and afterward, once the police had registered the suicide and removed the body to the morgue, it had been Charles's job to wash down the walls. "Alas, Yorick," he'd been unable to prevent himself from thinking as he sponged up cerebellum from between tiles, "Where be your gibes now? your gambols? your songs?" Which bit of brain had contained his brother's childhood memories, which his imperfect mastery of spelling, and which his existential despair?

When Charles returns to set the new bottles of wine on the table, Leonid is in the middle of a story. Everyone is listening attentively — even Katie, who knows her husband's repertory backward and forward but never tires of hearing it.

". . . the municipal swimming pool in Minsk," says Leonid. "At age fifteen I hardly knew how to swim, but there was this girl. What a girl. Valentina her name was. Valentina Sagalovitch. The light of my life. How can I tell you. A girl like this: nice blond hair, nice tan, very nice breasts in a red bathing suit, nice everything, and always she was surrounded by the big guys, the eighteen-year-olds, the MEN. They'd be there every day, making her giggle with their fat biceps and their deep voices, and I'd be sitting about ten yards away with my scrawny hairless chest, my skinny legs, my shaky squeaky voice, I couldn't even get close to her. It made me just DIE, the way she'd toss back her blond hair and adjust the straps of her red bathing suit and flutter her eyelashes at those musclemen and simper. Valentina, Valentina Sagalovitch. I dreamed about her at night, I dreamed she came into my bedroom in her red bathing suit and kissed me softly, softly, on the lips . . ."

"'And?" says Patrizia.

"Well," says Leonid. "So. In keeping with its bad habits, time passed. Lots and lots of time. And then . . . last month we had some plumbing problem and I called in a plumber. He comes in, he does the work, and on the letterhead of the bill I see — my heart jumps even before my brain has time to read it — Sagalovitch. 'Sagalovitch,' I say. 'Are you Mr. Sagalovitch?' 'Yeah, why?' 'Well, because . . . oh, it's silly . . . when I was a kid, back in Minsk . . .' 'What? You're from Minsk?' And so on and so forth, until we fall into each other's arms. Believe it or not, this guy is Valentina's *brother*. 'Whatever became of Valentina?' I ask him. 'How is she?' 'Oh, she came over, too,' he says. 'She's doing fine! Married to an American. If you like, I give you her phone number.' 'Sure,' I say. 'Why not?' Then I think about it. What do I look like? More to the point, what does my blond, red-bathing-suit Valentina look like? It's not five or ten years, it's *fifty-three* years have gone by. This is ridiculous. But I can't help it. I'm thinking about her day and night. I'm back at the pool in Minsk, listening to her giggle with the musclemen. Katie gets mad at me for not paying attention when she reads me her poems. So I call Valentina."

A rather lengthy pause ensues.

"So I call," repeats Leonid, heaving a sigh. "Of course she doesn't remember me, she never knew I existed. But she's glad to hear the language. 'I've got four children,' she tells me. 'What else is new?' I say. 'I've got six.' 'I've even got grandchildren,' she tells me. 'Sure,' I say. 'Me too. So let's make a date.'"

"Mistake," says Charles.

"Damn right," says Leonid.

"Always a mistake to visit the past," says Charles, without quite knowing how he knows this; no specific examples come to mind.

"So?" says Patrizia, thinking how unpleasant it has already become to run into friends who haven't seen her in two or three years. "What did she look like?"

"How shall I put it?" says Leonid. "Next to Valentina Sagalovitch — forgive me, Beth — Beth is Twiggy. Valentina, she weighs maybe four hundred and fifty pounds. She overflows everything. The only part of her that's not obese? Her eyes. They're not obese but they're crossed. Back in Minsk I never got close enough to see them. I don't know if they were crossed already or if they got crossed in the crossing . . . I mean, what can I say? I myself am no Leonardo DiCaprio, I'm not even Clint Eastwood, but . . . what can I say?"

"So what *did* you say?" asks Charles, feeling this story has gone on long enough.

"I forget," says Leonid. "I think I just gave her a box of chocolates and got out of there as fast as I could."

"And the moral of the story?" says Sean. "Listen closely, my dear Chloe: you must never grow old." He gazes at her with all the tenderness, admiration and charm of which he is still capable.

Chloe meets his gaze and instantly looks down at her plate. He doesn't know shit about me, she thinks, apart from the fact that I'm his best friend's wife, yet he thinks he can flirt with me. I hate his cynical toad eyes squinting at me through the haze of cigarette smoke, studying me, sizing me up . . .

Och, thinks Sean, won't be seducing this one. Doesn't happen the way it used to . . . Staring Lin into submission that evening over at Derek's twenty years ago — making love to her across the dinner table — and, later, in the kitchen, possessing her utterly by simply grazing her cheek with my finger while she was making coffee. She was mine to do with as I liked, though I never once removed her clothes. You can bring off that sort of thing when you're young, sure of your ability to knock 'em out and catch 'em as they fall — no more. Even Jody had to be persuaded, wooed and won, wouldn't spread her thighs until she'd read my poems, wouldn't marry me until she'd read my will, that's what happens when you start losing your hair and getting soft around the gut, you're obliged to make up for it in human kindness, prove your optimistic, constructive nature. As long as you've got your hair, a little sadism is acceptable, a drop of nihilism goes over very well. Lucky Hal. Who knows how long this new idyll of his will last, but who cares, what matters is that he's recently had the experience of touching and holding the body of a new woman and knowing he'd soon be making love to her. How long since a new lover and I ran along a beach hand in hand, tossing our cares to the wind, kissing madly, tearing off our clothes, rushing naked into the waves, throwing body against body? (Sean has actually never indulged in this sort of behavior, but he wishes to make his point.) It's all gotten so feckin' careful. You've got to be careful about AIDS, careful about pregnancy and careful above all about your partner's pleasure, women no longer want to simply soar off to cloud nine with you, they want you to take a six-week course in clitoral stimulation, and by the time you've done your homework and are ready for the exam, they've decided they can do just as well with another woman. (This has never happened to Sean either, but he enjoys the rhetorical effect.) Lucky Hal, lucky Hal to have found so simple and sweet a girl to wife.

XI

HAL

So far, I feel, I have been fairly magnanimous with this group of people. Most of them I've managed to pluck without their even noticing. The family triangle comprising Hal, Chloe and Hal Junior, however, will have rather a rougher time of it, I'm afraid.

Hal Senior, scarcely two weeks after the Thanksgiving dinner — a stroke. No, I won't take him yet. He's got some stock taking to do. (It may be appropriate at this point to mention that his real name is Sam, not Hal; he chose Hal when he determined to become a writer, convinced that there was a quasi-magical power in alliterative names — to wit, Walt Whitman, his idol. And he's right, Hal Hetherington is far catchier than Sam Hetherington, don't you agree?)

He returns from the hospital dizzy and confused. Chloe is shocked. Where is the person she so recently saw as solid, forceful, reassuring — the man she was counting on to protect her from the violence and craziness that had always been her lot? Overnight, her husband has metamorphosed from strong father figure into wheezing old geezer. He's unrecognizable. Unlovable. Scary.

She leaves him. Taking Hal Junior with her, as well as seven large trunks stuffed with clothing, furs and jewelry (all acquired since her wedding), she moves to London. She has unlimited access to Hal's fortune, all his bank accounts having been put in their two names and their marriage contract having merged their respective wealths — or rather, his wealth and her poverty.

Hal finds himself alone again. This has happened to him many times before, but never as an ill person. Now, from first dawn blink to last midnight flutter, each day is an unimaginable accumulation of awfulness. The worst is not the panting and the pain, the wooziness and the vertigo; the worst is the strangeness. He's a stranger to himself. Neither his body nor his mind are familiar to him. Not only have his wife and child left him, he's left himself. The person he is now forced to deal with is grumpy and lethargic. Indifferent to nature, poetry and music. He lies in bed wishing for nothing. Periodically, he's jolted to his senses by some pull of another time, another world. Carpe diem, warns his earlier self, in these moments, in anguish. You should be doing something! You should be writing! What's the matter with you? But the new self merely grunts and turns over in bed. His head is filled with weird buzzing sensations, electric twinges of despair and rage more frightening than anything he's ever known.

He lives in slow motion, watching himself stumble around the house, hating his sluggishness, his clumsiness, the obstinate refusal of his body to obey the orders of his mind. Every morning it takes him more than two hours to get through the ritual he used to dispatch with in thirty minutes. Each step of this hitherto smooth and automatic sequence of events — rising, shaving, dressing, having breakfast, clearing the table — is an excruciating labor. I'm like a character in a Beckett novel, he thinks, and it isn't funny in the least. He becomes hopelessly entangled putting on his shirt. Loses his shaving soap. Forgets to put water in the coffeemaker, so that when he turns it on the hot air blows coffee grounds in all directions and it takes him another half hour to clean up the mess. On his knees, sponging up coffee grounds from the linoleum, he starts to sob. Crumples into a heap. Howls as he hasn't howled since he was five years old, when his dog was hit by a speeding truck in front of his eyes.

He goes back to bed and lies there. Why do anything? What for?

Lying there, however, brings on another form of torture. Flotsam and jetsam from the past start bobbing up behind his closed eyelids and he is submerged by an undertow of chaotic memories. It's as if his brain, like his stomach, had forgotten how to digest, so that it now regurgitates every image and impression absorbed over fifty-five years of existence. Interminable Sunday luncheons of roast beef and potatoes up at his grandmother's house in Columbus, followed by stultifying games of Scrabble which he invariably lost. A pair of torn blue jeans he used to love, with a red patch on the left knee, also torn. His mother bursting into his bedroom when he was thirteen and bringing herself up short because he was coming with a groan, unable to stop, then not knowing what to do with the muck on his hand. His mother in curlers at the hardware store cash register, reading a beauty mag. His mother mussing his hair as she kissed him good night, then firmly wiping her lipstick off his cheek with her thumb. The plastic bags filled with uncolored margarine his mother used to buy at the supermarket — it was little Sam's job to press the bright orange button at the center of the bag, causing the dye to spurt out, then kneading the revolting white substance until it was uniformly yellow and looked like butter (indeed they called it butter; in their household the distinction was not between "margarine" and "butter" but between "butter" and "real butter," reserved for special occasions); then he'd snip a triangle off the corner of the bag and squeeze a revolting yellow spiral out onto the plate. A sailing trip out of Sandusky Bay with the wealthy family of one of his schoolmates, each detail of that day stamped as sharply in his memory as the sail's white triangle against the cobalt sky. Useless, all of it, useless for fiction. Playing with his turds in the potty and getting spanked for it by his mother. Driving tent pegs into hard earth, along with the six other adolescents in his group at a Scout camp out at Hocking Hills, blackening his thumbnail with a misplaced blow of the mallet, cringing at the chorus of laughter, detesting this and every other other chore he was required to perform, longing only to hole up in the tent, safe from mosquitoes and camp counselors, and read Evelyn Waugh and Stephen

Crane to his heart's content. Writing his first novel, at night, in Cincinnati, after delivering pizzas all day, soon hallucinating from lack of sleep, incorporating his hallucinatory images into the novel and later, at his agent's insistence, having to excise them . . .

Scenes from his life as a writer, too, come flickering through the jumble. His world travels, his career, his precious fame — in shreds. A bridge leading over a canal to a tiny church in Leiden, the image utterly still and peaceful in the autumn morning mist . . . A flayed sheep, hanging head-down in the Muslim market in Baalbeck, Lebanon, its tail a monstrous triangle of white fat. The lugubrious ballroom of Warsaw's Europejski Hotel in the 1980s, with its neon lighting, live Muzak, phony marble columns, trickling fountains, artificial greenery, dully dressed men and women dancing as slowly and sadly as if World War II had never ended . . . The Saturday-morning boys who so fascinated him in the Marais neighborhood of Paris — carelessly, naturally elegant young men with their cotton shirts tucked into jeans or corduroys and their hair still tousled from sleep, buying newspapers and sitting down to read them on café terraces, ordering coffee and croissants then lighting up Gauloises — God how he'd yearned after those Saturday-morning boys! The Kathakali dancers in Cochin, India, all male, whom he'd once observed in their four-hour daily preparation for a performance as they plastered garish makeup onto their faces, rolled their eyes, twirled their hands, twisted enormous crepe paper skirts round their narrow hips, prayed in time with the tabla and were gradually invested with the presences of male and female gods. Gerhard, the young German poet he'd met at a writer's festival in Barcelona and taken up to his room . . . but his nerve had failed him that time, as it did every time. All the young male students who'd given him aching erections over three decades of teaching, walking into his office for their individual conferences dressed in tight jeans and black writerly T-shirts, speaking to him in earnest about their characters, plots and writer's blocks, their feverish spurts of inspiration as he smiled and nodded his encouragement, controlled his breathing, counseled them about dialogue structure, symbolism and condensation, while imagining them rearing up behind him and perforating his anus to the soul. All the androgynous young prostitutes he'd paid for in cities around the world so as to fantasize they were boys, whereas with boys nothing ever happened . . .

It doesn't help, it doesn't stop or coalesce into anything meaningful; the memory machine simply keeps whirling around and around like a cement mixer, sadistically tossing up blobs of his past, this is your life, this is it and there's nothing you can do about it, you won't get a second chance, this is the sum total of your experience on the Earth — until, all but crying out in anguish, he heaves himself up out of the bed, forcefully drags his mind away from the frightening maelstrom of people and things he has known and lost — back to the present, the *hic et nunc* of his bedroom, the white rectangle of his bed — which he now resolves to make, smoothing the sheets, pulling up the blankets, readjusting the bedspread . . . a task so complex that it takes him over fifteen minutes, at which point he lies down again, exhausted.

Theresa comes in to clean for him twice a week, as she does for seemingly half the population of the town. Friends stop by — Sean, Rachel, Derek, Patrizia, Katie. When they're not around he feels desperately, shamefully lonely — but the minute they arrive fatigue washes over him and he's impatient for them to be gone. They bring him flowers, records, unusual things to eat. They tell him to be patient, "Just be patient, Hal, you'll get better, don't worry."

Hal isn't patient, but he gets better anyway. It takes about a year. He even toys with the idea of going back to teaching, though the university has offered him a retirement plan full of perks and frills. Then he has a second stroke.

And, shortly afterward, a third.

Now he's an invalid. Now he's in a home. The home is filled with other people who look very much the way he does from the outside.

But they're not at all like me on the inside, he tells himself. Most of them spend their time floating in fuzz, eating Jell-O, being wheeled down corridors, sitting openmouthed and apathetic in front of game shows on TV. As they've lost the habit of putting in their dentures, their faces have caved in, making them akin to the bald, hollow-cheeked monsterbirds of Hieronymus Bosch. Hal can't bear to think that all of them were once like himself, bright-eyed and bushy-tailed — and that some of them, despite appearances, might even have their brains intact.

"Hal Hetherington," a nurse says, glancing at his chart. "I dunno why, the name sounds familiar."

"Says here he used to be a novelist," says another nurse, studying his file.

"Oh, a *novelist,* are you?" says the first nurse, bending over him and articulating the words in a loud voice, as if to initiate a retarded Martian into the intricacies of human speech. "Well," she adds — this time as if he couldn't hear her at all, turning toward the other nurse with a wink — "you'll need a lot of imagination to have fun around here, I can tell you that much!"

Hal can hear. He can understand. But he can neither talk nor walk. The humiliation of being treated like an infant or an idiot makes him want to scream, as does the frustration of being unable to obey his own inner orders.

No one in the world can do anything about it.

But I can.

So I do.

XII

Second Helpings

"Which of the two is the *real* Valentina Sagalovitch?" says Leonid, sadly shaking his head.

"I feel the same way about Jordan," Beth blurts out. "I remember when Jord was about two years old, I took him for a walk down by the river and we saw this dead butterfly on the bridge. Believe it or not, there were dozens of butterflies gathered around it — beating their wings and fanning it, as if they were trying to revive it. And Jord was so moved . . . That night at bedtime, he said, 'Death is when you fall on the floor and the light breaks.' Isn't that incredible? Remember, Brian?"

"Yes," breathes Patrizia, sympathizing with Beth and trying (unsuccessfully) to recall what it was that her own son Gino had once said about death.

"I mean, was the beauty of that moment false just because we've come so far away from it?" says Beth. "Or the beauty of Valentina Sagalovitch?"

"Interesting question," says Rachel. "Is there any one point in our lives at which we can say: we are now, fully, ourselves? Or to put it another way, is how we evolve the *truth* of who we are?"

"Yes — *is criminality the truth of my son Jordan?*" says Beth, unable to restrain herself, willfully ignoring the way Brian's eyes are drilling into the side of her face, pleading with her oh Beth, please, don't talk about it, let's not wash our dirty linen in public . . . "Is *prison* his truth? Is it *now* that he's the real Jordan, filled with rage, spewing hatred — or was he real *before*, when he saw the dead butterfly, or when his eyes shone to bring me a starfish he'd picked up on the beach?"

I don't get it, thinks Chloe. Must have missed something. What are they talking about? Feel like I'm breathing in water. Water on the brain. Wish I could just slither down and hide under the table, the way Col and I used to do when we were little and the grown-ups would start hitting each other. When you look out at the world through the spray of holes in the lace tablecloth it's not as scary, it gets cut up into these itty-bitty fragments, like when you're dancing in some nightclub with strobes and everybody gets shattered into these jerky blinking bits . . .

"Jordan's your son, I take it?" says Charles. "Excuse me . . . I don't know . . ."

"Yeah, Jordan's our son," says Brian. "Black kid. We adopted him out of a hospital in Roxbury when he was two weeks old. His mother was in tenth grade; she couldn't keep him."

"I don't understand," says Beth, biting her knuckles.

"What don't you understand?" says Charles, keeping his voice low and gentle to contrast with the anger in his words. "You mean, given that you got him young and have exposed him to nothing but your own enlightened liberal values, raising him as if he were your own, you don't understand why he has thus reverted to his evil primitive black nature?"

"No, that's *not* what I mean," says Beth.

"White people shouldn't adopt black kids," says Charles.

"Right," says Hal, raising his glass. "Long live segregation! Blacks and whites should have separate schools! Separate sections in buses! Separate drinking fountains and toilets!"

"Racial hatred doesn't go away just because you make it technically illegal," says Charles, his voice still as mellow as a summer breeze. "Your Jordan gets it in the teeth every day in the outside world, and then he comes home and you expect him to pretend it doesn't exist, pretend he's just like you — can't you see the double bind he's in?"

"I'll have a little more dressing, please," says Leonid.

"Some turkey with that?" says Hal.

"All right — just a sliver."

"Anyone else want some more turkey?"

"Yes . . ." "You bet . . ." "By all means," say the others, and the bowls of vegetables make their second rounds.

"What's he in for?" asks Chloe, interested.

"Oh, nothing much," says Brian. "Just muggings. It's his seventh sentence for mugging in four years. I'm fed up with bailing him out. The first couple of times he was underage so I could look after his defense myself. But now it's out of my hands. He got six months this time. Hopefully it'll teach him a lesson."

"Sure," says Charles, seeing the brains of his younger brother Martin on the kitchen wall and gritting his teeth to block out the vision. "Young black men learn lots of interesting lessons in prison."

"Who does he mug?" asks Chloe.

"Oh, little old ladies, mostly," says Brian. "Real dangerous work. He and a couple of pals surround a little old lady sitting alone on a park bench, shake her up a bit, grab her pocketbook and run off with it. Very intelligent, very courageous. Little old black ladies, little old white ladies, little old Hispanic ladies, whatever. They're not prejudiced."

"Maybe he needs the money?" says Chloe.

"Yeah, right. He needs the money," says Brian, purpling with anger as, once again, the ringing in his ear rises to an unbearable level of stridency. "Because what we give him — rent and a monthly allowance — does not suffice. Jordan has lots of extra expenses. On visiting day last week, I asked him exactly what he needed the money for. You want to know the answer?"

Silence. Katie and Leonid are steeling themselves against the word *heroin*.

(It was Sunday morning, Katie remembers, and David's phone had been ringing busy since Thursday. Over coffee, after a sleepless night, the two of them had looked at each other and decided together, without a word or a nod, to go into town. They had to find out. They couldn't go on like this. They made the two-hour trip to Boston in silence, Leonid at the wheel and Katie staring straight ahead with her hands folded in her lap. As the day was hot and promised to get hotter, they drove with the windows rolled down, and at one point a large fly bumbled into the car and began hurling itself against the windshield — refusing to learn from its first or second or fifteenth failure, stupidly getting its hopes up over and over again — as if, perhaps, the *sixteenth* time the hard glass might give way and allow it to burst through to freedom. The repetitive, intermittent buzz of the ineducable fly was connected in Katie's mind to the busy signal she'd listened to a hundred times over the past three days — not counting the imaginary times, during her rare hours of fitful sleep. They parked the car on Dorchester and walked under the Skyway to Power Street. Climbed three flights of stairs to the top of a rickety, boarded-up building they'd never visited before, and of which their son was apparently the only resident. Already at this point Katie's every step was conscious, deliberate, momentous. Already at this point she was seeing herself from the outside. This day is going to change your life, she was thinking. Something enormous is about to happen and you'll never be the same again. This is a major, major crisis — the sort of event you've always told yourself the small crises were not. Alice's grades in Math — Marty's broken leg — Sylvia's lying and rudeness — your own rejection slips from poetry magazines — squabbling with Leo over the heating bill — don't worry about it, you've always told yourself, these are little things. Not tragedies. Not the end of the world. Today, however, is the real thing. There will be a before and after today. Get ready for it, sweetie.)

"A gold tooth," says Brian. "That's what he needs the money for. That's the sum total of the plans he and his buddies have made for the future. All of them are just dying to knock out one of their incisors and have it replaced with a gold tooth. And a gold tooth costs about thirty-two hundred dollars. So four gold teeth — thirteen grand. Lots of little old ladies."

"More turkey, anyone?" asks Hal again, unable to fathom why the conversation has to keep coming back to the subject of teeth. Can they talk of nothing else? ("All right, hand me my teeth . . .") Although . . . hm, this gives him an idea for his Klondike novel, yeah, not bad, the hero could become a murderer, he could knock off a bunch of other gold diggers, especially if they were old guys, it'd be easy up there in the vast wilderness of ice and snow with no law and order in sight, no witnesses apart from the sled dogs, he could stun them with an ax and leave them there to freeze, pulling their gold teeth with a pair of pliers, knocking the tooth part off and bringing the nuggets in to Dawson City, claiming he'd found them in the river, he could make a fortune that way, yeah, terrific idea, the only problem being the possible sensitivity of Jewish readers, they might take offense at the theme of gold-teeth pulling. Well, they don't have a corner on gold-teeth pulling for the rest of all time, do they? Have to think about it . . .

All demur, insisting they are fine, they are full, no more turkey thank you, they want to leave a little room for dessert. Katie and Patrizia begin stacking dirty plates and silverware, and there is a moment of vague discomfort — where should they go from here? If they ask Beth and Brian about their other child, Vanessa, they'll be expected to ask everyone else about *their* children, too, and risk getting bogged down in lists of grandchildren and studies and jobs, which they'll have forgotten about by morning.

Feeling a searing pain in his duodenum, Derek gulps down a few magnesium silicate and calcium carbonate pills and heads for the bathroom, so as to be able to contort his face uninhibitedly as he waits for the medication to take effect. He locks himself in, grabs the doorknob and screams silently with his head tossed back, mouth and eyes open wide. Even as he suffers, he notices a spot in the corner of the room, near the ceiling, where the wallpaper has been torn away and the hole around the water pipe enlarged, then sloppily refilled with putty — must have been some leakage — a new section of pipe has been put in — this reminds him of his selective vagotomy of six months ago: O brave humans that we are, he thinks, as tears of pain start from his eyes — tapping and scraping, repairing our homes and bodies, doing our best to stave off the encroachments of time — yet the rot marches forth — hair grays, skin wrinkles, rust and dust accumulate, wallpaper tatters and tears, feet grow knobby, wood warps, joints ache . . . After a while the pain subsides; Derek flushes the toilet and returns to the dinner table with a smile firmly established on his face.

"Cigar, anyone?" says Hal, getting to his feet. "Good for digestion. I smuggled six boxes of Havanas out of Canada." Halfway across the living room, he realizes he's quite drunk, and his mind lights on a way to conceal his unsteadiness from Chloe. "Ah, shit! Goddammit, Patchouli!" he says, coming to an abrupt halt in the middle of the rug and removing his left shoe. "For Chrissake, Sean, aren't you ever going to housebreak that damn animal of yours?" He opens the front door and wipes his shoe on the porch mat, causing all to protest as a gust of icy wind blasts across the table.

"Jesus! That's a fuckin' blizzard out there!" says Hal.

"What is this Patchouli thing?" says Chloe angrily.

"I told you," says Hal, sitting down next to her again and nipping, spitting, lighting his cigar. "He's Sean's dog."

"But where is he?"

"He's in a room with everyone else I love," says Sean. "My father, my mother . . ."

"You mean he's dead?" says Chloe.

"No . . . No, he's not dead."

Another silence.

When were the real experiences? thinks Sean. When was it that we were actually *living* our lives, rather than contemplating them as possible material for our writing, or as a dry run, or as a faint echo or a pale photocopy or a stale warmed-up leftover of the Real Thing? What happened to life? Wherever did it go?

"Do you have children, Aron?" asks Patrizia to defuse the tension. "I just realized I don't even know."

"I beg your pardon?"

"Do you have children?"

"Oh yes. Three daughters," says Aron, wondering which of them will exclaim, as countless acquaintances have exclaimed over the years, "Just like King Lear!" — but, their attention distracted by the desserts Katie is ceremoniously bringing in, Rachel's chocolate cake in one uplifted hand and her own pumpkin pie in the other, no one says it and his inner ear misses it — misses it so acutely that he ends up saying it himself, muttering under his breath, "Just like King Lear."

"How old are they?" asks Patrizia, and mentally kicks herself — that's stupid, she thinks; they must be grown up and long gone.

"Sixty, fifty-four and fifty-two," replies Aron compliantly. "And don't go thinking your parental woes will vanish as if by magic the day your children leave home. They last forever. Well . . . for as long as you do. My eldest daughter still costs me sleep at night."

"No!" says Derek. "At age *sixty?*" and mentally kicks himself — that's stupid, he thinks; as if Violet didn't have hypertension because of me . . .

"Yes of course," says Aron. "You keep wondering what you should have done differently. Wishing you could somehow slip in between them and life, take the blows in their stead. Disappointment, disillusionment, divorce . . . but of course you can't."

He tells them this, but he doesn't tell them his daughters were born and raised in South Africa; he'll never tell anyone about that half century of his life, in part because he can't stomach the black-and-white opinions of Americans concerning that country (its white inhabitants invariably being black and its black ones white), but also because he himself prefers to think about his life there as little as possible. (Ensconced all those years in his beautiful white villa with his beautiful white family in the beautiful whites-only neighborhood of the Berea, surrounded by bougainvillea and frangipane, twittering birds and piano music, earning a beautiful white salary for teaching at the beautiful mostly white University of Natal, sending his daughters to the best private schools and eating food prepared for him by the invisible dark hands of the maid . . . As a young man, he'd managed to placate his guilty conscience somewhat by choosing mind over matter — Anthropology over manufacturing — painful lucidity over convenient blindness. Revolting against the blatant materialism of his parents' milieu, then profoundly shocked by the professors who supervised his undergraduate work in Pretoria — quasi-Nazis to whom Social Anthropology meant the obsessional measurement of brain sizes to prove the innate inferiority of "Kaffirs" as compared to whites — he'd left in 1939 for Durban where the university was purported to be more liberal. This was where he'd met Nicole, recently hired by the Modern Languages Department . . . But then . . . well, then . . . they'd purchased the villa, founded a family and been compelled to lead the privileged and protected life that corresponded to their position. Of course they were sick at heart when apartheid became official government policy in 1948, but that same year Nicole found herself pregnant for the third time — and, given the increasing demands of their careers, they decided it was time to hire a "black mother" for their children. After interviewing and rejecting a dozen candidates, they happened upon Currie — a pearl. Both of them took to her at once. So gay, so energetic! She was just Nicole's age, thirty-five, and wore the same size as Nicole in shoes and clothing — an obvious advantage for everyone. Not only that but she, too, was pregnant at the time. The two women got on famously — when Currie brought tea into their bedroom every morning at six, she called Nicole not "Madam" but "Ma*dame*," proud of putting the accent on the second syllable, *à la française*. The system worked; it was so easy, so comfortable to go along with it. Naturally, Aron kept up with current events — barely a year after the new babies were born, for instance, he read in the papers about the violent clashes between Africans and Indians in Cato Manor, just behind the campus — but these events had no impact on his daily life. He was far more interested in the construction of the Memorial Tower Building, which would house a new five-level library. Like their villa, the university was triumphantly perched on the hilltop; it turned its back on the racial strife of Cato Manor and looked down toward the waterfront . . . Thus, the death figures in no way interfered with Aron's daily schedule of reading and teaching. Currie, too, had her daily schedule. She rose at five and spent the day nursing their baby Anna, cooking their food, scrubbing their floors, washing and ironing their clothes, singing songs and telling stories to Sheri and Flore, and long after nightfall she went out to sleep alone in her *kaia*, a tiny room attached to the garage, equipped with a cold shower and a squat-down toilet. She worked more than eighty hours a week and the salary the Zabotinskys paid her was better than the usual one, twenty instead of fifteen rand per month. As the trip from KwaMashu to the Berea took over two hours, on foot and in jam-packed buses, Currie went home on Saturdays and her own children were cared for by their granny. At Christmas, when the sweltering heat on the coast became unbearable, they gave her two weeks off and drove up to Pretoria to vacation in the cooler air of the mountains. All their colleagues lived this way, counting on brave, humming, efficacious black shadows to keep the home fires burning in their absence. It caused no resentment. They truly cared for each other. When Currie lost a nephew in the Sharpeville massacre of 1960, Aron gave her a whole week off to attend the funeral and even contributed a little money to the ceremony . . . He knew how important funerals were to the Zulus. He'd read books on the subject. One year, he'd even taught a course in Zulu Moral Philosophy in the newly created African Studies department . . .)

"Is she divorced?" asks Rachel to be polite.

"Who?"

"Your eldest daughter," says Rachel.

"Ah yes," says Aron. "Just a couple of months ago. It's tough, at her age."

(The girls grew up, moved out, moved away; before he knew it, Sheri, the eldest, was married and gone. Still Currie came and "did" for them, inherited Nicole's old clothes, lovingly coerced Anna into sitting still long enough to eat her meals . . . Never would Aron and Nicole have been so uncouth as to say she was "almost a member of the family!" — she simply *was*. Or so they thought. Then fate had struck. In 1964, improbable as it may seem, both women started displaying the same symptoms — heart palpitations, headaches, swollen lymph glands. Aron drove them to King Edward VIII hospital together, Nicole in the front seat and Currie in the back, and both were diagnosed as having chronic myeloid leukemia. Following this, each was given the medical treatment in keeping with the traditions of her people. Aron knew quite well what that meant, but he did nothing to intervene. He drove Currie — still in the backseat, always in the backseat — home to KwaMashu; it was the first time he'd actually entered a private home in a township and it was a shock to him, the plywood walls, the kitschy knickknacks, the pitiful two-room box-house in which this "member of his family" had lived for all these years. He knew Currie's husband would take her straight to the hut of the *sangoma*, who would give her *thakatha* remedies involving human fingernails and hair. Nicole, meanwhile, was flown back to France and treated to lengthy, expensive chemotherapy in the best Parisian hospital. Six months later, Currie was dead and Nicole had recovered. She remained alive for another full and happy fourteen years — long enough to see Anna become a passionate ANC militant and take part in the Durban strikes of 1973; long enough to enjoy the seven grandchildren born to Sheri and Flore . . .)

"Everybody's divorced nowadays," says Derek, glumly shaking his head.

"Hey!" says Charles irritatedly. "That was my off-word for the evening!"

"Oops! Sorry," say Rachel and Derek, hands flying to lips.

"What do I get to do to punish them?" Charles asks, turning to Sean.

"Er . . . You could tell a story in which Woody Allen makes a film about Saddam Hussein," suggests Sean.

"Forgive me," says Aron. "I started it."

"In Israel," adds Sean.

"You know the joke about the ninety-year-old couple that decided to get a D-word?" says Leonid.

"Oh, I love that joke!" says Katie.

"Their lawyer says, Are you guys sure you know what you're doing? I mean, you've spent your whole life together, is it really worth breaking things up at this late stage of the game? And they say, Listen, we wanted to do it half a century ago and everybody told us to stay together because of the kids. Well, so now all our kids are dead . . ."

There is a fair amount of laughter, Brian's especially raucous, Charles's through gritted teeth.

"That's a frightful joke!" says Beth — remembering how, as a child, she'd secretly dreamed that her father would divorce her mother and marry her.

(Like her own daughter Vanessa, Beth has always been ashamed of her mother. Not for the same reasons, though — it wasn't her body that made Beth cringe but her mind, her Boeotian brain, her crass and uncouth use of language. Beth's father Mark Raymondson had been a physician, and her mother Jessie Skykes was the daughter of a hillbilly pig farmer whom the good doctor had been treating for gout. How had they. . . ? Whenever she'd ventured to ask them about it, her parents had given her answers so evasive as to be meaningless. But somehow, having found themselves alone together in the house one evening — the rest of the family off where? at vespers? — they, the respectable thirty-year-old bachelor physician from Hammondsville and the dirty-haired, all-but-illiterate girl of seventeen, had conceived her. Beth. A fluke. A shameful mistake. But it was 1957, *Roe v. Wade* was years in the future and unwed mothers were a scandal, so Mark Raymondson had done the respectable thing and married Jessie Skykes, purchasing a small house on the outskirts of Huntsville in which to live with her and their future child. The truth was that the physician attached little importance to these facets of life — love, marriage, children . . . All he cared about was medicine — the latest developments in scientific knowledge about germs and genes, nerves and necroses, cancers and colics. From the time she was a toddler, Beth learned that the only way to get her father's attention was to show interest in his work. So by the age of six she could recite from memory the table of chemical elements; at ten she could take apart a complete human skeleton model and put it back together with every bone in place; at fourteen she could hold her own in a discussion of almost any article in the *New England Journal of Medicine.* She loved nothing better than to sit discussing science with her father in his study late into the night, long after her mother had finished the dishes and slumped away to bed. It wasn't that Jessie was not a kind human being — she was, definitely; but she was also stupid. Her body was firm and shapely but she had no idea how to wear clothes, style her hair, use makeup. Her uniform was that shapeless, colorless piece of patterned material known as the housedress. And though she was a peerless cook, she made no effort to prettify her "interior" the way other mothers did. Worst of all, in Beth's eyes, she had no ambition — no wish to improve herself, read books, gain insight into the world. She basically mulched around in the garden all day, grunting and getting red in the face as she drove stakes into the soil, weeded lines of vegetables, chased after chickens to break their necks, then sat on a stool plucking them, red-kneed and splay-legged, an obscenely vacant grin on her face. Beth avoided inviting friends over to her home, knowing how they might snicker if they saw her mother thus displayed. Or if they came into the house and noticed the plastic curtains, the fake-parquet lineoleum, the Formica countertops. She herself, Beth, craved culture. Breeding. Knowledge. Distinction. The world of libraries, universities, research museums and laboratories. Deep down, she could scarcely credit the idea that she was biologically related to her mother — and not the result, like Athena, of some miraculous birth from her father's brain.)

Meanwhile, she sees with a mixture of terror and delight, the dessert plates have come to rest in front of the eaters.

XIII

CHLOE

In London, Chloe will live off the royalties of her dead famous-novelist husband for a few years, then throw in the towel. I pick her thirty-year-old soul up off the sidewalk where her body splatted and take her home with me. She has never really had a home, poor thing. It might seem irresponsible for a mother to leap from the seventeenth-floor window of the luxury hotel in which she was living with her eight-year-old son, leaving the latter to fend for himself in the world. But as you know, Chloe's own life was snapped in two when she was eight, and the human unconscious often takes pleasure in producing this ironic echo effect.

She'd believed that Hal could be a home to her. And Hal's stroke had been the confirmation of her worst fears — that life was nothing but shifting sands, dashed hopes and vicious betrayals, that every place she tried to make into a home would turn out to be a fun house in some nightmare fair, a house in which floors slid and jerked beneath her feet, walls collapsed, doors slammed in her face, hallways turned out to be mirrors and roofs, sieves. She had no choice but to hightail it out of there with her little boy.

But . . . how build a life, even with money, when you have no idea what a life is? Money doesn't suffice. Chloe is no one. She was never allowed to be a child, so she has no idea how to go about being a parent. Living alone with little Hal, instead of mothering him, she discovers what childhood is supposed to be like. As Hal Junior begins to walk, then talk, run, learn, play with squirrels in Hyde Park, squeal in delight at rowboats, puppet shows, kindergarten songs and games . . . she measures the extent of her deprivation. She reels between time planes, losing the already shaky grip she had on reality. And the day comes when, swinging one leg then the other over the railing of their window balcony, she flips out of it altogether.

XIV

Dessert

*A*ron studies the eleven pairs of eyes around him — many of
them behind glasses, almost all of them now lowered. It's definitely a moment of discomfort, though just why they couldn't say;
he senses them casting about — yes, casting their well-strung rods
of thought for fat juicy topics of conversation — fish stories, tall
tales . . . This silence . . . Zulus never wonder what they should talk
about. They chat and chant and sing incessantly, whether they're sitting around drinking beer in the *shebeens* or taking part in political
demonstrations or mourning their dead, words bubble up from their
mouths as naturally as water from a spring. In all my years in
KwaZuluNatal, thinks Aron, I never once witnessed an awkward
silence among blacks. Here, even Charles Jackson has learned to
behave like a white man — learned to weigh his words; and the
white man's words are like stones — precious sometimes, but heavy.

All at once he feels his intestines begin to churn and gurgle — an
annoyingly familiar sensation, these past few years. Excusing himself, he rushes down the hallway to the bathroom, locks the door,
fumbles with his belt — blasted newfangled buckles, what was the
matter with the old ones, good Lord am I going to soil my underwear yet again — gets it undone at last and his pants dropped just
in time.

"Yeah," Hal is saying when Aron returns to the dining room.
"Yeah," he repeats, stubbing out his cigar and forking a hefty wedge
of chocolate cake into his mouth. "I heard about your mother, Sean.
Awfully sorry. It must have been rough at the end."

(Hal had known Maisie well because Sean had called on him on numerous occasions to help her "move." She was always "moving" — not changing houses, but endlessly rearranging furniture within the same house — surely the most overfurnished house on this overfurnished continent, thinks Hal. He'd always wanted to put a Maisie-like character into one of his novels but hasn't done so yet for fear Sean might take offense. Not that he's sure Sean actually *reads* his novels anymore; his comments tend to be enthusiastic but vague — "You've outdone yourself this time, man — *six hundred pages!*" or "Terrific cover illustration, man — where did you find it?" — and Hal is too proud to drill him on his reaction to specific characters or events in the book . . . But seriously, perhaps he could put a Maisie-like person into this Klondike novel, set her way over on the West Coast, make her chunky instead of rail thin, and Sean would chalk the rest up to poetic license, "the rest" being Maisie's madness, now that she's passed away he can be honest and call it that, even coin a term for her peculiar pathology — *accumulomania*, perhaps. Maisie Farrell had lived alone on the ground floor of a modest clapboard house in Somerville and her apartment was so tightly crammed with furniture, boxes, bottles, bags, stacked magazines, clothes, knick-knacks, canned food and junk of every description that there was no room in it for a guest to breathe, let alone sit down. Rail thin, yes, rail thin was the right and only term for Maisie, perhaps it would suffice to put her on the West Coast without making her chunky because rail thin she had *needed* to become in order to slither her way among the TV sets and refrigerators, extra sofas, reclining chairs and washing machines that crowded her sitting-dining-living room. "You could try sticking that over there, honey," she would tell Hal as he balanced a newly purchased futon on his left shoulder. "I hope it's not too heavy, luv?" — always flirtatious and ingratiating in her suggestions, as if the task had been set by him rather than by herself. The woman had scared him, made him clumsy, made him sad. It was a drowning: the total submersion of a human being in material possessions, a proliferating cancer of objects as in Ionesco's *Chairs*. A coupon she'd clipped out to save twenty-nine cents on a bottle of blue cheese salad dressing would be mislaid and an entire morning wasted sifting through drawers looking for it, deciding instead to put the drawers in order, coming across ancient yellowing letters and bills and checking account slips she had no idea what to do with, flipping through store catalogs looking for a new chest of drawers at a special reduced price, waiting on the phone to order it, tapping her foot as prerecorded pop music blared into her ear for half an hour, bewailing all the while the unsorted mail and magazines that had once again — stealthily, underhandedly — piled up on the dining room table while her back was turned. "Why don't you cancel your damn subscriptions?" Hal had longed to roar at her, or "Why don't you just chuck the damn mail into the trash can? It's not called junk mail for nothing!" — but he'd always managed to keep his cool with Sean's mother, reminding himself that it wasn't his problem or even his mother's problem, and that he loved Sean enough to do this for him — sacrifice a few hours of his own boring life to put some order into the still more boring life of Maisie Farrell. Meanwhile, having noticed that lunchtime was fast approaching, Maisie had hung up the phone and was leaning into her humongous refrigerator, opening and closing dozens of covered Tupperware bowls, sniffing at various leftovers for freshness and discarding those that had begun to spoil, until she found the three-day-old tomato soup she wanted, the rest of the afternoon then being spent looking for a special cleaning product to eliminate the scarlet stain the tomato soup had left on her immaculate white slacks. "Would you like a cup of coffee, Hal?" she'd asked him one day when, arriving at eleven in the morning, they'd found her still in her bathrobe and curlers, fussing over what to wear. "I know I've got some in the fridge, it'd be a cinch to heat it up!" "Love a cup!" Hal had exclaimed, spontaneously and truthfully, but Sean had kicked him in the shins. Ah yes, of course, for the task of serving him coffee would entail another mad flowering of choices

— which mug? reheated in the microwave or over the double boiler? with brown sugar or white? now where did I put that cream? I hope it's fresh — so he'd blurted out, "Cold is fine with me, Mrs. Farrell — I love cold coffee, as a matter of fact!" She'd poured him a cup and, bringing the dark brown liquid to his lips — not coffee at all, as it turned out, but beef bouillon, a nauseating surprise at that hour of the day — it had been all he could do not to expectorate it all over her piles of mail. He'd surreptitiously poured it down the sink, hoping he'd chosen the right drain among the numerous possibilities offered by her awesomely complex water purification system — but later that day, having come across the real coffee in the fridge, she'd sulked for half an hour about Hal's condescending concealment of her mistake . . . "And to think she was once a cheery, green-eyed Irish lass," Sean said to Hal as they drove away late that afternoon, exhausted, headed for one of the Irish pubs in nearby Cambridge. "Devout, what's more. Never missed a Sunday mass. Soft hands clasped in prayer — used to sing exquisitely, too, hymns and all . . . I mean, she's still a good woman, is she not?" "Sure she's a good woman," said Hal, raising his glass of Jameson's to meet Sean's over the table. "Just a bit — out of it, is all." "Last Easter," said Sean, staring at the ice cubes in his empty glass, "I offered to take her to church so she could sing the old hymns but she refused. Said she couldn't possibly get herself ready in time, though I'd asked her on Good Friday for the Sunday.")

"Mm," says Sean now, as Hal swallows his mouthful of chocolate cake. "She was in a home, as they call those places. Not far from here. I'd go over pretty much daily. But she could not get her bearings — without her, er, possessions, to put it euphemistically. Quite possibly her memory had stayed behind with them, gotten resold by Goodwill along with the rest. She was left with a limited repertory of phrases. Alzheimer's has interesting literary possibilities, if you're keen on the Gertrude Stein school. You know, *'All this time Melanctha was always being every now and then with Jem Richards,'* that sort of thing. After a while even that faded away and she could say only two things. 'What am I doing here?' and 'Where's the way out?' Especially 'What am I doing here?'"

"Good question," says Hal.

"Yeh, that's what I kept telling her. 'Good question, Ma,' I'd say. 'I wonder that pretty often myself.' And then she'd say, 'Where's the way out?'"

"So did you show her?" says Chloe.

"Well, I'd say, 'Shall we go for a stroll in the garden?' 'Oh, *yes!*' she'd say, so I'd help her put on her coat and meanwhile she'd forget all about the stroll, she'd think we were leaving the place forever, so she'd go around saying tearful good-byes to all her friends, 'See you next year . . . maybe!' 'Oh no,' the others would say, looking anxious . . . 'Surely before *that!*' 'Well, let's see . . . ,' Ma would say, and I'd watch her struggling with imaginary logistics. 'It won't be easy for us to get together . . . because, you see, I live in . . . uh . . . I live in Clonakilty . . .' She hadn't lived in Clonakilty since the Second World War. And they'd be standing there, listening desperately, trying to catch at least a shred of her meaning . . ." (Sean had shuddered to watch the floundering of these broken minds, searching for names and dates, reiterating the same phrases every few seconds with the same enthusiasm . . . "When are we going home?" "You live here now, Granny." "Could I have a cigarette?" "No one smokes anymore, Gramps." "And how are the kids?" "They have children of their own now, Mother." "What beautiful flowers! They're . . ." "Gladiolas, I already told you." "What line of work am I in, exactly?" "Well, you're retired now, but you used to be an engineer." "An engineer? Are you sure? I thought I was in publishing." "No, Dad, I'm the one who's a publisher." "You? Really? I could have sworn I was in publishing." "And how are the kids?" "What beautiful flowers!" "Could I have a cigarette?" Doing their best to emerge from the hell of pure present, and failing. Bewailing their own sluggishness, the blocked pathways, the sobbing labyrinth. Fighting to preserve a minimum of coherency.

The challenge was to follow a sentence, whether theirs or someone
else's, all the way through from beginning to end — and then, more
daunting still, to keep its accreted meaning in place. You could see
the anguish of it in their eyes.)

"No," says Chloe, "I mean, did you show her the *real* way out?"
She's coming down from the cocaine now and feeling slightly sick to
her stomach, so she tries to elicit the smell of gasoline. (This is her
favorite smell and has helped her surmount nausea on countless
occasions over the years. Not only the smell but the sight of gasoline
delights her — its glistening cold colors spilled on the pavement
near gas pumps, blue, purple, silver, iridescent as pigeon plumage.
Ever since she can remember she's taken pleasure in the sharply
delineated shapes of gas stations, used car lots and parking lots; she
loves their high rectangles of wire, festooned with triangular plastic
strips that quiver brightly in the wind. Cars, too, she loves. Driving.
The idea of going somewhere. She knows it's just an idea. You never
can get anywhere, Col. It's like the mirage of water up ahead on the
highway, always up ahead, up ahead, never reached. But you've got
to keep on chasing after it.)

That's youth, thinks Sean. Romantically assuming dying people
want to die faster. "She didn't want to die," he says. "She wanted to
get out of the bloody home was all. As simple as that. And as impossible." (He says nothing of the last time he saw Maisie, when she
truly had been dying, and perhaps knew it, and had turned to him
as he knelt at her bedside and stared him full in the face, reaching
out a skinny arm, stroking his balding head and whispering to him,
softly and sincerely, as if in amazement, "You're so beautiful" — the
words stunning him, plunging straight to his stomach, filling his
heart with pain and his eyes with tears. "You're beautiful, too, Ma,"
he'd told her then, contemplating her wasted stick body and her
straggly hair, her sunken eyes, her arthrosis-warped hands and feet,
and meaning it more ardently than he'd meant anything in his life,
"You're beautiful, too.")

"Katie," he now says, abruptly, "you must forgive our snide insinuations about your jack-o'-lantern this afternoon. This is the most delectable pumpkin pie that ever slid down my gullet. Hal, could you zip some whipped cream down to this end of the table?"

Beth intercepts the bowl as it passes, copping a heaping spoonful of the thick cream and plopping it onto her pie, telling herself, This is the last thing I'm putting in my mouth until the month of December. I swear, I swear. As in Brian's courtroom, I swear. So help me God. So HELP ME, God!

Rachel sees the move and all but hears the thought that accompanies it. Poor Beth, she thinks. Now where does that come from? *Poor Beth,* no, it's *Mad Bess* — a Purcell song?

Brian dives in to dispel the gloom. "And this, Rachel," he says, "is a Platonic Form of a chocolate cake. The paradigm. The Thing Itself."

Rachel gratifies him with a smile but Brian wishes he hadn't said that because he quite recently said it to someone else, not about chocolate cake but about *prosciutto con melone,* and repeating such things cheapens them, dissolves their specificity. (It was last June — a Civil Liberties convention in Ottawa; at day's end a dark-haired dark-eyed Canadian lawyer named Celia Torrington had come up to him on the steps of the courthouse and, after chatting desultorily with him about the Cuban trade embargo, invited him to share a late light supper at her house — a house from which her husband was providentially but temporarily absent. They'd set up a table in the backyard and as they carried out candles, wineglasses and chilled white wine, bread sticks and melons with smoked ham — "This, Celia, is the Platonic Form of *prosciutto con melone,*" Brian told her — he'd suddenly felt very sad. Would he remember this, remember the beautiful sadness that filled his soul that evening as he listened to the moan of the summer wind in the pine trees and watched Celia's white dress whip her narrow knees and cling to her stomach, knowing they'd spend the night worshiping each other's nudity, then kiss in the morning and separate and never meet again

— would he remember this single supper with Celia Torrington, its numbered, melon-sweet seconds — or would he remember the words? *Prosciutto melone, bread sticks, pine trees, white dress, narrow knees?* — words he'd selected, savored and cherished because they effectively summoned up this reality in his brain, but that, now, instead of summoning it, have gradually come to evince it ... *What is a memory?*)

"My mother also lost her memory," says Leonid. "It started right after my father died. I wasn't there but my sister wrote regularly to keep me abreast of her decline. It was almost as if she'd made a conscious decision to get rid of her past."

"Yes," says Katie (though she herself had never met her mother-in-law). "She just sort of ... tossed it away, you know? The way you get rid of excess clothing or baggage when you're toiling up a mountain path on a hot day."

"When people would come over to visit, my sister told me, our mother was always careful to pretend she still had a memory. Out of courtesy, you know, she pretended to recognize them, whereas she couldn't tell her cousin from a cow. But it was weird, my sister said ... Her memory loss ... ah, lightened her. She forgot all about the pain and disappointment she'd endured. Her children couldn't hurt her anymore, she didn't even know our names. Her husband's death she remembered for a while; then it, too, disappeared. She kept shedding her memories one by one, all the bitterness and resentment fell away from her, her eyes brightened and her smile got sweeter and more girlish by the day."

There's no point in telling him the reason for her euphoria, thinks Beth. Brain cell degeneration having made her incapable of getting her bearings in time, she no longer feared the future.

"And in the end," Leonid concludes, his voice hoarse with emotion, "one beautiful October afternoon, telling no one in advance, she went for a walk along the Berezina River, dropping her clothes as she went, like Tom Thumb's pebbles ... That's how they tracked her down . . . They found her lying among the leaves on the river-bank, naked as the day she was born, with a smile on her face."

"Isn't that an amazing image?" says Katie, whose own mother had died less romantically, of colon cancer, when she was thirteen. "It's as if she . . . I don't know . . . as if she'd levitated or something! I can just see her becoming more and more ethereal . . . transparent . . . and then just sort of melting away . . ."

You weren't there, Leonid tells himself. You weren't there, ever. (No, he hadn't gone back once, not until it was too late. As an art student in Belarus he'd had high hopes for himself as a painter, was sure he'd be among the happy few who leave their mark on the world, if only he could get to New York City. And here he is in his late sixties, choosing between orangey ochre and yellowy ochre for Mrs. Foster's new kitchen in Welham . . . some mark on the world! Having resolved to leave the country illegally, and the adverb was redundant, he'd borrowed money from his friends at the Minsk Art Academy to help him get started, then sneaked his way out of Belarus in the back of a munitions truck, bribing the driver to take him across the border into Poland, then hiding away on a boat from Swinoujscie to Malmö, hitchhiking to Stockholm, wandering around Gamla Stan looking hungry and artistic until Birgitta, a kind blond bookstore employee, finally took pity on him and married him. Disembarking in New York in 1960, he was twenty-seven and still firmly convinced his dreams would come true. But life in the States was disconcertingly difficult — he'd had to learn the language, scrimp to pay the rent and — hardest of all — strive to believe in his work amid the hubbub of family life. For Birgitta soon gave birth to twin girls, Selma and Melissa . . . Then, when the twins were five, their marriage fell apart and it grew even more difficult to make ends meet . . . Time passed and Leonid often thought with a wince of guilt about those he'd left behind to face the music in Belarus — those for whom the hassles of daily existence in a com-munist country had been exacerbated by his departure. Yes, people with relatives abroad were harassed and persecuted, suspicion and surveillance were intensified, restricted freedoms further restricted, privileges denied as they came due. Time passed . . . and it tortured him to think how the gap was widening between them. His little sister Ioulia grew up and married an engineer named Grigori and gave birth to a baby named Svetlana. His parents grew old, frail, ill. It wasn't that he didn't care — he did, terribly — but he still couldn't bring himself to go back, not even for a visit. In the first place it was risky — the government could detain him, retain him, lock him up for good; such was the stuff of his nightmares. But it wasn't only that. The thing was that . . . he now had responsibilities in America; he couldn't just up and leave. He'd met black-haired, vivacious, idealistic Katie at an SDS demonstration in 1968 and fallen in love with her as with no one since Valentina Sagalovitch back at the municipal pool in Minsk — except that this time the love was real and reciprocal. Despite their age difference (fifteen years), the two of them had leapt joyfully into wedlock, then parenthood — so that now, what with Birgitta's two and Katie's four, he had no fewer than *six* mouths to feed. It was a lot. Sure. Who could argue with that? No one, not even his sister Ioulia, whom he called each year on her birthday and for the New Year. True, as he admitted to her over the phone, noticing that his mother tongue felt clumsy on his lips and rang strangely in his ears, he wasn't exactly painting up a storm. It had been tougher than he'd expected to break into the Soho gallery world. He'd been forced to make a few compromises, and as a matter of fact he was now working full time as a housepainter. But the point was . . . here he hemmed and hawed and tried to think how to explain it to her — he'd become an American. Not an actual citizen, no — he still needed to renew his green card annually, but that was a mere technical detail — he lived, behaved and felt like an American; his wife and children spoke only English and had never been abroad. He'd been through everything in the States — Kennedy, Nixon, the Vietnam War, hippiedom, Watergate, Carter, yuppiedom, Reagan; his children had been born here and were growing up here and every facet of their lives was American, from school to sports to video games . . . how could he go "home"? And indeed, the more time passed, the more he dreaded going back to Belarus — less because of all that would have changed there in the meantime than because of all that would *not* have changed. His parents still lived in the house where he was born; his friends, recognizing him, would hold out their arms to welcome him back into their midst — and his decades of life in the United States would evaporate — Katie and the kids would melt into wisps of a forgotten dream — all his years of American striving, growing and changing would be annulled. Thus, as Ioulia informed him of their parents' inexorable decline year after year, he desperately tried to reassure her . . . knowing his phrases were trite even as he pronounced them. Eventually their parents grew so weak and sickly they could no longer fend for themselves, so Ioulia and Grigori reluctantly left Minsk and moved down to Shudiany, where Grigori was taken on as an engineer in the nearby nuclear plant.)

"You're lucky," Brian tells Leonid. "Your mom's the exception. My dad's the rule. He did nothing but get nastier as he aged. Paranoid, garrulous and despicable. Thought we were ripping him off. Spent five years screaming at my mother. Screaming at her. Not that he'd been a warm, loving sort of guy when I was a kid, don't get me wrong. But his behavior in the last five years of his life destroyed all the positive memories I had." Can see myself turning into him in the mirror, he adds to himself. Hate it.

Again a gloom of silence settles over the table, as the guests pay mental visits to their dear and less dear departed.

"Sounds like Tolstoy," says Hal at last.

"Sounds like my mother," says Aron.

"Was your mom like that?" says Rachel.

"Not was, is."

"You mean your mother's still alive?" gasps Chloe.

"I'm afraid so," sighs Aron. "I was born when she was seventeen; by the time she was your age she already had four children! Now she's a hundred and two and unfortunately still kicking. Lives in Jerusalem. *At* home, rather than *in* a home. Stubbornly refuses to enter an institution. It takes four full-time employees to keep her going — a cook, a housecleaner, a nurse and a secretary. But she's got money, so it could last a while."

"Good heavens!" says Beth. "Do you ever visit her?"

"Haven't seen her in twenty years," says Aron. "But we argue over the phone every Sunday."

"What about?" asks Derek.

"Politics," says Aron. "Fortunately I'm hard of hearing now, so her politics don't bother me as much as they used to." (Mrs. Zabotinsky had left Pretoria for Jerusalem when her husband died, taking his watch factory fortune with her. She now devoted all her time and money to the support of Israel's expansionist policies, its most reactionary political parties, its military occupation of Palestine, its incorrigible *chutzpeh*. In the course of more than a thousand transatlantic phone calls over the years, she and Aron have quarreled about these issues on a weekly basis without influencing each other's opinions in the least.) "No, she's still feisty. Her boyfriend died last year, but that doesn't seem to have taken the wind out of her sails."

"Her . . . boyfriend?" gulps Derek.

"Yes. He had a heart attack."

"How old was *he?*" asks Rachel.

"Oh . . . about sixty, I'd say. Could have been her grandson, but she was never one to worry about appearances."

"I find that admirable," says Beth.

"You do?" says Aron.

"Yes," says Beth. "You always hear about older men with younger women, never the other way around."

"True," says Aron. "When she started going out with him I figured well, at least she doesn't need to worry about contraception!"

"You mean they actually? . . ." says Rachel.

"Oh, I have no idea. It's not something I care to wonder about."

"My mother had a heart attack last month," says Patrizia, putting an end to a lengthy silence. "She simply can't relax; everything that happens to her children and grandchildren has to be turned into a major psychodrama. She's had high blood pressure for years, and now a heart attack . . . I'm worried about her."

"Of course you are," says Beth. "The heart is a very important organ."

"The heart is a very important organ," repeats Sean. "Do you never hesitate, Beth, before allowing such platitudes to cross your lips?"

"What have you got against platitudes, Sean?" says Katie, coming to Beth's defense. "Repeating commonplace truths is one of the oldest, most reassuring rituals of our species. Whatever would have become of the human race if we didn't have banalities to fall back on?" It's true, she thinks, recalling her gratitude for the clichés proffered by friends over the decades: "Don't worry, it's just the terrible twos," "Adolescent rebellion — what else is new?" "Takes all kinds," "You're not losing a daughter, you're gaining a son-in-law," "Our parents are becoming our children" — it's been going on for centuries, she thinks, and God forbid it that should ever stop. Clichés are magic wands that turn our private terrors into standing jokes.

"The heart's a very important organ," repeats Beth through clenched teeth " — for everyone, that is, except Sean Farrell, who neither has nor seems to need one. I also find it interesting," she goes on, appalled at the quantity of food she's ingested in the past three hours, "that Sean didn't invite any women writers to this dinner."

"Beth, please," says Brian in a low voice. "Don't start that."

"Am I the only one who finds that interesting?" Beth insists, feeling her cheeks redden and her voice go shrill but determined to make her point. "I mean, there just *happen* to be three writers at the table and all of them just *happen* to be men? There are plenty of terrific women writers on campus."

She can feel her heartbeat speeding up and her breath starting to come in short wheezes — please God, she thinks, don't let me have an asthma attack in front of everyone. (She hasn't had a full-fledged attack in years, not since those all-but-forgotten impressions of mildew and male sweat, back then, down there, her young uncle Jimmy's voice spurting deep and urgent into her twelve-year-old ear in the basement of her grandma's house in Decatur, his stubbly cheek rubbing her neck, reddening and inflaming it as he unzipped his fly, took out his thing and pressed it to her yellow Easter dress, kissing her shakily, then glancing up at her with eyes full of shining shyness, the clammy moldy dankness of saltpeter on the basement wall behind her mingling with the warmth of his breath on her face as he rubbed up against her, panting "Don't tell, Beth, don't tell, I can't help it if you're so durn pretty," rasping, grasping, his strong young hands on her almost-no-breasts-at-all and his prong now pressed hard against the cheap transparent yellow material of her dress — she was amazed at how big and somber and hairy it was, having seen until then only her baby nephew's white thumbthing, and when he'd gasped "Oh *God*" and fallen against her almost laughing, she'd stroked his head until his panting subsided and she could feel his heart beat evenly again. That evening she'd had her first asthma attack — wheezing, gagging, unable to squeeze air into her lungs, scaring her grandmother half to death — and ever since, on doctor's orders, she keeps an inhaler on her person at all times.)

"I'm fed up with ladies' novels," says Sean with a sleazy grin. "A century ago they all talked about gardens and matrimony; now the standard plot is: young woman, sexually abused by father during childhood, endures numerous vicissitudes including abortion but finds happiness at last in the arms of another woman, preferably a member of a racial minority."

"You're drunk, sweetheart," murmurs Rachel. "Why don't you go make us all some coffee?"

Sean coughs politely, then uncontrollably. When he manages to

catch his breath, he draws a handkerchief from his pocket, brings it
to his lips and removes the phlegm from his mouth with surprising
dignity.

"Brian," says Beth, getting grimly to her feet. "I think it's time we
headed home."

Katie glances at her watch. (Ah the many times she'd glanced at
her watch when their children were little and said, "We should be
going, Leo, it's late and we still have to drive the baby-sitter home"
— a good excuse for leaving, but now there were no more baby-
sitters, no more babies — Sylvia their youngest was nineteen and
already champing at the bit — she'd failed tenth grade the year
David died so was still at home with them but this was her senior
year and she was feverishly sending out applications to colleges in
Oregon, Colorado, Florida — what *is* it with this country, thinks
Katie in despair, that everyone so aspires to be *alone?*)

Brian has the feeling he and Beth have been in this identical situation countless times, she standing and he sitting, she impatient to
leave and he longing to stay — if her feminist outburst spoils the
evening this time, he thinks, I'll never forgive her. Ladies and gentlemen of the jury — he glances around the table, realizing he's had
much too much to drink and is no longer stringing his thoughts
together coherently — have you reached a decision or shall we consider the case dismissed? Come to think of it, there are twelve of us
here, we *are* like a jury — but sitting on what crime? Or else we're
the twelve apostles and this is the Last Supper — but then — who's
Jesus? Patchouli, maybe? Or little Hal Junior, upstairs? Oh God, I
feel lousy.

"Sorry about that, Beth," says Sean. "I take it back. Terrible taste,
forgive me. Do sit down again. I don't want anyone to leave until we
get this matter cleared up."

"What matter?" asks Leonid. "Did I miss something?" His lower
back is aching, aching, dragging him downward; when you're in pain
it's really *you* who are *in* the pain and not the pain that's in you, he

thinks, longing to return to the comfortable armchair near the fireplace. "What matter needs clearing up, Sean?"

"Yeah, Sean, what matter?" asks Katie.

"That," says Sean enigmatically, "is the question. "What . . . is . . . the matter?"

Stunned by Sean's apology, Beth sits down again, but just then Brian lurches to his feet.

"Scuse me," he says. "I need some fresh air. I'll be right back." (He knows the crime they're sitting on, this jury and every jury, he's in the jungle again, twenty-eight years earlier, aged nineteen, winding along the Sa Thay River. Jagged sunlight flashes through the greenery but the air is heavy — everything is heavy and waterlogged — their helmets, backpacks, weapons, boots; their hearts, weighed down by fear and by fatigue. They've been meandering along this ravine all day — seven of them, four blacks and three whites, plus a German shepherd named Zack — seemingly going in circles, as in a lush and deadly nightmare. The whole half year since Brian arrived in Vietnam has been one green writhing nightmare of roughness and rain, barked orders and stinking sludge, desperate running and diarrhea, marijuana and mosquitoes. Brian has forgotten all about the savvy political analyses of the war he and his draft-dodging pals in Vancouver used to come up with around tables loaded down with brown bottles of Molson's beer. His brain is clogged with clinging vines, bamboo shoots up and blocks off his inner vision, the stench of marsh and mud and blood stops up his nose. On outings like this, stalking Charlie, everything scares the daylights out of him — snakes, and sinuous light paths that appear to be snakes, and the sneaky filthy murderous Vietcong who behave like snakes, planting land mines that turn Brian's friends into piles of red and bubbling mush. He no longer cares a whit about his country's politics. The only thing he cares about is getting back to Los Angeles in one piece . . .) He staggers toward the kitchen, his stomach churning as badly as his brain, the shrill ringing in his right ear bringing him to the verge of nausea.

There is sudden squall from upstairs.

"Hey!" says Hal, glancing at his watch. "Way to go, kid. Right on time for his midnight snack."

Chloe swishes swiftly up the staircase — and, rising, all of them follow her with their eyes. The wailing of a hungry infant: a sound many of them haven't heard in years. All talk ceases and they strain, listening intently to this expression of open, unabashed, flagrant need — *come, please come!* their hearts plead, along with the baby's cry. *Come, Mother! Come, solace! Come, milk, honey, perfect appeasement! Come, comfort that will banish lack, fill gap, soothe wound, heal ill, right wrong, now and forever.*

Abruptly the crying breaks off and marvelous Chloe reappears; long blond willowy red-and-cream Chloe descends the staircase with the infant in her arms, at her breast, she's bared her curvaceous white breast and the child's lips are firmly clamped around its nipple, sucking — yes! Look! Its terrible total need is being met! Chloe sinks slowly to sit on the couch, and — moved, mesmerized — the other guests take their places in a circle of reverence around her.

Even Beth forgets she was on the point of leaving.

Then Brian comes stomping back from the kitchen, glasses fogged, beard flecked with melting snow: "Holy smokes!" he says. "There's something like two feet of snow out there and it's still coming down. The cars are practically invisible. You know what, you guys? We're snowed in."

XV

HAL JUNIOR

Like his mother, Hal Junior will be "placed." But unlike his mother, he'll have the good fortune to land in the home of a warm and loving foster family — a soft-spoken Swedish diplomat and her husband who, indeed, will end up adopting him. (Though no one will ever become aware of the coincidence, Hal's adoptive father happens to be second cousin to Birgitta, Leonid's first wife.)

This won't save Hal Junior from having to become an artist. He'll study theater and develop into a brilliant stage actor, one of the best known and best loved in the United Kingdom. Toward the middle of the twenty-first century, however, he'll start forgetting lines, mislaying props, confusing one play with another . . . Yes, another victim of Alzheimer's, sorry to say. But his slow decline into vegetablehood will be brutally interrupted at age sixty by a flamboyant case of prostate cancer. I'll whisk him off in a matter of weeks, thus sparing his public the distressing spectacle of a tongue-tied Macbeth.

XVI

Snow and Song

 *H*al Junior is still at the breast, his lips and tongue now playing with his mother's left nipple rather than actually drinking from it. Chloe, her eyes far away, is cradling his head in her hand but not smiling. They empty us, she thinks. They take and take and take. Drain us dry, all of them. We're vessels of sweetness. The milk of human kindness. Bullshit. They empty us. Babies, the lot of them. Big mean hairy hungry crybabies. Spank me, Mommy. Hurt me, Mommy. Punish me, Mommy. Kiss me fuck me give give give. Belong to me. I've paid for you and now you have to be all mine. You'll never get away again. I'll tie you up. Tie you to the chair, the bed, the table. Gag you. There. Now try and move. Now try and talk. Hands trussed feet trussed mouth stuffed up. Like the turkey. Hal says forget all that. Just draw a big black rectangle around those years of your life and — whoom! Trapdoor! Gone! Which years of my life, Hal? Where's the floor? I take a step — trapdoor. Another step — trapdoor. No wonder I get fed up with trying to walk and prefer to float, to fly. My little baby. My baby boy. And did she . . . did she . . . do you think our mother nursed us, Col? Nah. No way. How did she feed us then? Can you imagine her with a baby bottle? How did we survive? *Why* did we survive? True, you didn't. You ended up falling through the Great Trapdoor into eternity. One more month to go. Hal's idea, for me to nurse Junior until he's a year old. Says it'll save him from cancer. Statistically a sure bet. Worth the effort, isn't it? Twelve short months of breast-feeding and our son will be protected from cancer for the rest of his life. As if cancer is the only problem he might run into.

Hal Junior's hand moves to Chloe's other breast and fondles it, tweaking the nipple. Ah, thinks Katie. I remember what *that* felt like. A baby's soft round head pressed to my bosom, a baby's eyes searching out my eyes, its tiny hand stroking the other, unsucked nipple so it won't feel left out.

I never had enough milk, thinks Patrizia. (She remembers the time her breasts ran dry with Tomas still sucking at them, hungrily, then furiously, finally breaking away and hollering in red-faced rage as if to say, "You call this a *mother?* Mothers are supposed to feed their babies to satiation! This is a scandal! I won't stand for it!" — screaming more and more accusatorily as she ran with him to the kitchen — Roberto was out, she was alone in the house with their one-month-old baby and he was going to die, not of hunger but of apoplexy, his face now purple with rage as she waited in anguish for the bottles to be sterilized, each of his wails lasting so long that he ran completely out of breath and she was beside herself with panic, beseeching Jesus the Virgin Mary and all the saints to help him gather another gulp of oxygen into his lungs, even if it meant the unleashing of yet another siren scream . . . She remembers the last bottle, too — Gino's, some four years later, and four years is a long time but it's also nothing once it's gone — motherhood, a series of tiny deaths — never more the hand measuring out the powder in the plastic spoon, leveling it off and tipping it into the water, pinching the nipple and shaking and shaking the bottle, nevermore, darling Gino, your babyhood's behind you, nevermore will I have a baby and go through the baby gestures; it's done. Oh, how I loved it! I can't understand the young mothers I see nowadays, chatting on their cell phones with one hand as they walk their toddlers home from day care with the other — they haven't seen them all day and they *still* don't want to see them?)

"Oh, no!" cries Beth. "Don't tell me we're going to spend the night here!"

The men, all but Aron, get to their feet with a certain air of hesitation and leave the room. Shrugging into their coats, they go out to the porch to assess the situation. This is what men do, thinks Sean. They go look into things, check out problems, take stock of reality. It's up to them, always, still.

"You see?" says Brian, gesturing at the garden from which every detail has been effaced including the stone wall that marks its limits. "I mean, maybe if we spent the next two hours shoveling we could dig out the cars — but who knows when they'll send a snowplow out this way? I'm not driving thirty miles on a road like that in the state I'm in."

"Me neither," says Leonid. "Not even two miles. Not even in another state. Don't feel like shoveling, either. Got a bad back."

"Got a bad thumb," says Sean.

"It's just your left hand," says Hal.

"Ever try shoveling snow with one hand?" says Sean.

"Ever try shoveling snow?" says Charles. "Come on, Sean, tell the truth. How long since you last shoveled snow?"

"Coupla decades," says Sean.

"I don't think I've ever seen it snow like this in November," says Hal. "Not never."

"Reminds me of Joyce," says Sean. "The end of 'The Dead,' remember? Best short story in the English language. 'The snow falling faintly through the universe and faintly falling, like the descent of their last end, upon all the living and the dead.'" He'd never been able to convince his students of the genius of this ending. They thought it must be clumsy oversight on Joyce's part to have used "falling faintly" and "faintly falling" in the same sentence. They'd been taught to eschew that sort of repetition — whereas what Joyce's lilting, echoing phrase inimitably conveyed was the redundancy itself, each snowflake the same yet different, repeating, accreting . . .

"Reminds me of that Tolstoy story," says Hal. "'Master and Man.'"

"Beautiful story," says Charles. "Unforgettable."

"Don't count on it," mutters Sean.

Derek for his part is remembering a story by I. B. Singer that also ends with a sublime evocation of snow falling — *sparsely, peacefully, as if in contemplation of its own falling,* transforming Central Park into a vast and silent cemetery, but he doesn't dare quote it as he can't remember the title of the story; it was about a couple of elderly neighbors who hated each other's guts when they first met, then ended up getting married, and when the old man died . . .

"Just beautiful," says Charles. "Ah . . . Listen to that silence."

They stand there staring at the snowflakes as they lilt down and down through the golden lamplight, filling the air with gentleness and chill.

Sean lights a cigarette, coughs, clears his throat, says nothing.

"Snow used to scare me," says Brian. "We almost never saw any, growing up on the West Coast. I remember my first winter out East . . ." But he doesn't go on, doesn't know how to put into words what the fear was, not in front of these word men — snow had always seemed ominous to him, deceptive, each flake a weightless star, sparkling light and soft, melting on your tongue, your skin, whereas their accumulated weight was a murderous impediment, causing cars to skid, roofs to cave in, trees to topple, stopping everything, blocking people off from one another — like Time, he thinks, like Time exactly — each second weightless and imperceptible, a sweet shard of crystal that melted on your tongue, whereas their accumulated weight was a murderous impediment, the years driving you down and down, covering everything, shrouding differences, and how to shovel away the heavy drifts of Time? You tried to thrust them aside, pile them into mounds at the edge of the road in order to keep advancing, but on the road itself the snow had hardened into nasty ice, it caused accidents, killed people . . . whereas the whole thing had started out so innocently, one melting second at a time . . . I'm really drunk, he thinks.

"I don't mind shoveling," says Derek, "but I'd need a pair of boots."

"What size do you wear?" says Sean, not relishing the thought of Derek's feet poking into his boots. He got into my Rachel, he thinks, I don't want him poking into my boots.

"Twelve," says Derek.

"Nah," says Sean. "I wear ten."

Let it go on, let it go on, thinks Charles, let it never stop, let it fill the world, cover our ugly cities and ruined landscapes — oh another ice age yes, let us all freeze up in the midst of our grotesque goings-on, preserved in ice like the people of Pompeii in lava, let another civilization discover us a couple of millennia down the line and wonder at our odd postures, our quaint concerns, our silly wars . . . (That line of thought peters out and is superceded by another, he's remembering Randall and Ralph, five years ago, before Toni was born, the way they'd whined and sniveled at the snow in Canyon de Chelly. The four of them had hiked down to the bottom of the canyon together and there, at a remove from the inevitable displays of silver jewelry and phony fossils, they'd noticed a group of Navajo Indians standing around a small fire, warming their hands and talking together in low voices. Struck by the formidable wrinkled face of the old woman among them, small and squat and wrapped in robes, a gray braid of hair hanging to her waist, Myrna had wanted to take a photograph — but the woman had raised her eyes briefly, meeting theirs, and the look in them had said unambiguously *no*. Even your eyes on us are too much, her brief glare had said, you are an offense to the gods, and as the snow fell on their hair Charles had reeled suddenly, inwardly, at the arbitrariness of their presence in that deep secret browngold crevice of the earth — his ancestors having been torn from their villages off the west coast of Africa and dragged in chains to the United States, Myrna's having sailed here in mad hope or mad despair from Scotland and Sweden, so that now, a dozen generations later, having mastered the codes of modern tourism, the two of them had come to Arizona with their offspring and were gaping at the Indians who for centuries had been raising sheep and alfalfa here, making little cooking fires and talking to one another in low voices. He'd felt shame, and carried his shame with him in silence as his family toiled back up the path out of the canyon, the children whining and sniveling about the snow, "I thought we came here to get *away* from the winter, Dad!" At the park service tourist shop near the exit, Myrna had purchased a tape of synthesized Indian flute music and then, as they drove north, sighed at the beauty of these plaintive windy notes against the unearthly geometry of stark red rock laced with snow. For Charles, however, the day had been spoiled. Even hours later, amid the grandiose upjutting rock formations of Monument Valley, he'd refused to help Myrna whip up the boys' excitement about all the cowboy movies that had been shot there, from *How the West Was Won* to *The Legend of the Lone Ranger*. They were too young to know about those movies. This has got to be a poem, Charles thinks now. There *must* be a poem in it somewhere. The little fire, and the worn brown hands stretching out to it for warmth. The camera dangling around Myrna's neck — metal, plastic, click, clack, lens, focus, zoom — aggressive precision proof of superior civilization. And the Indian woman's contained fierceness as, arms folded over her chest, she'd lifted her eyes to meet theirs. No pictures. And the handful of other Indians standing by her, with her, protectively. No.)

"No way," says Derek. His hand moves to his chin, a professorial tic his students sometimes imitate behind his back. (What his students don't know is that his hand is fondling something just beneath his chin: a scar — the trace of that day in the Catskills when, aged eleven, he'd gone against his mother's wishes for the first time, flaunting his independence by tobogganing down a steep hill with another boy — Jesse, his name was. Derek recalls the thrill and flash of speed, the wind whistling in his ears, the keening of the flat board on sheer ice, the pure high white elation — and sure enough, as if Violet had put a curse on him, they'd hit a bump and Derek had gone flying headfirst through the air, landing on his chin on a protruding rock — a shock as if his cranium had burst — and spurting crimson blood onto the snow — *my blood!* he'd thought, staring at it in heady disbelief until he saw the fear in Jesse's eyes and realized it must be really bad. Violet had reprimanded him in the taxi all the way to the doctor's office: "How can you do this to me? I'm supposed to be resting and you can think of nothing better to do than give me a heart attack?" then the tamping, scoffing, tut-tut, stitching — and Derek's vow at that instant, even as the doctor's threaded needle pierced his skin, *never* to behave this way with his own children, always and only to love them, hold them, protect them and let them feel it, let them know how deeply they were cherished — and *why is it that this is impossible?* Marina baby, why don't you want to live? Fainting in class. Eating nothing. Courting chaos. Devouring narratives of the Shoah. Gorging on word death. Chugging down word blood by the gallon. And *why?* All because her mother walked out on her when she was three? A bomb so devastating that no amount of love could ever fill the crater it had carved out in her soul?) "No way," he repeats.

And, their thoughts as thick and swirling as the snow, the six men renounce the idea of shoveling in the middle of the night.

Hal moves down the steps and shuffles forward, abruptly immersed to his knees in the soft drift by the porch edge. Bending, he dips both hands into the white stuff, liking the familiar bite of cold on his fingers, shaping it — unthought, unmeditated reflex — into a ball, then spinning around and throwing it. Underhand for girls, overhand for boys: the snowball hits Brian smack on the ear — his right ear, his bad, permanently ringing ear — a conflagration in his brain — he sees red, sees stars, red stars.

"You asshole," he snarls. Berserk. Arms flailing, also without thought or meditation, he flings his body from the porch onto the hulking body of the novelist, battering it, knocking it down, whump onto its stomach in the snow.

"Hey!" says Hal. "Hey, it was a joke!"

Now Charles, Leonid and Derek have leapt to join the fray. Skidding in city shoes, shivering in thin sweaters, they grab snow and stuff it down each other's necks — yelling, roaring with laughter, pretending they're kids again, at the best time of their lives, whenever that was, reveling in the exhilarating sharp sting of wetness, waking up, shedding the stupor of food and drink, the torpor of the evening's talk by fire- and candlelight, answering the call of ancient ancestors in their veins, Old Norse warriors in bearskins, African warriors in leopardskins, the call to blind and mindless battle, rubbing snow in each other's faces, so cold it burns, giving themselves up to a no-holds-barred free-for-all, like barroom brawls in cowboy movies seen long ago — whack! a chair hits the mirror and it shatters — zoom! a table goes soaring into a wall of bottles — whizz! men slide headfirst down counters and crash into slot machines — playing cards scatter in the air — while, from the shelter of his porch, Sean shakes his head in wonderment at this American display of boys-will-be-boyishness.

It doesn't last long. Before Sean has taken the final deep drag of his cigarette, it's over and done with — for they are winded, pooped — rather aghast, in fact, at how badly they feel. Shooting pains flash up and down Leonid's back; Charles is on the verge of tears, having torn the black silk shirt Myrna bought him for his fortieth birthday; Hal is gasping for breath, terrified at the hammerthumping of his heart against his rib cage; Brian's ear has quieted down a bit but he wrenched a muscle in his shoulder trying to turn over when Hal was sitting on his back . . . One by one they break off, lumber to their feet, glower and grin at each other and move porchward, nursing their wounds, slapping snow from their trousers, feeling the clammy cold of wet clothes against their middle-aged skins.

"Buncha feckin' eedjits," murmurs Sean, as the others huff and hobble up the steps. "What we all need now is some nice hot Irish coffee. I'll get Rache to make us some."

∽

Life hadn't stopped inside the house while the men were gone, and when they return to the living room the ambience there is other. They hear strains of music and stumble into a Renaissance painting titled *Madonna and Child with Angel Musicians*. Beth, having caught sight of a guitar propped next to the bookcase in a corner of the room, is strumming it and singing *Where have all the flowers gone?* in a rich tremulous voice, while Katie, Patrizia and Rachel hum along in approximate harmony. Hal Junior is fast asleep on his mother's red velvet lap and Aron is rocking back and forth with his hearing aid turned down, entranced at the sight of Chloe's hands.

They're Bellini hands, he thinks. (Often at their home on the Berea in Durban, once the girls had gone upstairs to bed and Currie had finished the dishes and gone off to her *kaia*, he and Nicole would spend an hour or two poring over art books together — "Look at the *hands!*" she'd told him once, leafing through Bellini Virgins, whereas up until then they'd been exclaiming at the faces. And he'd looked, and been unable to stop looking. In the course of his lifetime, Bellini had sketched, drawn and painted hundreds of Virgin Mary hands, alive with reverence and wisdom, their long strong fingers curved around the body of her child — now newborn babe, now lanky gory corpse. Madonna hands, *Pietà* hands. Holding in joy, in succor and in sorrow. Who'll hold my body when it's dead? thinks Aron suddenly. He'd held his own father's, as the life went out of it and his mother prayed and wept in the next room. Sweet, stunning mystery of that instant, burned into his memory as with a branding iron — for *even when you're there,* watching desperately, attentive to the coming and the going of each breath, *you cannot understand.* This person. This large, powerful body you used to lean on, and count on — giving itself up completely, abandoning life or being abandoned by it, suddenly a mere slack mass of flesh to be stripped, washed, dressed and laid out, heavy to manipulate, on the bed. There; then there no longer. The shock of his absence, whereas you thought you'd been preparing and preparing and prepared. And the surge of energy that whipped through you then — as though, flowing out of him, his life had flowed into you, compounding your own. The savage urge to run, shout, eat, drink, talk — the urge to pray. O Kaddish! "My father is dead." More than thirty years have passed, and the sentence stuns him still. His father's body returns to him often in his dreams, chilling him with the intimate, tangible knowledge of his own mortality.

"*Long time passing*," sing the women.

"Ah, for Jaysus' sake!" groans Sean from the doorway. The song breaks off, and the women's faces turn to him in hurt surprise. Aron goes on rocking, oblivious, staring at Chloe's hands.

"That song was already a piece of shite when Dylan sang it," says Sean, "but now it's even worse, it's a festering old . . ."

"How come *you* get to legiferate, Sean?" says Beth. "Why should we all have to stop singing just because Dylan rubs *you* the wrong way? You've been ordering us around ever since we got here. What is this?"

"Beth," says Brian.

"I'm sorry but — I mean, if you know how everything's supposed to unfold, why don't you just tell us to line up and read the parts you've written for us in advance?"

"It so happens that that guitar is neither yours nor mine," says Sean as he lights a fresh cigarette, eyes smoldering. "And the fact that you're my dinner guest doesn't entitle you to simply — pick up — whatever comes to hand and — make free with it."

"It was Jody's," Rachel whispers to Beth, and Beth's face alters.

"Sorry. Sorry, Sean," she says. And manages to refrain from adding: I didn't know it was a sacred relic. Blushing violently in spite of herself, she replaces the instrument in its case and snaps the case shut.

"Oh, it's only her *old* guitar," says Sean caustically, expelling a stream of smoke through his nostrils and eyeing the whiskey bottle to make sure its level hasn't changed since his last dealings with it a

number of hours ago. "She took the new one with her when she left
— the one that cost me three months' salary."

A shocked silence meets this new enormity.

"Shite" indeed, thinks Beth. It's so pretentious of Sean to swear
in Irish when he's been living in the States since he was nine. "For
Jaysus' sake" . . . who does he think he's fooling?

"Hey," says Charles. "I think it's time we opened the champagne."

"Champagne!" cry Katie and Leonid. "Now that's talking!"

Sean sinks heavily into an armchair, pours himself a large glass of
whiskey, and stares at the bandage on his wounded thumb. (That
particular guitar, the one Beth sullied, was in Jody's arms when he
first set eyes on her. Bach — not pissy piddling hippie chants about
flowers and soldiers and young maids, but pure heavenly Bach rose
from the intricately strumming fingers of the woman in white. Jody
that night had been a holy, an unhoped-for apparition — lit up by a
spotlight in a corner of the coffee shop into which Sean had stumbled by chance, her every feature and gesture bespeaking bliss. You're
all I've ever wanted, he'd intoned to her in silence as he stared. You'll
change my life, make me whole again, I'm sure of it. We were meant
for one another . . . She was twenty-five and he, forty. She knew how
to do everything — cook, sew, hammer, saw, garden, dance, play the
guitar. He knew only how to drink and write. He had to have her,
had to win and marry her. She'd teach him how to live, he knew it
— her serenity would heal his bleeding soul. With her at his side
he'd be able to relinquish liquor, cut down on cigarettes, hit the
Nobel. He'd been waiting only for her, to become at last the poet he
was meant to be. His friends were skeptical. Brushing their caveats
aside, he'd courted Jody Robinson with flowers, poems, silk scarves,
French restaurants, the world's most prestigious concert recordings
of baroque music. He'd become a specialist on the baroque. Spent
hours choosing music for her in the record stores of Boston and
Cambridge. Penned odes, sonnets, villanelles to her beauty.
Introduced her to his mother. To Rachel. To Hal. Married her, with

Hal and Rachel as his witnesses. And at once plunged back into his acid-rain humor and self-destructiveness. "You've got to *help* me, Jody!" he'd told her one day, sobbing, when he hit rock bottom and saw her towering above him in her purity, lotus-positioned on the bed in her white nightgown, all eyes closed except the invisible one at the center of her forehead, palms upturned on thighs to receive the vibrations of the spheres. "You've got to help yourself, Sean," she'd replied, her lips curved in an infuriating Buddha half smile that made him want to slap her head right off her shoulders. "I wasn't born this way, you know," she'd added, referring to her spiritual superiority, which she flaunted in his face like a saber. Then she'd commenced a breathing exercise that divided her sentences into little floating koans. "You can't just snap your fingers — and be changed, Sean — it takes work — you have to work on yourself — I've been doing yoga — deep breathing and meditation — for seven years — it takes technique — training and discipline — humility and progressive mastery — if you really want something, Sean — that's the only way to get it." "That's not the way you get poems," pouted Sean. "Oh? How do you get poems?" asked Jody, breathing normally again. "You sink into the muck. Drink half a pint of gin. Breathe garbage. Chew linoleum. Embrace the dead. Vomit sentimentality. Life, in case you didn't know, is more than an alpha wave undulating through the cosmos. You're out of this world, Jode. You've got no connections to anything." "What are *you* connected to, Sean?" "Stop calling me Sean every time you open your mouth." "What do you want me to call you?" "I'm the only person in the room. I may be drunk but I can still figure out who you're talking to." "So what are you connected to?" Jody repeated, stretching her white arms high above her head and arcing her upper body superbly to the right, then to the left, bending as she exhaled until her hands grazed the floor next to their bed. "Feckin' *Christ*, can we no longer have a conversation without your needing to demonstrate how bloody healthy you are?" "I thought *you* wanted to be healthy too," said Jody, drawing her arms back into her lap with dignity and reopening her eyes. "That's what you told me when you asked me to marry you." "Well, I don't." "You don't want to be healthy?" "No." "You don't want to be whole?" "No. I happen to loathe whole people. What I like are little broken jibbets of people that go bouncing around all by themselves. Boing, boing. Disparate members. Time out of joint." "I can hear you, Sean, but I don't know how to answer you because two hours from now you're going to come to me and apologize and tell me just the opposite. What am I supposed to do? Think about it, Sean. Think about what you'd like me to do." He'd hated that sentence with a vengeance: *think about it, Sean.* "I'm your wife, Sean," added Jody, "for better and for worse, but no one gets to fuck with my mind. That wasn't part of our contract." Still in her nightgown, she picked up her guitar and started playing some fabulous morning *raga* she'd learned in the Rajasthan. Two hours later, Sean apologized. And all afternoon they made heart-wrenching, tear-filled love on Sean's wide bed, mingling their limbs and cries until they no longer knew which way was up. Months passed, the pattern repeating itself like the zigzag in the scarf Maisie knitted for Jody that Christmas, and which Jody refused to wear because its scratchy wool inflamed her neck. Then she became pregnant. She told him the news with an expression of sheer *Om,* sheer *Samadhi* on her face. And he swore that this — yes, *this* would transform him once and for all. That now — yes, *now* he'd be able to give up the cup, because at last he had something objective to look forward to — a *reason* to go on living — a future — a part of him that would extend beyond himself, far into the new century — his father's blood, revivified — his mother's joy, her joy, her joy. Then Hal rang up to pour out his latest woes — he'd been ditched by his fourth blond hooker in less than two years — so Sean met him for comfort at the tavern and came home at six-thirty the next morning, having been arrested for driving while intoxicated and spent the rest of the night in jail, where he'd hit it off with the cop who'd booked him —

an Irish kid whose folks hailed from Connemara and had raised him on a hearty diet of Gaelic public-house songs. "Fuck Bach," said Sean when he walked in the door that morning, seeing Jody sit up in bed and aim her serene, all-accepting gaze at him. "Bach has no balls!" he shouted from the shower, between verses of the obscene Gaelic song the cop had taught him. So Jody, as calmly and clear-headedly as she did everything else, killed their child, divorced him for mental cruelty, packed up her expensive new guitar and cleared out of his life forever.) "Mental cruelty," he mutters now, setting down his empty glass.

"Cheers!" say the others, raising their flutes of champagne.

"To the winter!"

"To Hal Junior!"

"To your health!"

"To hell with health!" grumbles Sean.

"Maybe Sean wants to go on pouting for a while," says Rachel.

"Yeh, I think I shall do just that," says Sean. "Cross my arms and hang my head and pout. I'm good at pouting, you know — it runs in the family. All my ancestors had huge, pendent, supple lower lips. My grandfather's was quite incredible, he could stick it out and touch his nose with it, you'd have sworn it was his tongue. So I'll just sit here and pout for a while if you don't mind, thanks very much, have to keep in practice."

"What's the snow situation?" asks Rachel.

"The snow situation is excellent," says Hal. "It's the road and vehicle situation that leaves something to be desired."

"What's the matter, Leo?" says Katie in alarm, seeing the gingerly way her husband is lowering himself into the leather armchair. "What's the matter, hon? Did you hurt your back?"

"No, no, I'm fine. Nothing another glass of champagne won't cure. You know the joke about the woman with rheumatism?"

"Oh, tell it!" says Katie. "That's a really funny one."

"Seventy-five-year-old lady, her doctor just told her she's got rheumatism and she says, But doctor, that's not possible, I've always been in perfect health — no one's ever told me I had rheumatism before! I see, the doctor says. And when would it be convenient for Madam to have her rheumatism?"

Hal and Rachel laugh the loudest this time.

XVII

ARON

As for Aron Zabotinsky, I'll have him die by fire, he who has always been obsessed with fire — *Maatla!* — from his earliest memories as a little boy in Odessa, watching his father, fat drops of sweat rolling down his wrinkle-riddled brow, stoke the oven in which he'd set his loaves to baking, to the hideous burning-tire punishments inflicted in Johannesburg in the 1980s by black militants on other black militants perceived as traitors to the Cause . . .

He's ninety-nine years old. He was hoping to make it to a hundred and three, if only to beat his mother's record of a hundred and two and a half. He knew this was childish of him, as she wouldn't be around to gnash her teeth at her defeat; still, he enjoyed the idea of this posthumous revenge and took fanatical care of his body to make sure he'd achieve his goal.

But this was not to be. Here is how I come to Aron Zabotinsky.

He's rented the second floor of a shoddy little house on Summer Street, just around the corner from the Main Street bakery he used to run single-handedly (and which is still called Tinsky's). That evening, the young couple on the ground floor have a run-in. She's opened a can of pork and beans for their supper. He's drunk and depressed, so he yells at her for being a lousy cook (his ancestors are Québecois, and he seems to recall that *fèves au lard* was the staple dish of the impoverished *habitants*.) "It stinks!" he shouts. "I'm not gonna eat that shit! It fuckin' stinks!" "Fuck off!" says she — adding, in an atypical feminist outburst, "Cook your own meal!" — and, matching gesture to word, she tears off her apron and dashes out of the house, slamming the door behind her. The man bangs out after her but his wife is running as fast as her legs will carry her, which is fairly fast (they're only nineteen-year-old legs) — and he, though not much older, is a heavy smoker so it takes him almost a mile to catch up with her; indeed he only manages to do so because, glancing back when she reaches the town limits and seeing that he is still after her, she pulls up short and bursts into a beery mixture of laughter and tears. They fall into each other's arms, slobbering and weeping all over each other, and then, feeling it is imperative they make it up on the spot, they duck into the woods and do not return home until later that evening, at which point they learn that they no longer have a home to return to.

Meanwhile, Aron, upstairs, peacefully rocking in his rocking chair and reading an early Richard Ford novel, unconsciously chosen because it had the word *fire* in the title, has heard nothing of the commotion downstairs because he is now stone deaf, and when the apron the young wife tore off and threw at the kitchen stove catches fire, igniting the curtains, rugs and furniture in quick succession, he remains oblivious because he's dreaming about fire and it seems only logical, only natural; he's coughing and choking but he does not wake up because he's still inside the book, inside the dream, and the sensations caused by smoke and flame, crackling and burning, singeing and stifling are part of the fire in the novel, part of the dream, part of that place in himself of the highest, brightest intensity to which he's always longed but never dared to go, he's back in Africa now, back in KwaMashu where Currie lived — a pile of cotton remnants has caught fire, a giant ball of flame is careering wildly across the township, setting fire to one shack after the other, whole families are being burned alive; Aron is standing there watching this, and at the same time he *is* the ball of flame, rolling, devouring, engulfing, laying waste to everything in its path . . .

XVIII

Drinking

*I*s it really impossible to leave?" asks Beth.

"Stop worrying," says Brian. "There's nothing to worry about. Jordan's safe and warm in his jail cell, Vanessa's happily ensconced in the most dangerous city in the world — and here we all are, snug as a bug in a rug."

"You're soused," says Beth. "What a silly thing to say."

("Snug as a bug in a rug" is the sort of thing Beth's mother used to say, with her exasperating gift for platitudes. "Just one of those things," she'd said, for instance, on June 26, 1975, when it turned out that Dr. Raymondson, detained by a medical convention in Frankfurt, would be unable to attend Beth's graduation ceremony at Hammondsville High School. "I'd gladly have flown home for you from anywhere in America, sweets," he'd told her over the phone, "but crossing the Atlantic twice in two days is more than my system can take." "Just one of those things," Jessie had said. Beth had left the house alone, on the pretext that she needed to be at school half an hour early, which was a lie, she simply couldn't bring herself to enter the school building at the side of a woman dressed in a puffy-skirted pink rayon dress, legs unshaven and stockingless, big feet squeezed into a pair of white pumps — Jessie's only "good shoes," purchased for her wedding day in 1957. So Jessie had come alone and taken a seat in one of the back rows of the auditorium. The black-gowned students had converged on stage — there were bands and banners, speeches and diplomas, salvos of applause, and then, at last, came the special mentions. Beth was the school's top student. To prove herself a worthy intellectual companion to her father, she'd gotten stunning results on the national achievement tests, surpassed every academic record in the memory of Hammondsville High — and now, now, she was being summoned back onto the stage — star of the year, climax of the afternoon — to have the highest honor award bestowed upon her. Waves of applause lifted her from seat and propelled her up the steps to the podium. The school principal smiled at her, energetically pumping her hand as he handed her the prize, a bronze medal with her name engraved on it. Then, turning to the microphone, he said, "Elizabeth Raymondson, congratulations! On behalf of all the teachers and students of Hammondsville High, I want you to know how proud of you we are. You may just be the one who puts Hammondsville on the map! Are your parents here with you today to share in the limelight?" "No," she blurted out. "I mean — I'm afraid they couldn't come" — blushing, mumbling, fumbling with her medal — "but it doesn't matter — it's all right!" "Of course it's all right, it's just too bad they couldn't come, that's all. Well, once again, our sincere congratulations. Let's hear it for Miss Raymondson, ladies and gentlemen!" Oh, the expression on Jessie's face, when Beth got home that evening . . . Her silence . . . But she'd been kind enough never to breathe a word to her husband of the affront she'd received at Beth's hands. Oh Mother I'm sorry, Beth thinks now. You were the best cook in the whole world. Your chicken-'n'-dumplings were simply scrumptious, even if you did have to splay your legs to pluck the chicken. I'm sorry, Mother. Thanks for all the blueberry waffles you served up to me, Sunday mornings in summertime. And your baby carrots, just drowning in freshly churned butter . . . No, I haven't forgotten, Mother, please forgive me . . . That fall, Beth had come East to commence her medical studies at Radcliffe; when her father died in a car accident the following year, she'd gone back to Alabama for his funeral; and then . . . returned three or four times over twenty years. Jessie Skykes Raymondson had been left to fend for herself, alienated from her hillbilly parents by her fancy house in the suburbs, and from her Ivy League daughter by her slack-wittedness. She hardly knew her grandchildren . . . Oh, Mother! I'll spend Christmas with you this year — I swear I will!)

"Come on," says Brian, pulling her down next to him on the couch. "We might as well make the best — "

"How 'bout some Shirley Horn?" says Charles, running his finger down Sean's stack of records.

"Yeah," says Patrizia, reentering the room from the kitchen where she's been scraping turkey bones and dried bread crusts and cold congealed vegetables from plates into the garbage can. "I love Shirley Horn." Kicking off her shoes, she does a series of unsteady two-step twirls around the room. "Matter of fact, I love all you guys!" she adds. "I'm so much nicer a person with you than with my kids."

"*What?*" says Derek. "What are you talking about? You adore your sons!"

"Sure I do," says Patrizia, losing her balance on the seventh twirl and toppling onto a cushion on the floor, "but I also mistreat them. Sometimes I remind myself of my own mother! I wonder if they see me the way I saw her — forever tense and hurried and preoccupied . . ."

"Don't be silly," says Katie. "I've seen you with Tomas and Gino. They worship you. Your almond cookies are famous throughout the county. You even know how to sew patches on their blue jeans."

"Patch?" says Sean. "Did somebody say Patch? Here, Patch!"

"I always preferred mine with holes," says Hal. "I even tore holes in my patches on purpose."

"Yeah, but I yell at them," says Patrizia.

"Don't worry about that," says Rachel. "Kids enjoy being yelled at every now and then."

"No they don't," says Patrizia. "My mother yelled at me and I hated it."

"Then why do you do it?" says Charles. (As a boy he'd been shocked by the verbal violence of some of his friends' mothers —

obsessed with dirt and danger, screeching at their sons for their table manners, hollering at them to come home from playground or baseball diamond — whereas his own mother had never once raised her voice to him, not even when he tore his pants or lost his jacket or spilled his milk. One of his worst fights with Myrna had been about whether or not they should read *Peter Rabbit* to the children — Charles was allergic to the moralistic mewling of Beatrix Potter.)

"Oh, for just about anything. Because one of them's in a bad mood, for example. I can't stand it when they're in a bad mood. Or because they take my eraser without asking. Or because my mayonnaise isn't coming out right. Or because Gino's got a tumor on his calf bone . . . I hit them, too," she adds, almost as an afterthought.

"You do not!" says Katie.

"I do, too!" says Patrizia. "I hit them! Not every day, but — "

"Stop boasting," says Hal. "Chloe will start getting ideas."

"Seriously," says Patrizia. "I disappoint myself as a mother. Motherhood upset the delicate balance I'd achieved in my adult life. I thought I'd made myself into a such a nice, wise sort of person . . . but the minute I had kids, my own childhood came surging up inside me, with all the screaming and confusion . . ."

"Italian mothers are *supposed* to scream," says Hal. "It's part of the image. *Mangia! Mangia!* Didn't you ever see *Amarcord?*"

"And I never feel like playing with them," says Patrizia. "I have to force myself."

"It's ironic, when you think about it," Aron puts in unexpectedly. (He recalls the countless evenings he and Nicole spent playing Monopoly and Scrabble with their daughters on the beautiful oaken table in their drawing room in Durban. They always stacked the games neatly away in the bottom drawer of the buffet afterward, so Currie wouldn't have to bother with their incomprehensible accoutrements: miniature houses and hotels, make-believe dollars, heaps of plastic letters.) "At first parents play games to humor their children, though they feel it's a waste of time — and then later, when the children come home to visit, they play games to humor their parents, though they feel it's a waste of time."

"Yeah," says Hal. "You see, Patrizia? Games are a drag, everybody knows that — *especially* with your parents!"

"Oh, let's change the subject," says Patrizia. "Can I have one of these, Sean?" She lights a Winston without looking up for his assent.

(She'd always been stymied, when the two of them were together, by Sean's ludicrous mixture of generosity and stinginess — he'd squander ninety dollars on a meal of steak and lobster, for instance, and then whine at her when they got home for taking a puff from his cigarette or dipping her lips into his nightcap. And when she teased him about it he stiffened up defensively — "I just like to know where I am in my tobacco and alcohol consumption, if that's not too much to ask.")

"Does anybody care I have emphysema?" asks Beth, not very loudly.

"Boy, can that Shirley Horn sing!" says Rachel. The voice makes her yearn to be naked and making love. With the first purred throat notes, she wants to *be* that way (a way she has in fact never been), languorous luscious and lascivious, lounging around in bed and licking her man, singing to him, moaning and crooning to him with the deep laughter of complicity. (A month or two ago, over a bottle of Muscadet, growing looser and more confessional as the cool white wine slid down her throat, Katie had opened up to Rachel about how shaky things had gotten for Leonid in bed in recent years. "We still love them, don't we?" she'd said at one point, ruefully shaking her head. "I mean it's still sweet and cuddly and all, that's not the problem, it's just that . . . oh, well . . . I always did like a hard-on," and Rachel had choked with laughter in the midst of a swallow, splattering Muscadet all over the table. But the truth was that — except with Sean who, there as elsewhere, had shared her darkness — she'd never been overly interested in sex. Embraces with Sean could be as lengthy and tangled and frightening as a child's nightmare ... "Orgasm is for hicks," he'd told her once, to make her laugh, as they fell back exhausted after several hours of love-hate-making. No, Derek's languishing libido was fine with her.)

"It's not that you don't have a nice voice, Beth," says Sean conciliatorily. "You have a very nice voice."

Nonplussed at hearing Sean apologize twice in the course of the same evening, Beth glances up at him and sees that he means it, sees also that his lips are somewhat gray, and is bizarrely reminded of the horses at her grandfather's farm, the strange feeling of their thick nibbling gray lips as they rolled over the palm of her hand and delicately picked up the lump of sugar or the clump of grass she was bravely, eagerly, apprehensively holding out to them ...

"I saw in the *Prattler* you did a stint at UCLA last summer," Brian says to Hal, eager to change the subject. "How did that go? How did you like my old stomping grounds?" He wants to give him the choice — not force him to talk about the teaching if he prefers not to — though that's what he, Brian, would like to hear about, on the off chance of gleaning some magical insight into the art of writing. (He's always been fascinated by writers and is secretly a little overwhelmed to be here this evening, rubbing elbows with personages whose names are known from coast to coast. He'd been struck speechless when, some five years ago, Sean Farrell in person called his office and asked him to handle his divorce. "It will be an honor, Mr. Farrell," he'd said, the ringing in his right ear growing louder as it always did when his pulse began to race, and since that time he'd handled not only the divorce but a number of other delicate legal tasks for Sean, most recently his last will and testament, a sad piece of paper indeed — "No, I'm afraid you can't leave it all to Patchouli, that just won't stand up to scrutiny in the courts" — so Sean had left his house to the town, which had long ago forgiven him his mortgage, and his archive to the university, which had been paying monthly installments on it for years. Were it not for the instant and mutual animosity between Sean and Beth, the two men might have become friends;

as it was they met only occasionally, for short manly drinks in the local tavern. And now . . . here Brian was, snowed in with the gods, eager to milk his luck, loath to see the night seep away in paltry patter. No calling, to his mind, was higher than the literary calling — he'd felt a thrill of it himself, as a pimply teenager back in East Los Angeles, and had passionately plowed through the American canon from Melville to Carver, confident of surpassing them all one day — I might have, too, he now mutters to himself, if the war hadn't wrecked my self-esteem. 'Nam veterans were antiheroes, despised and rejected by their peers. After his return to "the world," Brian had experienced a year of mental mayhem in the course of which he'd driven from California to the Yucatán, picking up a miserably wasted druggie along the way and getting stoned with her and stupidly impregnating her in a roach-filled motel in Chihuahua and deciding to face the music and marry her and live with her in Mexico for the rest of his life. But then, having run out of money and come down from his reefer high, he'd reconsidered his situation and skipped town, leaving his young wife pregnant and penniless. Perhaps to redeem himself in his own eyes, he'd gone on to study law at Harvard and practice it primarily in the slums, defending the poor under the auspices of the American Civil Liberties Union. This hadn't sufficed, however, to redeem him in the eyes of his jilted spouse, who'd tracked him down a few years later and sued him for not only divorce but also child support, forcing him to pay through the teeth for their unwanted daughter to whom she'd given the absurd name Cher, and whose acquaintance he was now compelled to make through the intermediary of snapshots, school report cards and especially bills, bills for dental work, dance classes and a costly private education in California, all the way through to her master's degree in Anthropology at Stanford. Since then — not a word.)

"Yeah," says Hal, scratching his belly. "They paid me fifteen grand. Came in handy, what with the new wing we're adding on to the house for the kid."

"Can you really, actually, teach people how to write?" asks Beth.

"No," says Charles. "But you can teach them how *not* to write, which is a start."

"Of course you can't," says Hal at the same time, in a louder voice. "But if they pay you fifteen grand for a three-week course, why turn it down?"

"He had a psycho in his class," Chloe puts in, in a blasé drawl.

"HA! Yeah," says Hal. "A change from the usual routine, that's for sure."

"What happened?" asks Brian, on tenterhooks.

"Oh, this guy . . ." And, for the nineteenth time in Chloe's presence, Hal proceeds to tell the story of the man who, when the time came for the rest of the class to discuss his short story, had bent down, drawn a gun from his attaché case and aimed it at his fellow students, saying "I'm warning you, this story is about my mother, and if anybody laughs . . ."

"No!" says Patrizia.

"Yeah," says Hal. "Damn dangerous profession, teaching writing!"

"But what was his story about?" asks Patrizia. "What did he have to say about his mother?"

"I don't know, something about how he used to rummage around in her dresser drawers, the scent of lavender and roses, stuff like that."

Patrizia loses herself for a moment in her own memories of rummaging through her mother's drawers; at about age seven she'd happened upon a box of tampons and spent weeks coming up with wild hypotheses as to how they might be used. Later, once she'd learned what they were really for: "Do you think they deflower you, if you're a virgin?" the girls at Gate-of-Heaven Junior High would whisper, going into gales of giggles. And later still, when she met with her confessor in preparation for her wedding: "I hope you've remained pure in body and in soul, my child?" — the image of being deflowered by a tampon had brought a most inappropriate smile to her lips. Incensed, the priest had launched into an endless speech about the

the mystery of holy matrimony that turns physical possession, by the grace of Jesus Christ, into purity.)

When she returns to the present, Hal has finished with his story and the friends, all but Chloe, are laughing uproariously.

"Whew!" says Brian, impressed.

"Yeah, damn dangerous profession," repeats Hal, wishing he'd drawn the tale out a bit longer and could go on reveling in the limelight. But Charles is already elbowing his way in.

"I never had any guns in my classroom," he says. "But back at Chicago, three of my students once laid waste to my office."

"What did they have against you?" says Brian.

"They weren't happy with the way I responded to their poems," says Charles. "So they overturned my computer, emptied my drawers on the floor, trashed my bookshelves . . ."

"Good Lord!" says Katie.

"Poetry matters, you see?" says Sean to no one in particular, perhaps to his dog.

"They belonged to this group of freshman Farrakhan freaks," Charles goes on. "Keep-up-with-the-Leroy-Joneses kind of thing. They wrote what were basically gangsta-rap lyrics about taking revenge on whitey, stuff like that. I told them the English language was comprised of more than seventeen words and they should settle down and try and learn a few of them before they started calling themselves poets. Read Baldwin, I told them. Read Shakespeare. Read Soyinka. Why don't you shut up and read for a while, until something starts happening in your head? I was in a bit of a bad mood that day," he adds, and the others laugh. (He'd been in a murderous mood, if the truth be told, because his mother had just been diagnosed with severe diabetes and he'd spent the better part of the morning shouting through the telephone at her doctor and her insurance company, incensed at their incompetence and beside himself with fear. Then, just before his class was scheduled to start, he'd tried to calm down with a cup of coffee at Dunkin' Donuts, but the electronic cash register was on the blink and the black cashier had driven him to despair by not knowing how to subtract a dollar fifty from five dollars. "Didn't you go to grade school?" he'd screamed in her face, regretting it at once when he saw her flinch and recoil in fright and realized he must be reminding her of any number of furious frustrated black men — her father, brothers, cousins, boyfriends — who'd been screaming in her face since the day she was born, and indeed his own father had been subject to the same sort of paroxysm, yes like that Christmas when, in the course of a stupid quarrel with his wife, he'd marched across the living room and sent their ceiling-tall, gloriously decorated Christmas tree crashing to the floor in front of the bewildered eyes of their four children — so Charles had apologized and cleared out of the place, leaving the three dollars and fifty cents behind for the cashier. "That'll teach her how to subtract!" he'd muttered to himself on his way to the car. Ten minutes later, confronted with these garbage poems full of *mothafucka mothafucka* and *slaves gon' kill you,* he'd lost it again.)

Wasn't it encouraging, at least, thinks Brian, that those gangsta-rap poets were at college and not behind bars?

"Want me to take the kid back upstairs?" Hal asks Chloe, whose silence is beginning to make him nervous.

"Sure," says Chloe indifferently.

Hal bundles the sleeping child into his arms and ascends the staircase — hey little man he thinks, lowering his son into his bed on the floor. Hey, Hal Hetherington Junior. I hope you'll be proud to bear that name. The name Hetherington didn't mean a thing when I came into it, a hardware store on Werk Road was all it was, my old man sold nails and masking tape and copper wiring while my mother, a kerchief over her curlers, sat at the cash register and painted her fingernails. Too bad your grandparents faded into the sunset before you came along, kid, but at least the name Hetherington means something now. That's an advantage — you won't have to pull yourself up by the bootstraps the way I did. The

Ivy League will fling its doors wide open to you and you'll never need to deliver pizza, pump gas, wonder where your next meal is coming from. Hey boy. Hey. Nothing but the best for my son.

As he rises from his squat to a standing position, his heart begins to thump again — not as wildly as it had after the tussle in the snow, but more noticeably than he'd like.

You'll see, he tells his son soundlessly. It's a big world out there. We'll travel all over it together. Every summer we'll hit a new Wonder, okay? The Great Wall of China . . . the Taj Mahal . . . the Pyramids . . . You have to be ambitious, kid. If you don't eat the world, it'll eat you. You have to whet your appetite. Like Walt Whitman. Now there's a man for you. A giant. The minute you learn to talk, I'll start reading you *Leaves of Grass*. You've only got so many years to walk the earth, kid. You have to make the most of them, get out there and grab life. Most folks are like pet mice, they don't even try to see what's beyond the limits of their cardboard box, they tell themselves oh so that's the way it is, this is my neighborhood, this is my church, these are the shelves of my hardware store . . . and life passes them by! They set their alarm clocks every night, do their weekly grocery shopping, send out greeting cards whenever Christmas rolls around, and before they've understood a thing it's time to jump into their coffins and good night. But you'll know how to *live*, Junior. Carpe diem. Suck the marrow out of every minute.

XIX

BRIAN

Brian will return to my bosom at age sixty-two, which means that he possesses a mere twelve years in which to bring his dreams to fruition — less time than he thinks, less than he's counting on, though were anyone to go to the trouble of asking him what his dreams are now (which they don't), he'd be hard put to say. One of them, a modest dream he thinks, but it's been years since he gave up hope of seeing it come true, is simply that the ringing in his right ear might someday stop. It never has. He's tried what the doctor told him was the only remedy for tinnitus: fighting fire with fire, he's added sound to sound, deliberately directing a slightly less shrill electronic ring into his left ear, then doing his best to revel in the sensation of control as he adjusts the volume of the intentional ring, in hopes that his brain might "forget" the unbidden, uncontrollable stridulation in his right.

Poor, plagued Brian. He doesn't sense me at his side as he enters a postcard shop in Paris — he and Beth are on vacation together, but when Beth curled up for an afternoon nap he decided to take a walk, stumbled upon this charming shop in the Rue Saint Martin just off the Rue de Rivoli, and began to scrounge around for an old card he might be able send to Vanessa, now living with her sound engineer of a husband in Des Moines, Iowa, and expecting her first child. Jordan they lost track of a few years ago and Cher (his daughter from his first marriage) he's all but forgotten since she stopped extorting money from him, but Vanessa he cares for with a vengeance — and so, leaning forward over the boxes of old cards (labeled variously as *"Monuments"* — le Moulin Rouge, le Palais du Trocadéro, le Sacré Coeur — *"Régions"* — Languedoc-Roussillon, Charente-Maritime,

Rhône-Alpes, names that mean nothing to him — *"Pays étrangers"* — Etats-Unis, Japon, Espagne — and *"Thèmes"* — Les Fleurs, Les Animaux, Les Bébés), he searches anxiously for the card that might make Vanessa's eyes light up, her heartbeat quicken, her lips soften into a smile at the thought of her faraway, gray-bearded old dad. But all the cards seem either trite, inappropriate, or too specific — or else they've got elaborate, incomprehensible messages scrawled across them — and as he leans forward, sweating now, panting, flipping more and more anxiously through the boxes, tiny platelets are accumulating unbeknownst to him in one of his arteries because an atheroma has gotten in their way. Suddenly the blood dams up, it pushes and pushes against the clot but can't squeeze past, Brian's face drains as if he'd just heard some very bad news, and indeed the news is bad but he hasn't heard it, he's getting pale, paler, palest, now he's white as a sheet and his features have gone slack, his brain is fairly crying out for oxygen — Quick! Hey! Let's get things moving here! — but his volition is like an impotent traffic cop waving his stick in the Callahan Tunnel at rush hour, no one's paying him the least attention and no one's going to get through, not even the panic ambulance, its siren wailing now, its revolving light flashing redly — no, the traffic is clogged once and for all, a definitive jam. Brian sprawls onto the card display, causing the table to crash to the ground. Involuntarily rolled onto his side by the sliding colliding boxes, he lies there amid Notre Dame cathedrals and Mont-Saint-Michel monasteries, simpering hand-colored geisha girls and snaking Great Walls of China, old black-and-white Brooklyn Bridges and stiff, silly poodles with their beribboned tails sticking straight up in the air, and dies. *"Merde!"* shouts the owner of the shop, clapping his hands to his head as he rushes over to take the measure of the mess, estimate how much of his precious time will now have to be spent — *"Merde! Merde!"* — first arranging for the body of this cumbersome tourist to be removed, then painstakingly re-sorting and restacking the hundreds of cards he has upset.

XX

Drifting

Proud of his little speech, Hal goes back downstairs — and is surprised to find that Chloe has vanished. For a second he imagines, insanely, that she's left the house and is walking homeward, defying the whipping wind and blinding snow like one of the characters in his Klondike novel. Then, more reasonably, he surmises she's gone to the bathroom. And finally, no — he sees her blond head bobbing up and down at the far end of the room — she's pulled a low stool up next to Aron's rocking chair and is nodding, blankly but politely, as he tries to tell her about the hands of Bellini's Virgins.

What *is* it with this guy? she's saying to herself. You'd almost think he was coming on to me. Unbelievable. Repulsive — his crabbed hands — scaly skin — wrinkled chicken's neck — white hair so thin you can see the pink of his scalp through it. I always hated doing guys over fifty, it took so long to get them hard. Hal's an exception. Being in bed with him is actually bearable, just as long as I keep my eyes closed when he gets undressed. He's so tender . . . and the rest of the time he takes good care of me, it's almost like he was my mother . . . Not our real mother, Col, but the one we used to invent for ourselves, remember? The one who read books out loud to us at bedtime and took us out for picnics on the beach.

"Hi, babe."

Chloe rises swiftly upon seeing Hal, grateful for an excuse to cut short Aron's ridiculous raving over the beauty of her hands. Nothing's beautiful, no human body is beautiful, apart from my brother's, all parts of the body are ugly including hands. (Once a client had offered her five hundred dollars if she'd simply sit next to him in a movie theater and hold him as they watched a film. "I won't lay a finger on you," he promised. "Sure," she agreed, indifferently. She'd seen porn before, though usually on TV screens in hotel rooms. "It's a true story," the client told her in advance. "And believe it or not, the heroine is from Vancouver!" So she'd sat there, sole woman amongst the scattered lonely men, and had done her best to glaze her gaze over, project some film of her own making onto the screen as the cute gullible waitress from Vancouver was drawn into the *Playboy* vortex — "Keep your eyes open!" the client warned her toward the end of the film, clamping her hand onto his swollen penis and guiding it up and down as the other men in the theater unzipped their own trousers and brought out their own penises and rubbed them in weird unison (like those symphony orchestras you see on TV, Chloe had thought, with their hundred violin bows sawing simultaneously up and down), watching Chloe watch the scene he knew by heart, seeing the images reflected in the pain in her face as the pretty waitress who'd dreamed of becoming a famous actress was attached to a machine by virtue of which every thrust of her lover's sex caused limb racks to tighten and sharp blades to slice into her flesh. It isn't really happening, Chloe kept telling herself, she isn't really dying — yes all this was make-believe of course, nothing but studio simulation, the film was a perfectly standard bit of porn, not actual snuff or they'd never have been watching it in an ordinary downtown theater — but it looked real, that was what mattered, and as the heroine bled to death with agonizing slowness, ejaculative gasps went off here and there around the theater — irregularly, unpredictably, no longer in unison, like the last damp afterthought fireworks on Victoria Day when Chloe was a child . . . Her hands had been forever corrupted by that experience. All of her body, part by part, had been corrupted, deadened, numbed. It was a matter of numbing and not, as Hal believed, of shame and scandal. The only scandal was that Chloe had not, like her brother Colin, met death

— that her body was still functioning — still able to walk and talk, dress and undress, shake hands make love and smile, even conceive a child, give birth, give suck — *that* was the scandal — whereas nothing mattered, nothing reached her, almost nothing in her lived.)

"You all right?" Hal whispers as she reaches him, and she shrugs, nods, rolls her eyes ceilingward as if to say *That old guy . . .* "You must be getting tired," Hal whispers lovingly, paternally. "Don't feel obliged to hang around. You can go up and hit the hay anytime you feel like it. People won't take offense. A nursing mother . . ."

Chloe shrugs once more — shrugs him off, almost — returns to her seat at the end of the couch and sinks her gaze back into the coiled colors of the rag rug.

She *looks* tired, thinks Hal. Her face is pale and pinched, and she has gray circles under her eyes. Sitting down next to her, he puts a bearlike arm around her but she shrugs him off again.

"This a photo album?" asks Charles, drawing a thick binder from a stack of books on the lower panel of the coffee table. "Can I take a look?" He's never been able to resist photo albums, though he knows they lie. (The one of his family's trip to Monument Valley, for instance, shows him standing in front of the famous rock formation known as the Mittens with a big grin on his face and a son under each arm. Click, clack.)

"Be my guest," says Sean. "It's an old one. Dates back to the 1960s. I dug it up when my ma was in the home. I thought it might . . . ah . . . stimulate her memory, as it were."

"And did it work?"

"Ah, no, she was back in the 1940s by that time."

Yes, thinks Beth, because the microscopic stigmata characteristic of Alzheimer's progress in reverse order to the myelinization of the nervous system. They attack first the rhinencephalon, then the limbic system, then the cerebral cortex — whereas as we grow into maturity, we develop first the cerebral cortex, then the limbic system, then the rhinencephalon. You never learned about this, Daddy, modern medicine was still in the dark about senile dementia when you died, but you would have been thrilled with these new discoveries — imagine the conversations we would have had! You were always fascinated by borderline areas, where it's impossible to distinguish body from soul — and what could be more borderline than the destruction of personality by beta-amyloid plaques?

"Who's this?" says Charles.

"That is my . . . ah . . . third stepfather, I believe. Mort, his name was. Silky mustache, big soft lips — used to kiss me a lot, to get in Ma's good graces. An unbelievable farter, too. Real military farts, like a drill sergeant playing the snare drum. Every morning after breakfast — *Taratatata, Atten-shun!*"

"Uh, huh," says Charles, laughing. "How old are you here, about ten?"

"No — that's '66? — I'm going on thirteen. Skinny little beggar, aren't I?"

From the other side of the room Katie looks at the men's heads as they lean forward and pore over the photos of Sean as a little boy and his mother as a young woman. All but Charles have gray or white and thinning hair, mottled foreheads, knobby hands . . . My goodness, she thinks in surprise, Sean actually has liver spots! I'd never noticed them before . . . And look how his hands shake as he turns the pages . . . Oh my darling David, the photo albums . . .

(Which registered first, the sound or the smell? she wonders. I think it must have been the sound. Most likely my brain succeeded in denying the smell until we were in the hallway, a mere few steps away from David's door, but there was no denying the barking of Cleopatra, the red Labrador bitch they'd given David years ago, when they first moved up to New England. Though old and half blind by now, Cleopatra was clearly beside herself, and the sound of her crazed and furious barking filled Katie's heart with dread. But it also filled her, and this was the hardest thing to admit, with . . . elation. She kept watching herself going up the steps, one by one, studying the cracks in each step, her sandaled feet, the way the nail polish was flaking off the big toe of her right foot, and thinking, *this is it. This is it.* Her heart was thumping fast and she noticed the difference between the two rhythms — her heartbeat and Cleopatra's sharp, repeated bark — they weren't going at quite the same speed but every now and then they'd coincide, like the ticking of two alarm clocks in the same room, in the olden days, when she was a little girl and alarm clocks used to tick . . . Then a third, much faster beat came to join the other two — Leo rapping on the door — but Katie knew beyond the shadow of a doubt that no matter how hard or how long he rapped, knocked, pounded on that door, David would never come to open it. *He's dead, honey,* she wanted to tell her husband in a reassuring tone of voice, but she didn't dare pronounce the words because she didn't want to shock him, see him blanch, break down and sob uncontrollably. *He's dead, honey* — she had the certain knowledge of it now, and wanted to protect Leonid from it. It'll be so hard on him, she thought. But she herself felt — what was it that she felt ? It was — undeniably, indescribably — relief. Release. It's over, she said to herself, as Leonid stopped pounding on the door and began heaving at it with his shoulder. It's over at last, she thought, as the flimsy lock gave way and the door banged open inward and Cleopatra came bounding out at them in a frenzy of crazed barking. "It's all right, girl, it's all right," she told the dog, doing her best to soothe her while at the same time solemnly telling herself: now you must turn your head and look toward the bed, and what your eyes will see when they get there is the lifeless body of your son — all this in an instant — but even before she had time to finish the thought, Leonid emitted a low cry and pushed her back out into the hallway and crushed her against the filthy brownish yellow wall, trembling violently, then leaning away to vomit, the dog no longer barking now but keening, whining, staggering around them, bumping into them and interfering with their movements, though neither of them any longer knew what they were moving for, or where they might move from here, or why.)

"Hey, your mom sure could wear a bathing suit!"

Bedazzlement, thinks Patrizia, caught up in the way the firelight is flickering in the champagne glasses and thinking once more of stained-glass windows in church. *Even as I child I took delight in everything that sparkled and spun, the tinselly little windmills that whirled when you ran with them in the wind, majorettes in a parade twirling their batons until they blurred, circus acrobats, cartwheeling weightless through the air, so fast their bodies became stars, ciphers, pure geometrical constructs . . . Diamond tiaras, sparkling jewels, precious stones, mica-schist. The words glimmer glitter gleam glisten glint glow. The word golden.*

"Yeh. That was the summer we spent up in Vermont, pretending we were an all-around normal wholesome American family. *We were dragged out to that lake by my second stepfather, Jack. Nervous guy, Jack. Very jumpy. Bit his nails to the quick. Tried to teach me to fish and hunt and cuss, make a man of me. It drove him up the wall to see me reading poetry. Slapped my ma around a lot. Off the wall, Jack.*"

"Looks crazed," says Charles. "A gleam of madness in those eyes."

"Yeh. You can see it, huh?"

Funny he should say gleam *when I was just thinking it,* muses Patrizia. *Wonder if he picked it up from me. Nice guy, Charles. If only he weren't quite so pompous.*

"Yeh," says Charles, remembering his baseball coach in high school, who'd had a similar gleam in his. *Mr. Rhodes — Jesus, I even remember the bastard's name. Haven't thought of him in years. Used to touch my rear end, accidentally on purpose, in the locker room. Wanted me to apply for a sports scholarship at Northwestern. "No, Mr. Rhodes, I want to study English." "Leave Shakespeare to whitey," he said. He actually said that. "Leave Shakespeare to whitey." My father could have said the same thing, albeit for different reasons. So disappointed in his sons, one a criminal and the other a professor poet. Neither involved in the struggle. But it was just that — my father's obsession with politics — that propelled me* into poetry. I didn't want to spend my whole life proving I had the right to live it. I wanted — everything, Dad. Everything life had to offer. My feet on the ground *and* my head in the clouds. The right to think about something other than black and white. New England, for instance — because I live here now and so it belongs to me, too — deep woods, deep snow, wild animals, *nothing in the fields / veins of ditches, snow spouts / lifting with the wind like hair* . . .

"Wonder why Maisie couldn't see it," muses Sean. "Ah! How about that trout, eh? Don't I look proud? Bloody awful day that was. Jack tried to make a fire to grill the fish on, but the wood was damp and the fire kept dying. He grew incensed and started yelling at poor Maisie, so she sat down and sulked. By the time the trout was cooked we were all too depressed to be hungry, so Jack flung the thing back into the lake and drove us home to Somerville, doing eighty miles on hour on the back roads, with Ma and me clinging to each other for dear life in the backseat."

"End of all-American vacation," says Charles.

"I've always wondered how the other fish felt when they saw that grilled trout plunge back into their midst."

The fish in the Pripiat, where my dad and I used to go fishing, thinks Leonid, will never be edible again. (His father had died first and then — nude, weightless, mindless — his mother, and even for their funerals he hadn't gone home. It took Chernobyl — the hideous, irreversible contamination of the rivers and forests and fields he knew so well — it took Grigori's death, Ioulia's mad grief, little Svetlana's thyroid cancer to bring him running back at last. Ah, yes. For Grigori's burial he'd gone back, only no one was allowed to get near the body. The coffin itself was radioactive, lined with metal sheeting, covered with huge blocks of concrete reinforced with lead, buried at a remove from the other coffins. In Leonid's homeland, even the dead now had cause to fear the dead.)

"Psychotherapy's just the opposite," says Brian, stroking his beard, which Beth knows is a signal he's about to make a speech.

"What are you talking about?" she says. "The opposite of what?"

"Photo albums," says Brian. "In photo albums everything looks hunky-dory and in psychotherapy everything looks tragic, and the truth is somewhere in between. Once I took Nessa sledding up in New Hampshire. What was she, Beth — about three or four?"

Beth merely sighs; she knows the story, knows it will last a while. Brian has begun to resemble his father in that way, whereas it was something he'd despised and derided in his father: the older he got the more verbally incontinent he became, overwhelming people with narratives that rambled all over the map, getting lost in digressions . . . Brian can still follow the thread of his stories, but they're getting longer and more disorganized and she fears that this might be just the beginning, and that twenty years down the line he'll be running off at the mouth like his father, incapable of listening, indifferent to whether or not his listeners have have already heard this particular story . . . As Beth finds this perspective genuinely frightening, she decides to go elsewhere in her mind. (To Miami.)

"It was during the Christmas holidays," says Brian. "Beth was on duty and Nessa said Look it's snowing, it's so beautiful, let's go tobogganing, daddy! . . . So I took her up to Mount Monadnock for the day. We spent the whole afternoon fooling around in the snow . . ."

(Beth is eating grilled pork off a paper plate, licking her fingers, drinking beer and laughing, sitting at a crowded picnic table at midnight in Miami's Cuban neighborhood with her Cuban lover Federico as smoke pours from the *braseros,* raucous rhythmic music rises from the radio, snatches of laughter and Spanish exclamations explode in the air around them. Federico is holding her bare white feet on his bare black legs and stroking them.)

"By four-thirty Nessa was getting tired, so I promised her we'd take the ski lift down. But when we got there, the last one had just left. 'Sorry, I can't send you down,' the guy said — 'we stop at sunset!' So there we were, stranded at the top of the mountain. Nothing for it but to sled all the way back down."

(Beth is taking a bath in her room in the Miami Hyatt, preparing for the evening with Federico. Catching a glimpse of herself in the mirror, she for once loves her body because Federico finds it beautiful, her curves seem bountiful instead of fat, her hair an enticing mass of curls instead of a hopeless tangle of frizz. Is she really going to make love with this stranger, is it possible, yes, she knows it will happen, she met him only two days ago, she'd wandered down to the beach after having been cooped up in her medical convention all day, and, spotting a little ice cream truck, had been unable to resist temptation. As he handed her her triple vanilla scoop, Federico had exclaimed, "Here you are, ma'am. Sure wish I could get slurped by such lovely lips!" and the kooky compliment had made her laugh out loud. Within minutes they were flirting openly and Beth realized to her astonishment that she trusted this stranger absolutely and would be prepared — no, delighted — to put her body in his hands. Never before had she betrayed Brian. She found her own attitude incomprehensible and was all the more electrified by it.)

"It had stopped snowing but it was getting cold and dark. I put Nessa between my legs and we started down — but she was getting the powder right in her face, and she started to cry. So I had this brainwave: I stopped the sled and switched places with her. That way *I* was getting the snow in my face, and she was sheltered behind the big warm wall of her daddy's back."

"Brilliant," says Patrizia, wondering how people have the nerve to tell such long stories. She herself, for fear of boring her listeners, rarely utters more than two or three consecutive sentences on evenings like this.

(They're making love on the smooth white sheets of Beth's enormous bed in the Miami Hyatt, in the cool breeze of the air-conditioning; palm trees are waving and a blue sea is sparkling beyond the window balcony; all the clichés of Florida have gathered to celebrate their embrace.)

"And then when we got home," Brian goes on, "Nessa threw herself into Beth's arms and said 'Mommy, oh Mommy we were on the sled and I got all the snow in my face and it was just *horrible* . . .' And I said, 'Hey, that's not the whole story!' For days afterward, every time she'd talk about coming down the mountain, she'd remember her suffering, which had lasted maybe one tenth of the trip, and forget all about her father's heroic solution to the problem, which had lasted the other nine-tenths."

(It's four in the morning, a nostalgic little waltz is playing on the radio and Beth is dancing with Federico on her hotel room balcony. She's stroking the tight curls of gray hair on his temples. She's sleeping in his arms. They're showering together, and Federico's lips against hers are wet with saliva and running water, his belly against hers is round and tight, his brown skin is smooth, his chest hairless. Brian is covered with hair from head to foot! She'd forgotten how different male bodies can be, sexually; it's the first time in years she's seen a real live man's naked body up close without needing to make an urgent medical decision concerning it.)

"I mean," Brian insists, his voice rising as he senses that some of the guests are actually listening to him now, "people go to shrinks and pour out their woes, feel sorry for themselves, beg for pity, blubber about how badly their parents treated them — and no one's there to give them a reality check — hey, what about the other four-fifths of the trip? What about that brilliant solution your daddy came up with so you'd stop getting snow in your face? I definitely think psychoanalytic theory should be revised on the basis of — "

"Och, who gives a shite about psychoanalytic theory?" says Sean, holding out the champagne bottle. "Brian, your glass is empty, do have another drop."

(Beth is in the elevator with Federico, it's the morning of her last day in Miami, she's wearing a formal sky-blue pantsuit, a wristwatch and a name tag, headed for the final meeting of the medical convention. As the doctor-filled elevator descends toward the convention room on the ground floor, Federico can't help snickering at their name tags — "Elizabeth V. Raymondson (Beth)"; "Joseph L. Black (Joe)"; "Doris R. Darlington (Dorrie)"; "Nancy G. Savitzsky (Nan)." When the doors slide open on the ground floor, Dr. Savitzsky stands aside to let them pass and Federico murmurs, "Thanks, Nan"; she leaps a foot in the air and then, ashamed of her own alarm, shouts "You're welcome!" after them as they glide across the lobby, weak with love and laughter. They exchange a final, fervent kiss in the glancing burning sun on the hotel's front steps, then part. As Beth walks unsteadily back into the dim chill of the lobby, she hears "For shame!" and starts in surprise, thinking no, she must be wrong, the words can't be for her, but they are, the eyes of Dr. Darlington are aiming a stream of contempt at her, puissant as a kick in the gut, and it takes her a moment to understand — ah, the kiss! Ms. Darlington is offended by our flagrantly sensuous, public, passionate, miscegenistic kiss. Beth returns to Boston that afternoon and never sees or hears from Federico again — though when, two weeks later, she learns she's pregnant, she plummets into a fearful but endlessly enticing fantasy that the child might be his, that its dark skin will give her away, and that the instant she gives birth Brian will collapse in tears or turn coldly on his heel and leave.)

It's such a pity, Hal muses to himself apropos of nothing. The brain's capacities are so spectacular and we ask so little of it. The brain is an eagle treated like a canary; encaged; compelled to flit instead of soar.

"No, he's got a point," says Rachel. "The same thing could be said about literature. It's darker than reality, because writers always focus on pain and conflict . . ."

"Darker than reality?" says Sean. "You must be joking!"

A few people laugh.

"Seriously though," Brian insists, "suffering is remembered out of all proportion to the time and space it actually occupies in our lives. The numberless experiences that are merely 'all right' go down the drain."

Everything goes down the drain, you dear dolt, thinks Sean. It all dissipates and disappears, which is why it's all so very beautiful. When Ionesco died — no, a bit before he died, for even the master of the absurd couldn't fax us his wisdom from the Beyond — Look, he said, at the poor dear hands of my wife, the hands I once fell in love with, such darling, delicate hands, look at them now, swollen with pain, stained with age — look, he said. It is all meant to finish. We go to school in order to finish school, we eat a meal in order to finish it and we live our lives to stop living them. But he was wrong, Sean goes on, cracking open a fresh pack of Winstons, the dear Romanian Rhinoceros was wrong because there *is* a point to it all and the point is this, just this, all this, the people in this room and in every room, the things we've said and done together, the endless, intertwining dance of our destinies, the dreams we've cherished and exchanged, the games we've won and lost, the facts we've learned and forgotten, the books we've read and written, and I love it. I love it I love it I love it — sweet, precious life — not the *least* desire to lose it, not the *least*.

"I rather like that story," says Hal — and Brian blushes with pride at having been cogent and coherent, gotten his point across, made sense to a novelist he admires. "You wouldn't mind if I used it in my new book, would you?"

"Are you sure they had ski lifts up in the Klondike?" says Beth drily.

"No, of course I'd change the details and all. I'd just keep the abstract structure of the story — you know. The gist of it."

"I'd be deeply honored," says Brian, already imagining how his name will look printed in the acknowledgments at the end of the book.

XXI

BETH

When Beth learns of Brian's demise, she's convinced that her time has come as well. The minute she returns from the police station to her hotel room on the noisy Rue de Rivoli, her eyes roll back, she convulses and begins to gasp. It's an out-and-out asthma attack — her first since that day of her yellow Easter dress in the mildewed basement back in Decatur. This day in Paris, however, she sprays and gasps to no avail, and were it not for the young policeman who (because Beth's hennaed hair and generous flesh reminded him of his dearly beloved mother) insisted on accompanying her back to her hotel and was therefore present when the attack came on and had summoned an ambulance on his cell phone by the time she blacked out, she might have come to me that day, too.

Such, however, were not my plans for Beth. No, with my inimitable sense of the arbitrary, I wished to pluck this flower with infinite mercy and dexterity.

Thus, many, many years later, when Beth is a replete complete fulfilled capacious sagacious and very elderly lady, overflowing with tales from the twentieth century, smiles and winks and good advice for her seven grandchildren (two of whom are Vanessa's and . . . five Jordan's!) and her seventeen great-grandchildren (never mind), she crawls into bed one night, in a quaint little inn in Rockport, carefully chosen by Vanessa for their vacation together, and starts reading the second volume of Jean-Jacques Rousseau's *Confessions*. She heaves a deep sigh of drowsiness and satisfaction as she turns out the light, and this is the moment I choose to come and extinguish her. Reaching out a hand, I melt through her mauve nightgown, the sagging wrinkled skin of her voluminous breasts and the bones of her rib cage — and clutch her heart. It seizes up briefly, palpitating, causing her to cry out in surprise. Then it stops. And it is Vanessa who, tiptoeing into her mother's room the next morning to see if she's awake, will gently close Beth's big blue eyes once and for all.

XXII

Sinking Somewhat

People don't realize the excruciating *work* involved in novel writing, thinks Hal. They think it's just a matter of jotting down on paper the things you've seen and done. Whereas — he tosses back his third flute of champagne and pours himself another — whereas it's *work*, man! It's like building a fuckin' *pyramid!* The champagne in his brain grabs at the image and decides to have fun with it. I am the Negro slave, he thinks, barefooted and barebacked, dragging blocks of stone over miles of burning sand. I am the pharaoh's corpse, mummified, laid out in the sacred hollow at the heart of the stone so that my soul may voyage to the land of eternal life. I am the architect and the foreman at the construction site; the treasure and the sweat; the food and the blazing sun; the desert and the mystery. Hm, that's not half bad, he thinks, his chest swelling with the divine breath of inspiration. Perhaps there's a chapter I could fit it into . . .

Chloe has slumped softly against him, eyes closed, palms upturned on the skirt of her red dress in a childlike pose of perfect trust. She looks about fourteen years old, thinks Hal. Dear child. Good thing I saved her from gutterdom before it could taint her lovely soul.

(She's not asleep, however. She feels ill. In spite of herself, she has gone back to that unforgettable afternoon with Colin . . . There they are, brother and sister, lying side by side on the bed. As the weather was warm, they'd left the window open — the faint breeze on their naked glistening-diamond skin had been a part of the wondrousness

of their loving a while ago. And now . . . a bird comes flying through
the open window. The naked beautiful brother and sister rise laughing from their bed, white-skinned and huge — still under the influ-
ence of the cocaine, still gods. What kind of bird is it? They haven't
the slightest idea, they're not versed in ornithology, but it's a sparrow.
"There is a special providence in the fall of a sparrow," as Hamlet says,
though they've never read Shakespeare either; *"the readiness is all."*
They corner the bird in the kitchen; Colin tosses a towel over it and
catches it. Laughing, he carries it to the table and sits down with it.
The fingers of his right hand circle its tiny trembling neck and Chloe
stares in fascination at its panic. Why fight for life? she says to herself. What does it matter? Now they cease laughing and grow deadly
serious — just as, ten years earlier, their mother's boyfriend used to
grow serious when he ordered them to pull down their underpants.
The light in their eyes grows extremely concentrated. Colin's thumbs
press gently into the sparrow's neck. The bird beats its wings help-
lessly and a thrill goes through the naked gods. They're united by a
shudder of pleasure — darker than the earlier, luminous pleasure of
their golden bodies on the white sheets. Irresistible. Chloe walks over
to her sewing kit and takes out a needle. Sitting down next to her
brother, she slowly sinks it into the sparrow's right eye. "Not too far,"
whispers Colin. "You don't want to hit the brain, eh? You don't want
to kill it." "Right," breathes Chloe. Under the table, the toes of their
bare feet twitch in time to the spasms of the sparrow. Chloe withdraws the needle and sinks it gently into the other eye. Does it matter? she thinks now, some four and a half years later, sitting quaking
and queasy on Sean Farrell's living room couch, eyes closed, remembering. The plucking, then. The slow plucking of the individual
feathers, as the living sparrow desperately chirped and twisted in the
giant hands of the gods. When, how did it die? And what did they
do with its lifeless sparrow body? She can't remember — dusk came
then to stab the day and a pall of blood descended upon them. She
recalls a knife — Colin's pocketknife slicing off the sparrow's wings

— and his eagerness for it to remain alive as long as possible. The first time it lost its sparrow consciousness, he even told Chloe to spatter its little head with droplets of cool water — and it revived, only to have its sparrow stomach gently punctured by the knifepoint . . . Oh, enough now; that is all; Chloe remembers nothing more . . .)

She opens her eyes.

"You fell asleep," says Rachel with a tender laugh.

"It's very tiring to nurse," says Beth.

"Don't you want to go up to bed?" Hal asks Chloe in the same amorous murmur as before.

"Leave me alone!" Chloe responds in a fierce whisper.

"Lucky you, to be able to nod off like that," says Rachel. "You looked so peaceful . . ."

"Rachel's addicted to insomnia," explains Sean.

Can't resist reminding everyone you've slept with her, can you? thinks Derek.

"I too used to have trouble sleeping," Aron puts in, "and I often found it helpful to listen to the radio." (During his final years in South Africa, he'd turned on the radio every night as he was getting into bed, in hopes of drowning out the screams of the young man he'd seen necklaced in Johannesburg: as the rubber tire doused with gasoline flamed red and green and blue around his neck and his hair caught fire and his eyes popped and his skin melted and his tongue fried, the victim had emitted desperate high-pitched inhuman nerve-jangling cries that haunted Aron's dreams for years . . .)

"Hey!" says Derek. "Don't forget there's a husband in the bed."

Can't resist reminding everyone you sleep with her, can you? thinks Sean.

"Well," says Aron, "perhaps she could . . . wear headphones or something?"

"Have you tried reading Kant?" asks Charles.

"Very funny," says Rachel.

"Sorry," laughs Charles.

"What about counting sheep?" Patrizia suggests.

"It's no use," says Rachel. "Every time I try counting sheep, one of them gets its fleece caught in the fence it's trying to leap over. It struggles to free itself and within minutes it's completely lacerated by the barbed wire. The shepherd comes along and finds it lying there, panting and bleeding, a quivering mass of mangled flesh, so he decides to put it out of its misery by whamming it over the head with a wooden mallet . . . How am I supposed to get to sleep?"

Almost everyone laughs, but Charles is appalled. Not hard to see where Derek's daughter gets her morbidity from, he thinks. He rises and selects another record, a selection of *Best Ballads,* walks over to the window — and then, realizing he is angry, but aware that his anger is also connected to the alcohol level in his blood, intent on controlling himself rather than ranting and raving as his father used to do, he decides to spare them all by holding both sides of the argument in his head.

(He begins by asking Rachel why Jews so love to wallow in suffering; following no logical order, he goes on to denounce the Jewish domination of Hollywood, which he holds responsible for the ineradicable racism of white Americans; getting carried away, he asks Rachel how it happens that the Soviet Union was internationally boycotted for having institutionalized class hatred whereas America's racial hatred was considered quite acceptable: European scholars, artists and scientists — including Einstein, the Jew genius! — kept coming over and shaking hands with American presidents, while segregation humiliated and harmed millions of innocent citizens . . . Finally, he masterfully sketches out the age-old antagonism between Jews and blacks in this country — the former a people of the Book, whose very identity was inseparable from memory, the latter an essentially oral culture whose memories had been totally wiped out . . . Should there be no compensation whatsoever for the descendants of slaves? And is pain the only heritage we care to pass on to our children? Ah! Charles feels better, having summed all these issues up remarkably within the space of five minutes and won a resounding victory over Rachel. It was Myrna who'd taught him to do this, let off steam without hurting anyone's feelings. People's minds are never changed by arguments in conversation, she'd told him, but only in silence and solitude — by reading, mulling over, muddling through . . . "That's why your writing's so important," she'd added, kissing him passionately . . . No one ever tells him his writing is important anymore.)

When he sits down again, the conversation has moved on to literature. How they got from dead sheep to literature he has no idea, but Hal is now speechifying about Tolstoy — the wild disparity between the man and the writer.

"The storyteller was wiser than the sermonizer," he says, "and the sermonizer was wiser than the man. After his religious enlightenment, Tolstoy grew more neurotic and insufferable with every passing year. He despised himself so much for not being able to give up crystal glasses and shtupping with Sophie that he took it out on everyone else by castigating material goods and preaching sexual abstinence. He even tried to prevent his own daughters from getting married! By the time he was in his eighties, he'd turned into a rigid, intolerant, rather loathsome individual."

Why so rigid, Myrna? thinks Charles. (He'd written his doctoral thesis on the subject of jealousy. Six hundred pages spent comparing the two great tales of wife murder in Western literature, Shakespeare's *Othello* and Tolstoy's *Kreutzer Sonata* . . . In this opus, an abridged version of which later became a chapter of *Black on White,* Charles had pointed out that whereas countless critics attributed the murder of Desdemona to Othello's blackness — "the triumph of his homicidal, inferior African essence over his civilized, Christian, European surface" — none ever dreamed of suggesting that Pozdnychev gave in to murderous urges because he was white. Naturally: because white is not a color, not a defining trait; Pozdnychev's gesture merely illustrates the tragic nature of human existence. And thou Myrna, white betrayed for black, thou in turn hast murdered me out of jealousy! *"Begot on itself, born out of itself. . . ."* Yet did I not give thee my all? How couldst thou feel threatened by my silly moment of weakness? Couldst thou believe that I would throw up all our happiness and run off to South Carolina with Anita Darven? O! Mad with jealousy, whether founded or unfounded, just or unjust, Des-De-Myrna has murdered He's-a-Jolly-Othello!)

"Yeah," says Leonid. "Bit late to start preaching abstinence when you've already fathered fifteen kids."

Katie laughs because she can tell from the tone of his voice that Leo must have cracked a joke — but she isn't listening to the conversation; her thoughts are still on Power Street.

(Now the smell was upon them — the smell of urine, excrement and rotting flesh. The flesh of their flesh, in a state of advanced decay. "It's all right, honey," she whispered to Leonid, wiping the sweat from his forehead and the vomit from his chin. "Everything's going to be all right." They clung to each other in the corridor for a while — and then, holding hands, they turned slowly to enter David's room. And saw. On the floor. The empty sheetless mattress. The phone knocked off the hook. And beyond that, sprawling, sprawled, lifeless, the body of their youngest son. Or what was left of it. For Cleopatra, locked up with her master's corpse — for how many days? maybe not just three, maybe seven or eight; when did we last talk to him? Let's see, thought Katie, struggling to do the mental arithmetic, I remember he phoned on Alice's birthday, July 24, that would make . . . — had chewed away his left shoulder, a large section of his left arm and part of his face. Oh, it's better this way, she kept saying to herself. At least he's not going to suffer anymore. You're happy now, aren't you, dear? she said to David in her mind. Leo bent over the wrecked, emaciated body, picked it up as if it weighed nothing at all, and slung it over his shoulder, the head and arms hanging down in front and the legs dangling behind. And then, as Katie followed them out of the room and down the hallway, she noticed that David's jeans had slipped down over his so-thin hips, revealing the upper part of his buttocks . . . It disturbed her; she wished she could pull his pants up for him the way she used to when he was a little boy, but didn't want to annoy Leonid by asking him to set the body down again for such a silly reason. So she followed them down the stairs, repeating, half aloud, "It's all right now, darling. Everything will be fine from now on." Her feeling of euphoria carried her all the way through the funeral, the condolence visits and the ensuing weeks, wholly given over to the liquidation of their son's interrupted life. It wasn't until six months later — one night in the heart of winter, in the no-man's-land between wakefulness and sleep — that she finally grasped the full extent of her loss. She sat up in bed and stared into the void, bathed in a cold sweat. When Leonid brought her breakfast in bed the next morning, he almost dropped the tray: overnight, her hair had turned from black to white.)

"I read a book by this really wonderful Russian author last month," says Beth. "Uh . . . It was called . . . What was it called, Brian?"

"Don't ask me!" Brian shrugs. He stopped following the conversation a while ago and is wandering along the Sa Thay River again.

(The sun has just begun its swift descent, setting fire to the surrounding mountain ridges, when suddenly Zack gets a scent. At last, something. Anything. An event. A hope for the poor fear-addled brain to latch on to. Not that we particularly want to catch *up* with Charlie, thinks Brian — but — anything — to bring the day a little closer to its end. A hundred and eighty days down, a hundred and eighty-five to go. Doug Johnson, the heavyset black lieutenant from Oklahoma who's holding the dog on a leash, beckons urgently to the rest of them. Within the instant, they feel each nerve in their bodies stretch to maximum awareness and tension, the breaking point of wakefulness, and then — incredibly, as always — a shot rings out. The noise is an apocalypse in their overprepared ears. They glance around in panic — to see who — which of them has his bowels tumbling out of his stomach this time — but no, it's the dog. Zack has been hit. Not fatally. But now, maddened with pain, he's leaping, straining, thrashing against the leash to get to where the shot came from. Doug lets him go. The dog bounds furiously toward a thicket of bamboo — two bullets hit him full in the chest and he drops like a stone. Then the impossible happens. A woman. A woman emerges from the thicket. Charlie's woman. Long hair, black. Dressed in a short-sleeved shirt and khaki shorts. Arms and legs half naked, badly scratched. She tosses her empty K59 in their direction, and for a minute they all stand there staring at each other, stunned. One Vietnamese woman and seven American men. Spellbound. As motionless as the air. Brian can read nothing at all in the woman's stare. Neither fear nor fearlessness, seduction nor bravado, despair nor defiance — nothing. Being unable to read your enemy's face is bad for you as a human being, but — as he's come to understand over the past six months — good for you as a soldier. Then she bolts. They follow her without a word, running lightly now, swiftly, powerfully — everything that was weighing them down a minute ago has become weightless. Despite her head start, there isn't the least doubt in their minds that they'll catch up with her — their legs are twice as long as hers — and within minutes, they do. Surrounding her, laying hands on her and wrestling her to the ground, they emit a collective roar of triumph. An unhoped-for trophy. A compensation for the agonizing day they've just endured. In Brian's memory, what ensues is bathed in a haze of unreality. He hasn't forgotten it and never will, but neither has he breathed a word of it to anyone in the world. Because. Because there are no words to speak it. The event unfolds in silence like an ancient ritual, learned not by individuals but by the species. Military hierarchy determines the order, which means that Doug will go first and Brian last. And as the sunlight dies and the surrounding jungle fades into nonexistence, arousal invades him. His every breath is arousal, his heartbeat a throbbing jewel of ecstasy. Nothing's left in the universe apart from the sacred circle of black and white men with the yellow girl at its center. The girl cries out once, when her own center is pierced; she bleeds, and Doug, his shaven black head glistening with sweat, mutters a delighted oath at finding her a virgin; then words subside once more and all that remains is movement. Unhurrying, unspeaking, they let the darkest forces of the human species flow through their bodies into hers. Here, woman, beloved, abhorred, take, take my life seed, die! When Brian's turn comes he's already so immersed in this communion of real flesh and blood that the time he spends in the girl's body is brief indeed, scarcely has he entered her than climax shoots through him, turning him into a mere electrical conductor, all thought and personality are annulled and for the space of an instant he actually blacks out. When he comes to, stumbling to his feet and pulling up his pants, dizzy and disoriented, the other men laugh at him, jostle him, mock him for fucking a corpse. He glances down uncomprehendingly — and Doug, still laughing, empties a machine gun cartridge into the girl's head. It's now fully dark and they're convinced the day is over but it's not. Not quite. One more event still has to take place. A hand grenade explodes in their midst, tossed by one of the Vietcong the girl had been guiding through the Sa Thay River ravine — and whom she'd successfully protected, knowing at what cost, by shooting the dog. The blast kills three GIS on the spot. Both Doug's legs are ripped from their sockets. But Brian . . . well, somehow, Brian comes out of it unscathed. The only aftereffect is this little ringing in his right ear . . .)

"Anyway, it was a really beautiful book," Beth insists. "It was called . . . ah, *Medusa's Children,* or something like that."

"Don't you mean *The Laugh of the Medusa* by Hélène Cixous?" asks Patrizia, who has photocopied the latter work many times for female professors of Contemporary French Literature.

"No, no, that's not it at all, I told you the author was Russian."

"Beth," says Brian exasperatedly, "if you can't remember either the author or the title, we're going to have a hard time — "

"*Medea's Children*, that's it! Not *Medusa's Children*, *Medea's Children!*"

"Medea murdered her children," Rachel points out reasonably.

"Yes, I know," says Beth, "but it's not about that Medea, it's just an ordinary woman who lives in Crimea and whose name happens to be Medea, and as a matter of fact she doesn't have any children . . ."

"Come to think of it," interrupts Leonid. "I used to know a woman called Medea, back in Minsk."

(When he arrived at the Mitino Cemetery, his sister Ioulia stared at him blankly and said nothing. Nothing. But on the way home, her best friend Natasha — the flabby, wrinkled, retired librarian whose still-sparkling black eyes Leonid remembered vaguely from Young Pioneers summer camp half a century before — took him aside. Your brother-in-law suffered agony, Natasha told Leonid . . . and went on to describe the disintegration of Grigori's body, omitting not one of the gory details. Only when Ioulia injected pure vodka directly into her husband's bloodstream could he forget himself and disconnect. The whole country is steeped in vodka, Natasha told Leonid. The morgue employees, theoretically inured to every imaginable form of horror, invariably requested vodka when they came to pick up a Chernobylian. The men flown in to decontaminate the area were told that only vodka could help combat the effects of radiation, and instructed to drink as much of it as they could . . . Thus, they'd wandered about the countryside in a permanent alcoholic stupor, shooting dogs and burying them in mass graves, laying waste to carefully tended vegetable gardens, rolling up the topsoil like a rug, murdering millions of insects, burying the earth in the earth. It's world of madness you've come home to, Leonid, said Natasha. Of course, the Chernobyl catastrophe wasn't his fault, as Katie repeated to him ceaselessly when he returned to the States and sobbed in her arms night after night. And yet — and yet. Had he only made an effort — had he been a better son — had he moved heaven and earth to bring his elderly parents over to America — or at least set

them up in a nursing home in Minsk — none of this would have happened. Grigori and Ioulia wouldn't have needed to move south, Grigori would have been spared, Svetlana would still have a father .
. . Ioulia wouldn't be insane with fear for the health of her child, and the health of her child's children, and so on down the line, for the fourteen billion years it takes for thorium to lose its deadly potency.) "Did you, dear?" says Katie. And the conversation fizzles out, Beth having failed to convey anything of the state of wonder in which she'd waded through the pages of Ludmila Ulitskaya's novel with its sad, munificent peasant heroine — a woman who'd spent her life lavishing care on her nieces and nephews, cousins and aging sisters, all the while nursing an ancient secret sorrow.

"Don't worry," Derek tells Beth, "Rachel and I do that all the time. Our conversations are beginning to sound like the Watergate tapes, with the proper nouns deleted instead of the expletives. Remember that film we saw in, uh, beep-beep, you know, the one by beep-beep, starring beep-beep, wait a minute, wait a minute, it'll all come back to me . . ."

"What will we remember, do you think?" says Sean.

KATIE AND LEONID

The Korotkovs' deaths won't be as clean and harmonious as Beth's — far from it — but at least they'll go down together. A pearl of a death, really, for a couple as amorous as they. Each would have been utterly helpless on this Earth without the other. So here it is — a plane crash. Six years down the line.

They actually could not quite afford this trip to Kiev — they'd had to borrow money for the fare — but, they agreed, the occasion was important enough to warrant splurging: Leonid's young niece Svetlana was getting married! To another "firefly," of course (as radiation victims are called over there) — a young man by the name of Vadim.

Both Svetlana and Vadim were children at the time of the "accident." Svetlana's father Grigori worked in the Chernobyl plant and lived but a stone's throw away from it, so when the fourth reactor caught fire he summoned his wife Ioulia, gathered sweet Svetlana in his arms, and they all went out onto the balcony to admire the sight. A truly grandiose display of pyrotechnics, more dazzling than the Fourth of July in Manhattan, more awesome than the Northern Lights in Nunavut. A miraculous luminescence, an unearthly incandescence, a blazing raspberry glow. By car, by bicycle and on foot, people traveled miles to admire it. They crowded onto the balconies facing the plant, jostling one another for standing room. Everyone stood there wide-eyed and openmouthed, oblivious to the black dust they were inhaling. "Look!" Grigori whispered to his little girl. "Look! You'll remember this for the rest of your life."

I was on the rampage. Wreaking havoc with people's chromosomes. Carrying off several million potential inhabitants of Belarus and Ukraine in one fell swoop. Grigori would be called in the next day to help dig a tunnel under the reactor. Nice guy, Grigori. Glad to have him. Oh, yes, I took care of those liquidators lickety-split. The others, however, I allowed to linger on Earth for a while, just for the novelty of the thing — to see what happened when I combined my radioactive and my human elements. I just love to experiment.

Svetlana rapidly lost all her hair and had to be hospitalized; she spent the remainder of her childhood in and out of hospitals, mostly in. But having survived into her late twenties, she decided to take the chance of marrying Vadim and trying to have children.

Here, then, are Katie and Leonid Korotkov in the DC-10, on their way from Prague to Kiev. Just as they're approaching the eastern Carpathians, the electrical system of their rather ancient, bumpity-jumpity plane (dating back to Czechoslovakia's Velvet Revolution, to a time when there was still a country known as Czechoslovakia) experiences a short circuit; fire breaks out in the cockpit; smoke seeps into the cabin and the aircraft begins to pitch. As the weather is clear and sunny, it's rapidly apparent to all that they won't be gaining sufficient altitude to make it over this particular eastern Carpathian. And down below there's nothing but dense pine forest — not the ideal terrain on which to effect an emergency landing. Brains start tearing around in all directions, looking for an exit. But there is no exit, as Jean-Paul Sartre would say. Mmmmm, oh, yes, now I am cradling all those passengers and crew members in the palm of my hand. Most of them jump up from their seats and start screaming at the poor, paralyzed flight attendants. They eventually fall to their knees simply because their leg muscles give way, but once they find themselves genuflected they begin to pray, jabbering incoherently in my ear, imploring me to perform a miracle that will get them out of this predicament. No way! This plane is going down, my friends. It's hurtling earthward, headed straight for the mountain wall. If Katie's hair weren't white already, it would turn white now. She and Leonid aren't taking part in the pandemonium, however. They've unbuckled their seat belts, turned to one other, slid their arms around each other's necks and closed their eyes. Now they're talking in low voices. Their conversation is predictable and repetitive, but at least there's nothing hysterical about it. Leonid is saying, "I love you Katie." He's remembering her almost continual arousal during pregnancies. He thinks of them one by one, Marty Alice David and Sylvia, at the time nothing but anonymous little merpeople swimming in her deep; he clasps his wife to him and recalls the way they explored all sorts of positions for their embraces, as he couldn't put all his weight on that swelling lifebelly of hers — and how, no matter what the position, Katie would moan and swoon in a seemingly endless pouring forth of bliss. Now Leonid is hugging Katie and Katie is hugging Leonid and thinking of the stories he always liked to tell in public, all the stories she's heard him tell repeatedly in their nearly four decades of married life, she knows them by heart but has never tired of listening to them — "I love you Leo, I love you," she says, softly, then a bit more loudly, because the ambient noise and temperature have risen all of a sudden, windows are beginning to explode here and there, the aircraft is groaning beneath the weight it can no longer carry — and so it happens that, halfway between Tirgou Mures and Piatra Neamt, these two individuals — definitely on the decline, yet quite endearing in their attachment to one another — come to me through swathes of smoke, joined at the lips, their brains extinguished long before they melt.

XXIV

Remembering

"What will we remember, do you think?" says Sean.

"Do we have the choice?" asks Derek.

"I mean, do you think we remember the things that are worth remembering, or is the selection fairly . . . ah, random?"

"I always tell my students: you can't write unless you accept the fallibility of memory," says Hal.

"I forget my students!" says Rachel, kicking off her shoes and then, quite drunk, slipping down from her chair onto the rug between Sean and Derek, the two men she loves. "I forget everything about them. Not only their names and faces but our meetings, our discussions, everything. I run into them even a year later, they tell me, Hey, I've got this great idea for a book on such-and-such, based on a suggestion you made — and I've got no idea what they're talking about."

Charles laughs. Having browbeaten Rachel into oblivion a few minutes ago, he now feels nothing but magnanimity toward her. "I forget my kids' birthdays," he says. "At least I used to, when I was living with them. Now I can think of nothing else." (He'd give anything to play ball with his boys again. His palms press into one another, tense with the urge to hold the bat and feel the hard ball smacking into it — crack — *ah, right!* — you know it's a good hit without even looking, know you'll get at least two bases out of it. And the elation, as a boy, of running fast, no resistance whatsoever in his legs, his elbows whacking his jacket from left to right, whack, whack, quick, quick, his breath regular and untiring . . .)

"I didn't ask what you forgot," says Sean, "but what you thought you'd be likely to remember."

"I remember a summer evening in the city of Bath," says Hal. "England," he adds for Chloe's benefit. "Must be thirty years ago, but for some reason the memory's indelibly imprinted on my brain. Swallows wheeling in the sky at dusk . . . and behind the abbey, a solitary violinist playing Irish dance tunes, distorting them, filling them with a wincing nostalgic dissonance. I remember the soft mauve of the sky, the way the stones of the abbey shaded yellow-ward in the fading light . . . and how peaceful everything felt."

"You wrote that scene in one of your novels," says Brian. "You know, the one about the two young Pakistanis who meet during the guided tour of the Roman baths . . . What's it called?"

"Bath Time," says Hal, half embarrassed and half flattered.

"Yeah, that's it," says Brian. "Maybe that's why you remember it — because you wrote it down."

Patrizia has drawn her nylon-stockinged toes up onto the couch next to her, revealing a few more lovely inches of thigh.

"I remember," she says, "how my grandmother used to make me hot lemon and honey when I was sick. I'd be sitting at the kitchen table and feeling so happy because she was doing it *just for me,* I'd watch her move around the kitchen — heavy woman, light step — and it was so marvelous, you could tell there was nothing else in the world she'd rather be doing than making lemon and honey for her granddaughter's sore throat . . ."

"Yeah," says Derek, "we remember moments. I remember when I first discovered the idea of *moments.* It was my birthday, I must have been fourteen or fifteen and my folks had taken me to Staten Island to spend the day at the fairgrounds. It was a Saturday, but for some reason my dad had to leave at noon to check something out at his factory in the Bronx. I remember standing on the pier and waving good-bye to him as the ferry pulled out. I looked around at the crowd, everybody was waving to some person on the boat, and I suddenly realized this was a *moment*. You know . . . The waving. Hands held high in the air and moved back and forth to say — We love you. We're still with you. We can still see you. The ferry pulled out, maneuvered, turned in the harbor, gathered speed. We kept on waving. My dad was wearing a red sweater that day, so he stood out in the crowd on deck. We could see his little red arm moving up and down, getting smaller and smaller as the ferry receded into the distance . . . The moment lasted, it lasted a little longer . . . and it came to an end. The wavers' arms dropped to their sides; they'd ceased being a group. On land, singly, they turned away and dispersed; on the boat, they sat down and unfolded their newspapers . . . And that was it. Never again would we be waving good-bye to my father from the Staten Island Ferry dock on August 18, 1969."

A long silence ensues, in the course of which the *Best Ballads* come to an end and Charles resolves to stop playing disc jockey for the white folks. *Ain't gonna be your monkey man no mo'!* he thinks, smiling inwardly at his own joke.

"Ever since that day," Derek goes on, but for Katie the remainder of his lecture is swallowed up by the shimmering of a luscious spring day in a small town in western Pennsylvania, 1960, she's thirteen years old, standing in the graveyard next to the church with her father at her side, his firm grip on her elbow is literally holding her up; right now they're listening to the priest but soon they'll have to step forward, they'll go first and the rest of the group of family and friends will follow, filing past her mother's tombstone to the pace of the organ music they've just been listening to in church, stepping up to the grave one by one and bending to lay flowers on it, Katie can feel the moment approaching, the priest's speech of murmured comfort is drawing to a close, there's a brief silence and now it's here, she's stepping forward but she still has the flowers in her hands, as long as the flowers are in her hands her mother won't be completely dead, but now she's bending forward, now her hands are stretching out to lay the flowers on her

mother's grave, she breathes in their scent and sees their colors
dancing through a blur of tears and the impossible thing happens,
her hands release the flowers, it's such a soft and gentle thing to do
but there's no way to make it last, and once the flowers have been
been released her body will have to straighten up, take a step backward, then move away from the grave, yes, that's what it's doing
now, with her father gripping her elbow more tightly still, and now
the moment's over, she's released the flowers and taken one, two,
three steps away from the grave, it's done, done with, her mother
is dead.

"I remember when I was a senior in high school," says Beth after
another silence. "Every time they played 'Those Were the Days' on
the radio I'd listen to it with all my might. Because . . . it was before
I reached 'the days' she was talking about, you know? I was teetering
right on the edge of the period I'd be able to miss and feel nostalgic
about later on, and I kept trying to grasp the irony in the woman's
voice — forgive me, Sean . . ." She breaks into song. *"Those were the
days, my friend, we thought they'd never end / We'd sing and dance forever and a day / We'd do the things we choose, we'd fight and never lose /
For we were young and sure to have our way!* And I swore I wouldn't
squander my youth, I'd take advantage of it, because I'd been warned
in advance . . . and now . . . well . . . I wonder whether those days
ever came. I can't remember having gone through a period of feverish joy and illusion and dancing and struggle . . . Did I, Brian? No,
nothing like that. Just . . . just sort of . . . And now, doing my shopping at the supermarket, I sometimes hear a Muzak rendition of that
song, and . . . it tears me apart."

"Yes," says Rachel.

"I remember," says Brian, now thoroughly inebriated, "the day I
set fire to the garage, and my dad took off his belt and whipped my
bare ass till it was raw. I remember the day my pet hamster died, and
when I cried about it my dad taunted me and slapped me around
and called me a sissy . . ."

"Though as we all know," says Sean, smiling, "negative memories take on far too much importance in retrospect . . ."

"I remember how I used to hate being sent away to camp every summer," says Charles.

As always when she hears the word *camp*, Rachel needs to correct herself inwardly, remind herself that the person is *not* referring to a concentration camp, no no, not at all; Charles had not been sent away to camp the way millions of European Jews had been sent away to camps, to be tattooed and shaved and beaten and starved or gassed or shot to death, here in America there were nothing but camps for fun and games, healthy hearty outdoor activities designed for building muscles and community spirit; she and Sean had always shared a certain mistrust of these activities, Rachel because she found them reminiscent of Nazi propaganda films filled with strong young Aryan bodies whose goal was to conquer every mountain peak, win every relay race and exterminate every Jew, Sean because he saw them as bespeaking the American preference for primitivism as opposed to civilization — Americans so proud of wolfing down bloody hamburgers and raw vegetables, hiking through forests rife with hungry bears and poisonous snakes, sleeping on rocks in the icy or mosquito-filled night, barking at each other in monosyllables — whereas comfortable beds and automobiles and refined cuisine and exquisite poetry had been invented ages ago — *"Why is it,"* Sean had asked Rachel once, shaking his head, "that yuppies on vacation behave like bloody cavemen?"

"All I ever wanted to do," Charles goes on, "was stay at home, hang out with my family and friends and gorge on comic books . . . but every year they'd send me off to live with a bunch of strangers, on the pretext that I needed fresh air and exercise or some damn thing."

"Me too," says Hal. "Me, too. Jesus, did I ever hate going to camp."

A summer camp, thinks Rachel. Not a concentration camp.

"I remember," says Aron, "how sad I felt when my first daughter Sheri was born. I came home from the hospital and listened to

Bach's *Magnificat* on the record player as the morning sunlight came flooding through the window . . ."

"Why were you sad?" asks Chloe, who has been following the conversation intermittently, stitching its images of ferries and supermarkets and hamsters into the fabric of her dreams as she drifted in and out of sleep.

"Because everything was perfect, and I realized I could only lose from there on in."

(He also remembers the day in the summer of 1939 on which he and his bride Nicole conceived Sheri. Nicole had insisted on taking him home to Brittany to meet her parents, a grueling honeymoon trip that had lasted six weeks because of travel restrictions, border mania, searching and interrogations. Safe in their bubble of bliss in a world on the brink of disaster, they'd ferried across from Lorient to the wild rocky island of Groix. It was late afternoon — oh *sheer beauty*, that afternoon of our arrival! Sea's edge, ledge of gray rock under gray sky, and the gull that kept flinging itself at us again and again, riding the wind down then up then down, its blind mad instinct stirring awe in me. Nicole was simply elated, homecoming, but I was dumbstruck, awestruck by this landscape, the sun piercing the cloud bank and the shining shale, mica-laced stones glistening in layers, a *feuilleté* of old gold with the sea glittering beyond in a million crinkles of wind. Picking up fish skeletons and gull feathers, staring at their intricate geometries, instantly satisfying to eye and brain, marveling at life's endless, ingenious effort to renew itself, its unrelenting talent for form and beauty, its supreme indifference to the borders we men trace and retrace endlessly, our iron bars and barbed wire, our protective guns and identity checks, our free and occupied zones . . . Before long, the inhabitants of Groix would build an ugly cement bunker beneath the very ledge on which we were standing, but that day we were entranced with the horizon, the fishsmell and gullcry, the scurrying rabbits, the heady fragrance of heather and honeysuckle amid clover, fern and bramble, the thump and pump and lubrication of our own bodymachines as we walked, arms locked, hair and hearts buffeted by the wind, then sank to the ground and made love in a brilliant yellow field of waving chamomile.)

"I remember waiting six hours for a plane connection in San Diego," says Sean.

"Dead time," says Rachel.

"Och, no," says Sean. "You have to be somewhere."

"Katie!" says Leonid. "Do you remember the parking lot at Dorval Airport, that time we went up to visit Alice in Montreal? Spot No. c52, wasn't it?"

"Unforgettable!" says Katie. "And remember that gorgeous exit ramp off Highway 84 — you know, on your way down to Manhattan, right where you have to switch to the 684?"

"O, incomparable exit ramp!" says Leonid. "Yeah, we took it once in '72, and then once in '85, and then practically every year throughout the 1990s. And what about that hospital corridor — oh, hahaha, that charming old vomit-colored hospital corridor we waited in for four hours at Boston General, remember, the day Marty crushed his finger in the waffle iron . . ."

"Yes," says Katie, "and the gas station — remember that cute little Exxon station about halfway between Metuchen and Newark?"

"You bet!" says Leonid.

"I know that one!" Derek interjects.

"Remember the time you took the 79th Street crosstown bus, sweetheart?" says Katie. "You know, in 1967 or thereabouts, when we were living on Amsterdam and you were working over on Third?"

"Yeah . . . uh . . . but I'm not quite sure I know which time you mean," says Leonid. "Since I took the same bus every day for eleven years."

"Oh, but you *must* remember! It was this hot, stuffy day and the bus was jam-packed, it got stuck in traffic, people were sweating and trampling all over each other."

"Okay, now I've got it narrowed down to forty or fifty possible days," says Leonid. "Go on, go on."

"Well, and — I know! It was the day I made frozen fish sticks for supper!"

"Ah, okay. Sure, it's all coming back to me . . . Yeah, yeah, yeah. Fish sticks with ketchup, right?"

"Exactly! And I served it all up with Wonder Bread and margarine, you remember?"

"Got it! I got the day! Uh . . . Alice cut her toenails that day, too, isn't that right?"

"Exactly!" says Katie triumphantly.

"And the rest stop," says Leonid. "That really picturesque rest stop on the 2A, you know the one I mean? Remember taking Marty to the bathroom there when he was three?"

"I'm not sure," says Katie, feeling her neck begin to burn again, the heat rising in waves to suffuse her cheeks and forehead, and hoping that people will chalk it up to embarrassment over her faulty memory.

"How could you forget that rest stop? About two miles past the Burger King, right before you get to Ames . . ."

"Oh, Ames! That Ames!" shouts Hal, not wanting to be left out. "The one with the bubble-gum machine next to the cash registers, right? Boy, I count on being able to buy my underwear in that store when I get to heaven."

"I remember Daniela Denario's wrists," says Patrizia, her voice thick with liquor. "Does anyone else remember Daniela Denario's wrists?"

"Sure," say half a dozen voices. "Sure . . . How long has it been? . . ."

"Six years already," says Patrizia. "I can't believe it."

(A week or so ago she'd had a vivid dream about Daniela — the Lucca-born professor of Classical Italian Literature who, improbably, had taken a liking to *her* — her, Patrizia, mere department secretary, third-generation Italian from impoverished South Boston. Daniela had asked her questions about her life, invited her out to the local Starbucks for a poor imitation of cappuccino, then to her home for a real one, befriended her. For two years they'd met several times a week to chatter in Italian, smoke cigarettes, sew curtains, share campus gossip and pasta recipes — and also, once, clumsily but unforgettably, a long, tremulous kiss. Only to Daniela had she confessed how, as a teenager, she used to filch money from the collection plate when it was passed around at the end of mass — a quarter or two a week for several months — and then, when she'd accumulated ten or fifteen dollars, slip out of her room on a Saturday night and join up with Conchita her best friend from Gate-of-Heaven Junior High, swagger boldly into the local disco club, and — amid throbbing strobes and ear-splitting vibes — dance their Travolta-crazy hearts out until dawn. "I could never bring myself to confess it to the priest," she told her new friend, laughing. "That's nothing!" scoffed Daniela. "That's a piddling little sin compared to mine! You know what *I* did once? When they paraded the Virgin Mary statue through the streets of Lucca on her feast day, I stole a bunch of ten-thousand-lira bills that were pinned to her dress! I made as if I were pinning on more bills but in fact I was ripping off the Holy Virgin!" How can she not exist anymore? thinks Patrizia. Brain cancer. Started getting lost in the streets of her own neighborhood . . . Blind at the end. Oh, Daniela . . . How can it be such a long time since you died? What's left to me of you? The softness of your skin. How sleek and small and whimsical and elegant you were. Your incredibly delicate wrists. The way you wore your hair pulled back from your face. And how well you loved me. Thank you, Daniela.)

Poor Patrizia, thinks Sean. Daniela must have been be one of her first important deaths. She doesn't know what's in store for her, what it's like to be surrounded by ghosts, first the ghosts of your parents and then your friends, dropping off the edge of the abyss into blackness one by one as you stand there, awed, helpless — no, no, not *you!* no, not *you, too!* — thinking, always, the pain will be too great; the world will stop rotating on its axis or at least you'll go mad, but no, it doesn't and you don't, you simply go on taking the blows in the gut, having the breath knocked out of you and pursuing your daily existence in cowed silence, shamed by the force of inertia that allows you to go on living despite the loss of virtually every person whose love you thought enabled you to live . . .

"I remember my father's last words," says Rachel. "I was thirteen years old, my mother and I went to visit him in the hospital and he said, 'Is the furnace working all right?' He'd spent the past four days in a coma and that was the first thing he thought of when he finally came to, 'Is the furnace working all right?' It was mid-January, fifteen below outside; we'd just had a new furnace installed in the basement. 'Yes,' my mother said, stroking his hair. 'Yes, Baruch. The heat is lovely.' 'Good,' he said. 'Because I don't want you ever, ever to be cold.' It worried me to hear such endearing words between my parents. Usually they bickered from morning to night about everything from Yasir Arafat to how to fry an egg. Then my father relapsed into a coma. And when we arrived the next day he was gone. I took his hands in mine and they were cold." (Do they hear me? she wonders. He didn't want us to be cold, and then . . . I'm not going to spell it out for them.)

"What about you, Chloe?" says Sean at length, heaving a sigh. "Anything worth remembering?"

"Not much," says Chloe dreamily. "But I remember sleeping with my older brother once."

"Your *brother?*" says Hal.

"Oh my God!" breathes Beth, and her exhausted mind having once again brought her back to her uncle Jimmy in the basement, but also her own unavowable wish to marry her father, she unexpectedly bursts into tears. She snuffles and snorts, gasping for breath . . .

Unkindly but involuntarily, Rachel marvels at how rapidly Beth's face is made hideous by weeping: red nose, blotchy cheeks, features convulsed into a grimacing, repulsive mask of despair.

Brian moves from where he was seated on the rug to go over and comfort his wife, but as he rises one of his beefy thighs upends the coffee table, causing everything on it — ashtrays, bottles, glasses — to teeter, tip, topple, slip and crash to the floor.

"Hey, hey, hey, hey!" says Charles.

"Oh, shit!" says Patrizia, who has just received a copious splash of champagne on the lacy front of her white blouse. And, getting up, she pads off to the kitchen in her stocking feet to fetch the broom and dustpan.

"I get the feeling this party is drawing to a close," says Rachel.

"It was an accident," says Aron. "I saw it happen; he didn't mean to knock the table over, it was an accident."

Though no one can really understand why, Beth is still weeping uncontrollably, her head buried in Brian's shoulder, and Brian is rocking her and stroking her hair as if she were his daughter.

"I was just kidding," Chloe whispers to Hal, who has led her over to the foot of the staircase and is firmly gripping her pointed little chin between his thumb and forefinger so that she has no choice but to look him in the eye.

"You don't have a brother?" he says.

"Nah, of course not. I just wanted to shake them up a bit."

"Well, if that's what you wanted, you sure found the way to do it," chuckles Hal in relief and reluctant admiration.

Sean lights his last cigarette of the day as Patrizia sweeps the burned butts and broken glass into the dustpan and Katie uses paper toweling to sop up what she can of the champagne on the rug.

"Let's call it a night, all right?" says Derek.

"It was still a good party, Sean," says Patrizia, slipping her shoes back on. (To celebrate her First Communion, she recalls, her mother had for once bought her exactly the pair of shoes she wanted — black patent leather shoes so shiny you could see your face in them; every time she glanced down she felt a rush of pride at how spiffy they looked, with the strap and buckle sharply set off against her white ankle socks.) "It was fun. We just had a bit too much to drink, that's all."

"C'mon, man, time to hit the hay," says Charles, patting Sean on the shoulder the way he used to pat his younger brother Martin on the shoulder when they were still in their teens and the worst tragedy that could befall them was getting a D in math or losing the ball game or not being allowed to go to the movies . . .

"Here," says Rachel, her arms now laden with a heap of blankets, cushions and quilts she's fetched from Sean's linen closet. "Everybody grab a blanket and find a corner to curl up in."

But instead of complying at once, they all stand there motionless for a moment, together yet apart. The ensuing silence is longer than all the other silences combined; their eyes rove across the rug at random or stare at arbitrary objects — as thoughts, words and images go sliding confusedly through the convolutions of their brains. It is three o'clock in the morning and their bodies are heavy with food, sleep, alcohol, the years of their lives . . .

Our friends are all we have, Derek is thinking. They're the people we live with; they're like our families; we've got no choice but to accept their faults along with their qualities. Even if the latter seem to fade and the former to intensify with every passing year. Hm. That feels like some sort of insight, but I probably won't see it that way in the morning. The trouble with enlightenment is that it's temporary. Buddhist writings claim that when a master pronounces a koan, the scales suddenly fall from his disciple's eyes. What they *don't* tell you is what happens to those eyes the next day, or the next year. Personally I've had the scales fall from my eyes any number of times. I see; then I go blind; and then, ephemerally, I see again.

God invents man and man invents God, reversibly, back and forth *ad infinitum*, thinks Hal apropos of nothing.

The deer are running rampant this fall, thinks Katie, mentally writing a letter to her dead mother. Wreaking havoc in the gardens . . . eating bark off the trees . . .

Never could we have dreamed how rough adult life would be, thinks Charles . . . Dammit, Marty, you never had time to find out. You cashed in in 1985. I carry this picture of you around with me in my head, the years keep passing and the picture never changes — do you realize you're beginning to look a bit ridiculous, man? Why don't you get rid of that stupid Afro? People don't wear their hair that way anymore, don't you know that? You're just a kid, Marty! Why don't you grow up?

The most important things are missing from all the books we write and teach, thinks Rachel. So few of them tell of the waning of desire. Of uglification, fragility and fear. The pain that stops up our throats.

Oh the dawning aching lucidity, thinks Leonid, as we begin to glean, truly glean, the rules of the game, watching our parents weaken sicken die, our children wax in insolence and strength — it's their turn now, their turn to blush and flirt and giggle . . .

Sean is staring silently at the Chivas Regal bottle, now pitilessly empty, and wondering what it will be like to die. In his mind, he makes the rounds of those to whom he owes apologies. Sorry, Da. Sorry, Ma. Sorry, Hal. Sorry, Patrizia. Sorry, Jody. Sorry, Rache. Sorry, Derek. Sorry, Leo. Sorry, Clarisse. Sorry, Katie. Sorry, Zoë, if that's what your name was. Sorry, Chloe. Sorry, Charles. Sorry, Aron. Sorry, all my dear and diligent students. Sorry, all my brave colleagues and compatriots. Sorry, Patch . . . But och, in spite of it all, I wrote some feckin' good poems, didn't I?

XXV

SEAN

The death of Sean Farrell isn't as imminent as you might think. He's got a good two years ahead of him. Well, "good" . . . manner of speaking. Not the sort of years people like to have ahead of them, as a general rule. The sort of years they definitely prefer to have behind them. As far behind as possible . . .

So, Sean. Losing his hair, just like sweet Svetlana — except that he's lost a fair amount of it already so his baldness isn't as upsetting to his loved ones. They'll stick by him, all of them, the way busy Americans stick by their friends at the beginning of the twenty-first century — that is, a bit distractedly. With more phone calls than visits when he's in the hospital, more jokes than questions when he's out. The single exception being Rachel, who will stay with him to the end . . . like the sister Sean had always dreamed of having.

He'll do a lot of thinking in the final months of his life. About his father, for one thing. He can't get used to the idea that he's now older than his father was when he died. (The dear man came to me all yellow, yellow every inch of him including the whites of his eyes. Cirrhosis of the liver, forty-four years old.) Whenever he thinks of his da, Sean still feels like a little boy — still sees himself in the pubs of Clonakilty, Kinsale and Courtmacsherry, slipping a small hand into his da's big paw and looking up at him, listening to him chortle and guffaw and talk politics with his chums, admiring his gift of the gab. Blarney, yeh. He'd taken Sean to see the castle at Blarney and kiss its famous Stone — which, it was said, could make a man eloquent on the spot, he couldn't quite remember how. "Buncha baloney," said the uncouth Americans — confusing, conflating in their usual loathsome melting pot, the Irish Blarney (with its magical gift of verbal prowess) and the Italian Bologna (with its fat-spotted mortadella specialty).

He'll also spend a great deal of time weeping. Men who are deprived of their fathers at an early age tend to be tear-prone, I don't know if you've noticed that. After a year or so of living at close quarters with the thought of me, the least little thing is liable to make him burst into tears. A sparrow pecking at bread crumbs on the windowsill. Or "The Thrill Is Gone" as sung by Chet Baker, the boy with the girl's voice, so soft, so sad. Or the cheap flashy engagement ring on Janice-the-supermarket-cashier's left hand, which reminds him that she has a future whereas he does not. Or the sight of Daniel the gardener, ten years his senior, chopping wood, trimming trees and lifting heavy stones to repair the wall as if it were a breeze — whereas he, Sean, grows dizzy from the mere effort of bending over to tie his shoe or pick a daisy. Straightening up, he feels flushed and nauseous, has to sit down, sits down, weeps. Or dreaming about his mother — a dream in which Maisie was young and lively again, and speaking to him with great animation, smiling, explaining, gesturing, but he couldn't hear her — her lips kept moving and he kept straining to make out what she was saying, but there was no sound at all in the dream. Is this death? he wonders, waking up and bursting into tears.

Thinking and weeping are run-of-the-mill activities for people who have got an appointment to meet me in the near future. Sean Farrell being what he is, however, he also writes poems. These will be collected after his demise in a slim volume titled *Dolce Agonia*, which will sell better than all his previous collections combined and even earn him a couple of posthumous awards.

But I mustn't get ahead of my story.

In the final month of Sean's life, he and Rachel are inseparable. One day, he takes her with him to visit his mother's grave (Rachel, as we've seen, has tombward leanings herself and is always glad to drop in on friends and acquaintances beyond the Pale). After standing there for a while lost in thought, Sean puts an arm around the scarecrow figure at his side and says, "My da used to tell me about the Wisdom Bell."

"The Wisdom Bell?"

"Yeh. It was a large, solid bronze church bell in some town up in County Kerry where he was born. Folks with problems used to go there to ask its advice, and always it answered them well. 'How far should a man walk, O Bell, to get a smile?' said one man. 'Mile,' answered the bell. 'How long will it take, O Bell,' said another, 'for my sweetheart's love to flower?' 'Hour,' said the Bell. And so forth. Da and I would spend hours making these things up and laughing at them, of a Sunday afternoon. 'What would it require, O Bell, my awful thirst to slake?' 'Lake.'"

Rachel laughs.

"Later, though," Sean goes on, "I came to see that the Wisdom Bell was more than just nonsense rhyming — it was a lovely metaphor for God. Man shouts out his questions, hears the echo of his own voice, and blindly gratefully follows the advice thus received."

Rachel nods and waits.

"And now, you see, I've just asked the ultimate question. 'Why this malady, O Bell, what is cancer?' And the Bell has just told me: 'Answer.'"

Rachel laughs, then stops laughing. They stand again in silence, staring at the plain granite block with its etched letters, MAISIE FARRELL NÉE MACDOWELL.

"I feel like singing something to her," says Rachel at last, "but I don't know what."

They cast around for an appropriate song, reject "Molly Malone" and "Lay Lady Lay" in quick succession, finally settle on "I've Grown Accustomed to Her Face." They sing it very earnestly, standing there at Maisie Farrell's graveside, refraining from looking at each other so as not to crack up, and by the end of the song Rachel can sense that the increased weight of Sean's arm across her shoulder owes less to grief than to fatigue.

Driving home, he mutters, without taking his eyes off the road, "I'll be dead within six months."

"Don't be silly," says Rachel.

"Bet on it?"

"All right," says Rachel. "But no cheating, huh?"

"No cheating."

"Promise?"

"Yeh, promise . . . Shake on it?"

"Put it there, Bud."

His left lung is removed, and a few months later a new nodule appears on the right. He tells Rachel about it over the phone.

"It might just be a lump, you know," she says. "An ordinary, bumpy sort of lump. Like a pimple or something."

"I never had pimples," says Sean.

"Well," says Rachel after a thoughtful pause, "we could always pray for each other, I guess."

"Och, now that's an idea," says Sean. "What shall we pray for?"

"I'll pray for your new nodule to be benign, and you pray for my book on Kant to be accepted by Harvard University Press."

"Right."

But I choose to fulfill neither of their prayers.

Three weeks before I waft him away, Sean invites Rachel over for lunch. She hasn't set foot in his house since that memorable Thanksgiving dinner of two years before, hasn't been alone with him there in over a decade. Between ghastly fits of coughing, Sean grills lamb chops for the two of them — Rachel sets the table — Sean uncorks a bottle of California Cabernet — Rachel makes a salad — and they sit down to lunch. Sean coughs. Rachel eats and drinks, savoring.

"The wine's delicious," she says, raising her glass, staring at Sean, not even attempting to hide the fact that she's intent on recording the exact beauty of his dark burning gaze so as to be able to hang on to it forever. "The meat's delicious," she says, knowing full well that my presence in the room is what's making the food and drink taste so good. "Everything is absolutely, absolutely delicious."

"There's but one thing missing," says Sean, "for this moment to be perfect."

"What's that?" says Rachel.

"A cigarette," says Sean.

He walks her part of the way home afterward, very slowly, stopping off at a florist's shop on Main Street and buying her a modest array of black and purple pansies in tiny plastic boxes. Rachel has always been fond of dark flowers. These will outlive their giver. When she kisses him good-bye, she smells me on his breath.

A week later he calls her from the hospital. His voice has changed. "I'm sick to my stomach, Rache," he says. "I'm sick to my soul, Rache."

"Must be the chemotherapy," says Rachel.

"No," says Sean. "They haven't started the chemotherapy yet. Jaysus, what will it be like when they do?"

Rachel doesn't know, so she doesn't say.

"Man in my room died last night," says Sean. "The wife was sitting in the armchair next to his bed, watching an old *Seinfeld* on TV."

"Which episode was it?" says Rachel.

"You know, the one where he tries to convince everyone he was only rubbing his nose, not actually picking it."

"Oh yes, I remember! That's one of my favorites."

"Anyway, the man was dying. His eyes were closed, his head was thrown back, you could literally hear his death rattle, and his wife kept saying 'Is it loud enough for you, dear? Want me to turn it up?' *I'm done for, Rache,*" Sean blurts out suddenly, in a very different tone of voice. *"I'm done for!"*

She remains on the line for him, wordless, loyal. Finally he hangs up.

The next day he has an embolism in his left brain. Speech lost. Right, writing hand lost.

Rachel sits with him and watches as his left hand scribbles clumsily on the notepad next to his bed. A heart appears, a warped yet recognizable heart shape with their four initials in it.

"You love me?" says Rachel.

A nod.

"I love you, too."

A series of other letters, T-H-R-I-L-L, slowly and painfully formed.

"I don't understand." says Rachel.

Sean sketches two eighth notes above the word.

"'The Thrill Is Gone'?"

A nod — and Sean falls back onto his pillow, exhausted.

That night, late that night, I come to deliver him. Like an obstetrician, really, only in reverse.

While I am at it, I scoop up Patchouli, too.

XXVI

Dreaming

*I*t ends, their uneasy gazing into inner space. Snapping out of it, they stand glancing about, blinking at one another — and then are pulled downward at once by a heavy wave of fatigue — the wish to give up, go under — yes, succumb now to sleep, nothing but sleep, now there's nothing for it but to sleep.

"Uh . . . where do you suggest? . . ." says Leonid, looking at Sean for ideas as to how to share out the house's possible resting spaces — but Sean is in the throes of another violent coughing fit. Hunched over in his chair, hacking, wheezing, tears in his eyes, he waves a hand at the women to say could you take care of this please, women should handle this sort of thing, bed making, bed dispatching . . .

"Hey," says Charles, patting Sean on his hunched and heaving back, "nasty cough you got there, man," and Sean nods, coughing, coughing, coughing. "Anyway," Charles goes on, addressing the others, "you can count me out of the bed problem — I feel a poem coming on. I'll just hole up in the kitchen and see if it will consent to lay itself nicely down on the page between now and tomorrow morning — which can't be that far away anyhow, what time is it getting to be?"

"Three-thirty," says Patrizia. "Still a good five hours till sunrise. Sure you've got a five-hour poem coming on?"

"Oh," says Charles, "I can drop off any old where." (It's true: as a teenager he'd learned to sleep through church services with his eyes wide open, and later, whenever tiny Toni had a fever, he'd fall sleep on a chair at her side, his forehead pressed up against the metal railing of her bed.)

"Well, let me at least clear off a corner of the table for you," says Patrizia, remembering how her *nonna* used to clear a space for her homework on the kitchen table, right next to where she was chopping onions and tomatoes for the evening meal.

"Nah, that's okay, I'll do up some dishes first myself," says Charles, heading for the kitchen. "Help me get my brain in gear." And he vanishes.

Patrizia looks after him, crestfallen. I love being coddled, she thinks. Why don't people want to be coddled anymore?

Katie, despite her fairly muddled thought processes, is struggling to master the logistics of turning Sean's house into a dormitory. "You guys get the guest room," she tells Hal and Chloe, "since your kid's already up there. That much is obvious. Straightforward."

"Brian and I don't mind crashing on the floor," says Beth, to Brian's dismay. "We can sleep right here with a couple of quilts under us — take us back to our hippie youth."

"I'm fine right where I am," says Aron. "As long as no one steals my rocking chair while my back is turned . . ." And he pads off to the bathroom for a final confrontation with the demon Diarrhea.

"The couch opens out," gasps Sean, recovering from his bout of breathlessness and lurching to his feet.

"You guys take the couch," says Rachel to Katie and Leonid.

"No, you take it," says Katie to Rachel and Derek.

"No, you," Rachel insists. "It's more comfortable than the twin beds up in Sean's study, and Leo's got a backache."

"How do you know I've got a backache?" says Leonid indignantly.

"Hard not to know, given the weird angle you've been holding yourself at all evening," teases Rachel.

"Where does that leave me?" asks Patrizia, who's removed her shoes again because her bunion is hurting her. My *nonna* had a bunion, too, she thinks.

"That leaves you, my dear," says Sean, "right back in my arms where you belong."

"Oh, Sean, I was hoping you'd say that!" cries Patrizia, flinging her arms around him in delight. "I'll be good, I promise."

"No, I'll be good," says Sean.

Good night good night good night good night good night . . .

And so it is. Six of them climb the stairs and six do not; all undertake a minimal preparation for a minimal sleep. Belts are loosened, bras unhooked, shoes and glasses set aside, noses blown, medication swallowed, feet rubbed, and bladders emptied, but makeup and underwear are not removed; real and false teeth are not cleaned; prayers are not pronounced.

"I've been dying to do this all evening," says Sean, kissing Patrizia's pelvic bones through the white silk of her slip, lingeringly and in turn. "Your breasts may have changed shape somewhat over the past few years, but your pelvic bones are immutable."

"Are you sure about the breasts?" says Patrizia drowsily, putting her hands on either side of Sean's balding head and drawing it upward to where she can kiss it. He turns it to the left, to the right, nuzzling her nipples through the material, then starts to cough. "I brought you a glass of water just in case," Patrizia murmurs, reaching for it on the bedside table and handing it to him.

"Thanks."

Sean swallows a sip of water, then turns out the light and lies down on his side with his hunched back to Patrizia. She wraps her body around him, slipping one leg between his two just as she used to do long ago, when they were lovers. Within a few seconds she's walking up the stairs to the opera house behind her mother, and then the situation is reversed: she is ascending the staircase in front of her mother, in neither case does her mother see her, she's in a hurry as always, rushing and hysterical because the show's about to start, no, it's already started, they can hear snatches of throaty contralto floating through the air: *calvo dentello, calvo dentello* . . . How lovely, thinks Patrizia, that means a lace cape, doesn't it? Och, would that water could help me, thinks Sean. Would that water were all I needed. The crossing. Water, endless expanses of rough gray heaving water — first your da dies and then you leave him, perhaps if you hadn't left him he wouldn't have died, how can you have done that, put endless expanses of rough gray heaving water between you and your da, it was pouring rain the day they buried him, rainwater sluiced into the waiting tomb, turning the soil to mud, rain slid from the hats of the mourning ladies and down the noses of the gents, you couldn't tell if they were crying or not because everything was wet, our shoes were soaked through, the earth was brown and shitlike, thud, thud, the shovelfuls of mud on the coffin like the shovelfuls of manure being hefted by Leonid's father in Shudiany — he's got such powerful biceps and such a thick, bristly mustache — by the end of the day his face and neck are bright red from working in the fields under the sun, so his wife sits him down on the porch, brings a basinful of cold water and plunges a rag into it, then douses him, slapping the rag lightly across his burning neck and forehead so that the water runs down his sweating torso — laughing, Leonid's mother is laughing as she washes down her husband after his day of toil, the weather is scorching, the earth spins on its axis, the weather is glacial and the snow swirls and swirls, enveloping the house, rising beyond the window frames, Charles studies it from where he's sitting at the kitchen table, absently, sees it without really registering it, then bends over his page again, oh but I wanted to work out that next verse, ah, *The silence of a man asleep. / In the last light a deer will flash / through the ravaged woods like a face. . . .* Don't you know, Myrna, can't you see I love you, what Moor do you want from me? "Excellent wretch! Perdition catch my soul But I do love thee, and when I love thee not, Chaos is come again." *A branch will crack by itself / swinging its claws into the drifts,* I like that, the claws make the branch come alive, turn it into an animal, *and the tracks of men and wolves / will cross like something else.* No, "something else" is weak, especially as a final line. Got to find . . . something else. Hahaha. *Veins of ditches, snow spouts,* that's good, that can stay, but *lifting with the wind like hair* I'm less sure of — a poor, vagrant, empty-handed metaphor. "Can't see it? Can't say it" is the rule, and whose hair is lifting in the wind, anyway? Not mine, mine doesn't lift, even in the midst of a Kansas tornado it stays put, stays pat, in South Africa that's how you could tell if a kid was black, the pencil test, they'd take a strand of the kid's hair from above the ear and wrap it tightly around a pencil — if the pencil fell to the floor the kid was white, if it stayed put he was black — Anna came home from school in tears one day, Aron remembers, rocking gently next to the dying fire, because her best friend Hetty had been expelled for being black, no one had ever noticed her blackness before but the Boer teacher had performed the pencil test — then performed it again, triumphantly, in front of Hetty's parents, the school principal, and a committee of town officials — and there it was, undeniable, the pencil had remained imprisoned by Hetty's strand of hair, which meant that her mother had committed a monstrous crime and her father was not her father, what year was that? wonders Aron — 1957 or thereabouts, Anna would have been eight, was that the day the seeds of her revolt were sown, seeds that would later flower into spiky thorny Marxist rhetoric — for Anna had become a militant, an organizer, an intractable unreachable spouter of dogmatic truths, as rigid and unforgiving as the men who, decades earlier, had provoked the flight of Aron's parents from Odessa, the same words, the same angry concepts, the same punishment and constraint for your own good, for the good of the country, the people, the freedom movement, yes, *sjambok* beatings, torture and murder and ANC concentration camps, it goes on and on, thinks Aron, rocking gently as the snow eddies beyond the windows, the cycle of hope and despair, rampant destruction and ruthless renovation, good Lord what's going on here, he's in the streets of a Palestinian village filled with wreckage and ruin, armed Israeli soldiers with Uzis and sunglasses are striding up to people in the burning sun and demanding to see their papers, there are roadblocks everywhere, stacked sandbags, barbed wire, heaps of broken glass, concrete and stone, you have to leap over them somehow, not easy, not easy at my age, how will I ever make it through, the regular creaking of Aron's rocking chair is keeping Beth awake, she can't stop listening to it, it's a ski lift, hauling her up an absurdly steep slope, how can it be so steep, almost ninety degrees, almost vertical — her head is thrown back and her skis jut up in the air in front of her — when they reach the top there's an unbearable, interminable pause, and then she's hurtled into the descent, plunging down and down, head forward — how do you brake, she wonders, are you supposed to bend your knees or straighten them, she can't remember, she clutches Brian's arm convulsively and he turns over in his sleep, puts his arm around his wife, pulls her to him, oh the flesh, the so familiar flesh, the warmth, his body already aching from the hardness of the floor, they're not hippies anymore, bombing their way through Mexico, surviving on beer and Mary Jane, they can no longer flop down to sleep just anywhere — beach, forest, *zocalo,* city park, city hall — "Ladies and gentlemen of the jury . . . No, I wish first of all to address the judge directly." Turning, he's dismayed to see that the judge is his own father, immense and imperious in his black robes. How could I not have noticed it was him? thinks Brian. Now his father's eyes are drilling into him. "Go on!" he roars. "What have you got to say for yourself?" and Brian recoils in fear, madly casting about for his argument, shuffling through the sheaf of notes in his hand — where on earth is his argument? How will he make his case if he can't find it? "Go on!" repeats his father, pounding his gavel, "we can't wait all day!" Then the courtroom vanishes and the two of them are in the backyard of their home in Los Angeles, Brian is trying to set up the barbecue, the sheaf of papers in his hand is now the instruction booklet but there seem to be several metallic parts missing and he can't figure out how the thing fits together. "For the love of God," his father fumes impatiently. "Can't you do *anything* right? Come on, *get with it!*" At this Brian bursts into tears and his father leaps on him. "Mommy's boy! Mommy's boy! You little sissy! Crybaby, crybaby . . ." The harder Brian cries, the more enraged and sadistic his father becomes, he's like a madman, dancing around him, flicking a wet dish towel at him, slapping, pinching, mocking — "Poor little boy! You just can't figure out how to put the barbecue together, can you? You nincompoop! You good-for-nothing!" At last he grabs Brian by the shoulders and gives him a shove that sends him flying into the half-constructed barbecue, which collapses onto the lawn in a clash and clang of metal, but in fact it was only the pot that Charles, in the kitchen, was trying to extract from amid a pile of other pots and pans in the dish rack to heat up some water for a cup of tea. Poem's progressing not too badly, but *the silence of a man asleep* sounds flat. Too self-evident. You've got to find a way to to make them *hear* the silence of the winter landscape. Rhythm's good, though. *The SI-lence of a MAN a-SLEEP.* The words are quickening in his brain, standing out, becoming powerful vibrant living things the way they always do when he manages to immerse himself in poetry like this, in the depth of night, in the kitchen, with Myrna and the kids asleep in the house around him, *the silence* (the long *i*, stretching upward like a grain silo) *of a* (soft and chuffing, like the comforting chug of a train) *man* (opening out, stretched flat like the palm of a hand) *asleep* (suddenly curled up like a gently closed fist), Patrizia pounds her fist on the table. "I won't stand for it!" she screams — and, dumbfounded, Gino and Tomas look up at her in fear. "Why did you have to draw on the floor?" "The color was so nice," says Gino quakily. "The blue turquoise." "Don't worry, Mommy," says Tomas. "It's just linoleum, it'll wash off." Another child is there, too, in the background, a little girl, half invisible, Patrizia can only see her out of the corner of her eye. "Why don't you ever see me?" asks the little girl. "Of course I can see you, darling!" says Patrizia, her heart filling up with dread. "No," the child insists, "even now you refuse to look at me!" Patrizia collapses onto the table, sobbing, burying her head in her arms, and Gino and Tomas rush over to comfort her, "It's okay,

Mama, it's okay," they say, stroking her head and shoulders, her arms, but gradually their words degenerate into twitters and chirps, their hands are birds, fluttering and skittering about Patrizia's head and shoulders. All the birds are asleep, fast asleep, the forest is still and the snow is beginning to abate, the flakes are falling more slowly now, tiredly as it were and intermittently, it's the dead of night but the house is very much alive, athrob with the dreams of its occupants. Hal Junior releases a stream of urine into his diaper and revels in the sensation of lush mush, inchoate images go sliding across his brain, colors and intensities, jagged flashes of joy, sparse syllables, *Ma, Ma, Hal, ba, bo,* sweet fragmented possibilities of the English language, as concrete and sensuous to him as apple juice or oatmeal. Rachel is lying stiff and straight and sleepless, alone in her narrow bed — like Mrs. Dalloway, she thinks, and, propping herself up on her elbow, she swallows a second sleeping pill and her mind lets go at last, sinking, the claws of anxiety momentarily loosening their grip on her soul — but she has a class to teach and it's very late, how can she have allowed it to get so late, she starts running toward the university but there are snowbanks everywhere, slippery and treacherous, impeding her progress, she scrambles over them as best she can but as she's wearing a tight skirt, nylon stockings and high heels, she keeps slipping and scraping her legs on the ice, now she's completely overwrought, on the verge of tears — I'll never be able to teach in the state I'm in! she thinks, and, drawing a tube of Xanax from her handbag, she gobbles down a handful — No, no, that's too much — it'll knock me out — turn me into a zombie — I won't be able to put my ideas in order — so she starts coughing them up again — spitting them out into the snow, trying to calculate how many Xanax she should swallow in order to be calm but not numb . . . Her anguish is so acute that it awakens Derek, in his uncomfortable narrow bed on the other side of the room. He strains his ears and eyes — is there something? . . . No . . . all is calm, apparently . . . but he feels awful. Heavy head. Burning stomach pain.

Shouldn't have drunk that champagne, in addition to the wine, in addition to the punch. Oh God, don't want to go through another operation . . . "What are you complaining about?" says his mother Violet. "Your father's dead, you cared so much about him that you weren't even there to say good-bye, your mother's got phlebitis and rheumatism, high blood pressure and gout — and you're complaining about a little stomach pain? Old age, schmold age, you don't know what you're talking about. Come and see me when you turn seventy-five, then you can tell me about old age." "I can't do that," says Derek. "Why not?" demands his mother, and he doesn't dare tell her the reason, namely that when he's seventy-five she'll be dead. "It's all right, Violet," he says, "everything's all right, I'll come and visit you as soon as I can, I've just got this one article I want to finish, I'll be in touch soon, I promise." "Promises schmomises, I know you," snarls his mother at the back of his neck as he toils up a hill in a familiar yet deeply foreign city with cobbled streets and ramshackle brick houses . . . Katie, too, is in a foreign city, though how she got there is a mystery — she'd boarded the 79th Street crosstown bus with her daughter Alice but the bus came to a halt in a place she'd never seen before, and the driver simply got out, went to sit down in a sidewalk café and ordered himself a drink — "I like it fine right here," he said, by way of an explanation. Indeed, the neighborhood is breathtakingly beautiful, and some sort of carnival is going on — he's right, thinks Katie, why would we want to go any farther? She's enchanted to be sharing this with Alice; arm in arm, they start heading for a gypsy camp when — lo and behold — Katie's *mother* appears! "Mother!" Katie exults. "I thought you were dead!" "No, no," her mother laughs, "I didn't want to be in the way, that's all. Isn't it marvelous here?" A smile plays on Katie's lips as she sleeps, then floats across the room to where Beth's body is intertwined with Brian's on the floor, the smile hovers around Beth's head for a while but is impotent to dissolve the frown on her forehead because on the other side of that shell of bone, in her sleeping yet active brain, Beth is undergoing major surgery. She's both the patient, lying unconscious on the operating block, and the surgeon, articulating the names of the various instruments she requires the nurses to hand her. Her stomach is wide open and there's something inside it — Beth strains to see but she can't quite make out what it is amid the swarming green-clad arms of the other doctors and nurses — it's quite large, though — nestled between stomach and liver — and it's squirming — what can it possibly be? A fish? They must get it out. Squirming there — under the brightly flashing surface of the Pripiat River — yes! — he's got it! Leonid has got it! He scrambles excitedly to his feet on the rock and his father, standing behind him, holds his hips to help him keep his balance as he reels it in — it's a *big* one — thrashing — a fantastic feeling, the frantic movements of the panicking fish conveyed through line and rod to Leonid's skinny arms — he's got it! Wow! Wow! The sun is starting to set, the day is drawing to its close but the instant is so exquisite that he's loath to hear his father say they should be heading home. *In the last light,* writes Charles. Now *that's* good; that much I'm certain of. *The last light.* Two monosyllables — so similar — glinting off one another. That's fine . . . *a deer will flash / through the ravaged woods like a face.* Can you see a deer flashing like a face? Yeah, I know what I mean. When you come upon one in the woods — that glimpse of sudden recognition — that flush of excitement — ah! — then gone. The problem is that *ravaged* resounds with *face* — it's more often faces that are ravaged than woods. And one line ending *flash* and the next *face* — that's ugly, man. Real bad. Jesus . . . nasty cough Sean has got there. Maybe take him up some tea? But I wouldn't want to bust in on his night with Patrizia. Cute kid, Patrizia. Nice lady. Upstairs, drawn briefly from her sleep by the sound of Sean's coughing, Patrizia slips a hand beneath his navy blue T-shirt and strokes his back, "Hey, that's a nasty cough, sweetheart," she whispers between hacks. "You should go see a doctor." All at once she remembers the dream she had about the opera — *calvo dentello,* the cape of lace —

no, she realizes now, *calvo* doesn't mean cape, it means bald. Bald lace . . . now what could that possibly mean? "I did," says Sean. "Didn't he give you some medicine or something?" — but Sean's answer is mangled by a fresh volcanic eruption of coughing and Patrizia gradually subsides into dream, turning the cough into the bark of a dog as she approaches the cathedral of her childhood, or rather, four walls surrounding a garden space in which a number of men and women, dressed for mass, are gaily shoveling dirt from a series of raised mounds that are the tombs of their ancestors. "What are you doing?" Patrizia asks them, as the dog barks and barks. "We're turning this cemetery back into a place of worship," they inform her, and she sees that on one of the walls a man is deftly redrawing the branches of the rose window that used to be there. "That's terrific!" she exclaims, filled with elation. Looking up, she sees that the sculpted cherubims on the capitals are alive, gently sliding and twisting around one another, winding tendrils of stone flowers through each other's heads and bodies. "That's terrific!" she repeats, and the dog goes on barking and the snow has now stopped falling completely and indeed, in Chloe's mind in the guest room at the far end of the hallway it's summertime, a sunny day, bright and brittle as a knife blade, she's brought her baby to visit someone in Los Angeles and has set his basket on the lawn in front of the house — Hal Junior is younger than his age, exceedingly small and frail — slowly the basket overturns and the baby spills out onto the grass, and then, though no shots ring out, two big black crows drop down from the sky — dead, bleeding, chock-full of cartridges — one on the front steps and the other on the baby. The dead bird on the living baby. Chloe wakens with a start and looks around her in dismay — where am I where am I where am I, all she can see are walls of books, where am I oh yes I'm in Sean Farrell's house, what do these people need so many books for, they think books can protect them from the world but they can't, can they, Col? Nothing can protect you, nothing can help, books try to turn life into stories but that's not the way it is — remember the turtles, Col? Where did we get those turtles, anyhow? Remember how weird it felt when you'd hold them by the soft-sharp edge of their shell and they'd swish their little legs against your fingers, like, "Hey! What happened to the ground?" And the pretty brown-and-yellow patterns on their stomachs — a surprise when you turned them over, their shells were so drab and gray. Remember how we used to race them? We'd each of us grab a turtle, plunk them down at the edge of the lawn and say, "On your mark, get set, go!" then release them. But instead of dashing across the lawn in a straight line and trying to win the race, they'd just go wandering around any which way. That's life, huh Col? People act like it was a race and you could try and get somewhere, but the truth is we're nothing but a bunch of stupid turtles. We've got no idea where we're going, or where the finish line is, and even if we found it there wouldn't be any prize. Don't you know that, Hal? What good's all your education if you still don't know that? She turns over in bed, unwittingly pulling the comforter away from Hal, exposing his large body to the chilly air of the room (as Sean is anxious to economize on heating bills, the temperature in the house drops automatically at night from seventy to fifty degrees). Hal shivers, and immediately embarks upon a dream he will later incorporate into his Klondike novel — a dream in which a gold digger freezes to death and is discovered by a group of Eskimos and thawed out and chopped up and turned into stew. I hope the Eskimos won't take offense, thinks Hal, waking up and scribbling the dream into his notebook on the bedside table, using a pencil flashlight so as not to waken his sleeping wife and son. The Inuit, I mean. I hope the Inuit won't take offense. If they protest I'll tell them it was just a dream — in the mind of your average white man in the 1890s, all nonwhites were tantamount to savages and cannibals. It's the nightmare of a racist, that's all, not the author's personal point of view. Jesus Christ, it's freezing in here. He gently pulls the comforter away from Chloe until it covers him again. *And the tracks of men and wolves,* murmurs

Charles to himself for the seventy-fifth time in the past half hour, but then the words blur in front of his eyes and, laying his head on the scrawled and scribbled page, he falls asleep. Meanwhile the fire has died out in the grate next to Aron's rocking chair; a shudder goes through the old man's sleeping body, his hands and feet are numb with cold and his mother is rubbing them, reciting Pushkin's "Pilgrim" to him as she does so; when she gets to the part about the fire — *Nash gorod plameni i vetrom obrechën* — she blows on his hands to warm them, then slips them beneath her armpits, they brush against her breasts and a violent thrill goes through him that is part pleasure, part disgust — then she slips his feet between her thighs and squeezes them — "Now you're my prisoner!" she says, teasing, laughing, but he believes her and is desperate to break free. The harder he tries to pull away from her, the more firmly she retains him. Finally — scared now, whining, straining — he yanks himself free with all his might and she releases him so abruptly that he goes flying backward, waking up with a jolt in his rocking chair, lost, brought back to reality by the soft, regular snores of Leonid on the couch, Brian on the floor, Charles in the kitchen: Good, good. He slips his hands between his own two thighs and rubs them there for warmth, then drifts back into another dream.

It is morning, early morning and the friends are all asleep, their eyes are closed but their lives are moving onward, the earth continues to spin on its axis and soon it will expose the section of the North American continent that contains this little house to the slanted, nearly transparent rays of the winter sun; the snow has ceased and the clouds have thinned out, grown wispy, evaporated, dawn is starting to break, the morning of a day called Friday in a month called November in a year which, ludicrously enough, also bears an identifying number — but as the friends are all asleep, none of them will witness the golden flash of Apollo's sublime chariot as it breasts the horizon to the southeast.

A while later, Katie opens her eyes and sees a wan, tentative light sifting through the curtains of the living room. Leonid has flung a heavy arm across her chest, pinning her down. She turns her head toward the darkness that is her husband's sleeping face and stares at it in the slowly whitening light until its features become distinct: the large nose first, then the heavy lips, the sagging jowls, the bushy white eyebrows . . . A prickly flush of warmth inflames her face as she remembers how, awakening thirteen years ago in Ioulia's house in Shudiany, the morning after Grigori's funeral, they'd made love on the living room couch — and how, locked and rocking in careful silence with her man as their love swelled to bursting and over-flowed, she'd wept with joy at the thought of receiving his seed — yes, *you, here,* my darling, in your country at long last, the place you came from, the land of your ancestors, your dead parents, your living sister and niece, oh I thank you Leonid, for being alive, I thank this land for having made you, I love you Leonid, want to prolong you forever in and through my body — it wasn't the wish to conceive another child, oh of course not, it was, rather, that morning, the acute awareness that their coupling was a chord in the echoing music of generations, a link that connected them, by chance and by choice, to those who'd come before them and to those who would come after — whereas in Shudiany, though they hadn't yet fully real-ized this, the chain had been snapped forever . . . And here we are this morning in Sean's house, she thinks, wiping beaded droplets of sweat from her forehead and turning her gaze back toward the sky, now pale blue — alive, our animal hearts beating beneath the warm skin of our aging bodies, in the silence of a solitary house buried in snow, in the hubbub of a frenetic culture, on this continent, on the cusp of a new millennium . . .

Upstairs, a second brain has bobbed up into wakefulness — the brain of baby Hal. Sentences haven't entered there as yet; no experi-ence is engraved there as a memory; his mind is a space of large loose intelligence over which images and sensations form and disintegrate, briefly coalesce and then dissolve. Waking into unfamiliar surroundings, Hal looks around, increasingly startled and upset. He's on the verge of crying out for help — but then the smell of his parents' bodies reaches his nostrils and reassures him. Soundlessly, he bunches his knees beneath his stomach, maneuvers his body into a standing position, seizes the bedsheets in his little fists and starts to kick and flail, stabbing his pajama-clad legs out behind him, wagging his cumbersome wet-diapered bottom from left to right — and, after several fruitless attempts, manages to clamber up onto the bed. Eureka! There they are! Both of them! He's about to hurl himself upon them, awakening them to be held and hugged and nourished in the harsh smoky sweatsmell of their morning flesh and the vibrating thrum of their voices, one sand the other velvet, when suddenly his gaze is attracted by a sharp light.

He turns his head — and there, beyond the window — *oh, there* — *what?* Crawling over the deeply breathing heaps that are the bodies of his parents, he grabs the windowsill with both hands and hoists himself up to look out — *oh, there* — *what?* The whiteness — *what?* white, *what?* white — oh such whiteness, oh sheer thrill — his eyes widen, his slobbery, all but toothless mouth drops open and he can only stare, stare in dazed amazement at the world that, since he last saw it, has been inexplicably, totally transfigured and is now — *oh, now* — nothing but pure, blinding, sumptuous whiteness — *thrill* — as far as the eye can see — *yes, now* — sparkling silent in the sunlight — a blank page — untouched — perfect — new.

Lux fit.

THANKSGIVING

I owe the title of this book to my friend the sculptor Pucci de Rossi — who, though he may some day use it for a short-story collection of his own, has generously agreed to share it with me.

The idea for a book titled *Black on White* (on race relations in America) belongs to Haitian playwright and poet Jacques Rey Charlier.

The Pushkin poem Aron remembers is "The Pilgrim" (1835), English translation by John Coutts in *The Complete Works of Alexander Pushkin,* vol. 3, "Lyric Poems: 1826–1836," pp. 233–5. Published by Milner and Company, Ltd., England.

The passages on Chernobyl are inspired by Svetlana Alexievitch's book of reportage, *The Supplication.*

Hal Hetherington's state of mind in chapter XI owes a great deal to May Sarton's *After the Stroke.*

The Gertrude Stein quote on page 122 is from *Three Lives,* Vintage, 1936, p. 222.

The film referred to on page 168 is *Star '80.*

The snow-in-the-face story was told to me by German novelist Peter Schneider.

Eugene Ionesco's thoughts on aging were published *Le Figaro,* 1 October 1993.

"Those Were the Days, My Friend" by Gene Raskin, © 1962 and 1968 Essex Music, Inc., New York.

The Sa Thay River scene is recounted (from a different point of view) in Bao Ninh's novel *The Sorrow of War.*

To these and more, many more, all those who have shared their stories with me over the years, my heartfelt thanks.